When *Push* Comes *To* SHOVE

YEADON PUBLIC LIBRARY
809 LONGACRE BLVD.
YEADON, PA 19050
(610) 623-4090

EARL SEWELL

When Push Comes To SHOVE

WHEN PUSH COMES TO SHOVE

ISBN-13: 978-1-58314-641-5
ISBN-10: 1-58314-641-5

www.kimanipress.com

Printed in U.S.A.

It's not the load that breaks you down.
It's the way you carry it.
—Lena Horne

For my aunt, Layuna Sewell

CHAPTER 1

Cynthia sat nervously in the waiting area of the emergency room at Jackson Park Hospital. She couldn't stop gnawing on her fingernails or bouncing her leg up and down rapidly as if it were a jackhammer busting up concrete. Cynthia was a worrywart and during high-stress times such as this, her worst thoughts, fears and insecurities had a way of taking control. She tried to keep her worrisome imagination from running away with her, but she was losing the battle. She decided she needed to move around so she stood up and began pacing the floor. She massaged the back of her neck with her fingertips, then exhaled a few times. Cynthia paused at the nurses' station to ask if there was any news from the doctor about her mother, Elaine, who'd been rushed in because she was experiencing chest pain.

"They're still working on her. As soon as I hear something I'll call out your name," answered the nurse, who continued about her business of typing on her computer. Cynthia wanted to ask the nurse to double-check, but she decided to try to be patient for a little while longer.

She walked back to the waiting area and sat down on

one of the hard and uncomfortable plastic chairs. Her leg started doing the involuntary movements again, and the scent of alcohol and disinfectant wafting through the air was making her stomach turn. She hated the smell of hospitals.

Cynthia attempted to distract her mind by watching a rerun of the program *227* that was playing on the television in the waiting room. Comedian Jackee Harry was making jokes about how the men in her life weren't any good in bed. Under different circumstances, Cynthia would have laughed at the humor, but right now she couldn't. Nothing was funny to her at the moment and adding to her frustration was the fact that her life was in a wild and crazy state—nothing was going the way she'd envisioned it. *My husband isn't any good in bed, either.* Cynthia smirked at the truthfulness of her thoughts and how well she could relate to what Jackee had just said.

Cynthia had chosen to get married early instead of going to college. She had thought marriage was the best way to escape from the poverty and poor living conditions of her mother and brother. If she got married, she had believed, life wouldn't be such a struggle and she and her husband could build a better life for themselves. Now, after having her first child and with continual money problems, she realized the marriage might have been the worst mistake of her life.

Cynthia began to think about her older brother, Victor, whom she was upset with at this point. She'd phoned him well over an hour ago and left word about their mother having to be rushed to the hospital. She'd even left the number of the hospital front desk where she could be paged but he still hadn't contacted her.

"Typical Victor," she muttered to herself as she once again began to pace the floor. *He doesn't think about anything or anyone except for himself. If something doesn't have a direct impact on him, he could care less.* Cynthia was even more upset with him because she'd loaned him fifty dollars which he had promised to repay in a week. It was now three weeks later and when she had confronted him about it earlier that day, he'd yelled at her.

"You're worse than a damn loan shark, Cynthia. When I get your money I'll give it back to you. I don't have it right now. Besides, you don't need it right this minute anyway."

Cynthia cringed at the memory of the argument and the shouting match that followed. She hated fighting with Victor in front of her mother, but she had no choice since Victor still lived at home but refused to meet her somewhere else to talk. Elaine had become very upset with them for fighting. She'd gotten so frustrated that she'd begun shouting at both of them for ruining her quiet afternoon. Eventually, Victor had stormed out. A short while later, Elaine had started experiencing chest pains and had to be rushed to the hospital.

"I feel guilty as hell about this," Cynthia muttered. "If I hadn't started the argument with Victor, I wouldn't be in here with my mother."

"Mrs. Cynthia Clark," Cynthia heard someone call. She rushed over to the nurses' station.

"Yes, that's me, I'm Mrs. Clark," she informed the nurse.

"Come with me. I'll take you to see your mother and the doctor will give you an update," she said and escorted Cynthia through a large wooden door and back toward the E.R. They walked to Bed Seven, where Elaine was sitting upright and fastening the buttons on her shirt.

"What's going on?" Cynthia asked, relieved to see that Elaine appeared to be okay.

"Nothing," Elaine answered, and Cynthia knew right away that she was still in a foul mood.

"The doctor will be over in a moment," the nurse said and then left them alone.

"How are you feeling?" Cynthia asked. "I was worried sick about you."

"It was just a little heartburn that's all." Elaine paused as she fastened her last button. "But you know how these doctors are. They want to poke around in your ass until they find something."

"Mom, it had to be more than heartburn. The way you were complaining of chest pains made me think you were having a massive coronary. You had a different look in your eyes, too."

"I didn't have any kind of look in my eyes," Elaine argued.

"Yes, you did. You were just staring at nothing, like a doll does. Your eyes were open but I didn't think you could see, and then you fainted. I've never heard of heartburn making a person faint."

"I did not faint and I wasn't acting like that. I just felt a little tired, that's all. I just got a little dizzy from the heartburn. Now I wish this doctor would come on so I can get the hell up out of here. All they did was place me on a cold-ass table, in a cold-ass room, and stick and pinch me for two hours. I'm ready to go!"

"Elaine, lower your voice," Cynthia said soothingly. "Now, what did the doctor say?"

"The hell if I know. Like I said, all they did was strip me naked so that they could stick me and take some of my blood."

Cynthia sighed a frustrated sigh. Talking rationally to her mother when she got into one of her cynical moods was impossible.

"Hello. Are you her daughter?"

A male doctor came over. He was a nice-looking man, Cynthia thought. He had pretty brown skin, a bald head and a nicely shaped mustache.

"I'm Dr. Weaver, the cardiologist on staff tonight." He extended his hand and Cynthia shook it.

"So, what happened to my mom?" Cynthia asked.

"Thankfully nothing has happened yet, but her test results indicate that major changes need to be made."

"Changes like what?" Elaine snapped.

"Mom, don't be difficult," Cynthia said through clenched teeth, glaring at her mother. Cynthia wanted her mother to know that she wasn't about to put up with one of her classic tirades up in the emergency room.

"For one, the smoking has to stop. Her cholesterol

level is extremely high and initial tests are showing signs of vascular disease."

"Vascular disease?" Cynthia asked. "What exactly is that?"

"Oh, Lord! Now the man is trying to tell me I got the damn—whatchamacallit." Elaine folded her arms across her chest and began to rock back and forth on the edge of the hospital bed. Cynthia was an expert at reading her mother's body language and knew that Elaine wasn't ready to hear or accept what was about to be said.

"When high cholesterol goes untreated, it clogs the arteries and restricts the flow of blood. Blood not flowing well can lead to a variety of medical problems, including a heart attack."

"Did she have a heart attack?" Cynthia asked.

"I don't think so. I'm certain that her shortness of breath, chest pain and dizziness are warning signals that her body is having a difficult time." Dr. Weaver picked up a nearby clipboard and began jotting down information. "Elaine, I want you to follow up with me later this week. I want to run some more tests, place you on a diet and work on your addiction to nicotine."

"Addiction! Man, I don't have an addiction!" Elaine shouted. That was the way that Elaine handled things when they didn't go her way—she'd explode, and Cynthia hated when she did that. Cynthia shot threatening daggers at her mom with her eyes. "Mom, you need to relax," Cynthia quickly spoke out.

"The man is trying to say that I got some damn

vascular thing and an addiction, and all I had was a little heartburn. I know what I had, and I don't need someone like him to tell me that I got something else. All I need to do is take some of my roots and herbs and I'll be just fine." Both Cynthia and Dr. Weaver remained silent until Elaine ran out of breath and began coughing uncontrollably.

"Go on, Dr. Weaver. Tell me what needs to be done and where she needs to go and I'll make sure she gets there." Cynthia focused on Dr. Weaver's instructions; she'd deal with fighting and dragging her mom to his office later. Right now, all she wanted was to get the information and get Elaine released before she caught her breath and continued hollering about what Dr. Weaver did and didn't know.

"I can't believe the way you acted up in there," Cynthia scolded her mother as they drove down Stony Island Boulevard back toward Elaine's apartment on Fifty-First Street and King Drive.

"Those doctors don't know everything, Cynthia. They were in there running a bunch of tests so that they could get paid, that's all." Elaine rolled down the car window and allowed the crisp winter air to blow into the car. She then opened her purse, removed a cigarette and lit up. She inhaled deeply and then blew the smoke out the car window. She also positioned her cigarette near the window opening so that the smoke wouldn't circulate inside the car.

"Dr. Weaver just told you that you need to stop." Cynthia was annoyed by the fact that her mother wasn't taking the doctor's findings seriously.

"I'm going to stop when I finish this pack," Elaine said. Cynthia didn't believe a word of what she said but made a mental note to work with her to kick her habit.

"Where is Victor?" Elaine asked.

"I don't know. He never showed up and he never called me back," Cynthia answered bitterly. If there was ever a moment that Cynthia anticipated an outburst from her mother, this was it. Instead, Elaine was silent for a long moment and then she began to sniffle. Out of the corner of her eye, Cynthia saw her quickly wipe away tears. Cynthia knew that Victor's absence had hurt her feelings.

When I see Victor, he'd better pray that I'm in my right mind. It's not right that he didn't at least call to see about his mother's well-being.

"I'm going to get on his case. Don't worry," Cynthia said trying to make her mother feel better. Elaine didn't speak a word; she just continued to sniffle and smoke.

"That's okay. I'll be all right. I just can't believe that my own son didn't come to see about me."

"Maybe we should give him the benefit of the doubt," Cynthia offered, thinking that might ease the sting a little.

"Now you know as well as I do that Victor is going to come back with a million excuses as to why he didn't come see about me." Elaine took another drag and then exhaled. “One of these days, he’s going to run out of excuses with me,” Elaine said and then remained silent for the rest of the drive home.

CHAPTER 2

Cynthia's black Chevy Caprice gave off a high-pitched sound as she pressed down hard on the brakes in order to bring the car to a halt. She was at the corner of Sixty-Third and Western Avenue on Chicago's South Side. She jerked the gearshift into Reverse, twisted herself around to look out of the rear window, and then went about parallel parking the car. Once she got the mid-sized sedan situated, she cut off the ignition and glanced out at two men who were loitering around the door of the currency exchange she was about to enter. She needed to get several money orders to pay her bills.

"Look at them," she said to her mother, who was lost in a magazine article about singer Michael Jackson and the problems he was having with his skin color.

"Look at who?" Asked Elaine.

"The hooligans hanging around the front door of the currency exchange," Cynthia said with displeasure. "Why don't they go somewhere?" she asked her mom. "I mean why is it that wherever black folks are the urge to just loiter in front of somebody's place of business just consumes them? If it's not a gas station, it's the liquor store or beauty salon. When their triflin' behinds get tired of loitering around there, then they move to the grocery store parking lot or some fast-food joint. Why do so many of our people just congregate like they don't have shit else to do?"

"Maybe they're going somewhere. Maybe they're just waiting on the bus. I know that sometimes when I go to a burger pit to order my food, if the place is too crowded I'll stand outside. That way I can at least see what the hell is going on."

"So you just stand around the front door, waiting?" Cynthia asked.

"Yeah, what's wrong with that?"

"I don't know. I guess I just hate coming over here to this currency exchange. I get tired of having to squeeze past people in order to take care of my business," Cynthia griped.

"You say that every month. If you hate it so much, there's a First Chicago Bank right over there across the street. You can go in there, open up an account and handle your business," Elaine reminded her as she studied the young men a little more carefully. "I don't know why you just don't get a bank account. If you did that, you wouldn't have to be bothered with coming to the currency exchange every month to get money orders to pay your bills."

"You know that Butch doesn't like dealing with banks. He says that they play with your money too much. For example, if you go below the minimum balance they charge you a fee. Now what kind of sense does that make? I mean, if you have to take your balance down to zero in order to pay your bills, why should you be charged for that? Bankers are stupid for charging a minimum balance fee. It should be obvious to them that you're broke anytime you have to take your balance down to zero. If bankers could, they'd probably charge you a fee just to walk in the door."

"Would you just go and take care of your business and come on back out? I'm tired of hearing about how brilliant you think Butch is. A man without a bank account doesn't sound too bright to me, but hey, that's just my opinion."

"Butch is very smart," Cynthia said in defense of her husband. "He has so many plans and ideas that are going to provide us with a good life."

"Yeah, right. A good lifestyle doesn't start with a job as a clerk at an auto parts store. You could have done so much better. With your striking looks, you could have had any man you wanted. You could have easily married the wealthy man of your choice. But no, you wanted to plant roots with the likes of Butch Cassidy and his grand ideas."

"That's not his last name, Mom." Cynthia didn't like her mother's sarcasm. Elaine's honesty just fueled Cynthia's anxiety about the choice she'd made to get married at an early age.

At that moment, Cynthia's one-year-old son, Anthony, who was buckled down behind her in his car seat, began making cooing sounds. Cynthia tuned around to look at him and noticed that he was creating spit bubbles with his lips; it was a new trick that he'd learned from her mother.

"Why did you have to teach him how to do that?" Cynthia complained.

"I didn't teach him anything that he didn't want to learn," Elaine said quickly as she focused her mind back on the magazine article she was reading.

"Of all the things you could have taught him you choose how to make spit bubbles."

"Look, are you going to sit here and whine all afternoon or are you going to go take care of business? You're starting to irritate me, Cynthia, and I just don't feel like hearing you complain about every damn thing." Elaine's short fuse had just been lit and Cynthia knew it. Cynthia stared at her, trying to understand why she was in such a foul mood.

"I'll be back." Cynthia exhaled in frustration as she searched her coat pocket for her brown mittens and matching hat. Once she had them on, she grabbed her purse, which was sitting next to Anthony, and headed toward the door of the currency exchange.

When Cynthia returned a few minutes later, she noticed that her mother had a sour expression on her face.

"What's the matter with you?" Cynthia asked as she got back inside the car.

"Don't you smell him?" Elaine said, wrinkling her nose. "He needs to be changed. He's stunk up the entire car. I want to roll down the window but I don't want to give him a cold. You're going to change him, aren't you?

I can run across the street to that spot right there and pick me up an order of hot links and rib tips while you do that. I can pick you up an Italian beef heavily dipped in hot sauce if you want me to."

"Now you know that you don't have any business eating that type of food. We just came from your follow-up visit with the doctor and he just placed you on a strict diet. You sat up in there and promised him that you'd stick to the diet and start working out."

"Shoot me, I lied. I feel just fine and if I want to go over there and get me an order of hot links and rib tips with my own money, I'm going to do it. I've got a taste for it, and my mouth is all set to have some of it. I can't eat that dry tasteless food he wants me to eat. Hell, he doesn't eat the shit his damn self. I guarantee you that if I went back to Dr. Weaver's office with a half order of rib tips soaked in barbecue sauce, he'd be smacking his lips and just waiting to dig in. I'd bet he'd be licking the barbecue sauce off the boat with his fingers."

"Why do you make everything so difficult?" Cynthia whined because her mother was so stubborn.

"I'm not making anything difficult." Elaine raised her voice. "All I'm saying is, doctors don't know every damn thing. They go around telling people stuff just to keep them on edge and to keep them coming back to see them so they can juice the insurance company. I know how they think. They're just trying to scare me, that's all."

Elaine suddenly had a coughing attack that she couldn't control.

"See there," Cynthia said as her mother struggled to regain her breath.

Elaine stopped coughing and was silent for a moment. "I need a cigarette."

"No, you don't. Dr. Weaver was serious. You can't keep doing the same things that you were doing. You need to get more exercise so that you can drop a few pounds, which I'm sure will help you deal with your stress better."

"Well, tell all of that to my damn taste buds because they're the ones telling me to go across the street to get some hot links and rib tips."

Cynthia could tell that her mom was wound up because Elaine couldn't have things her way, at least not while she was with her. Cynthia knew that despite her efforts to change her mother's habits, Elaine was going to be Elaine and sneak off when she wasn't around to get her order of food.

"Are you going to change Big Stinky back there?" Elaine asked, referring to her grandson's growing odor.

Cynthia sighed. *Why is she like this?* Cynthia turned around in her seat and looked at her son, who seemed happy. His little legs were kicking in and out like small pistons.

"Look at Mama's precious baby." Cynthia began talking to him and got him so excited he began making grunting sounds.

"That baby is trying to tell you something. What are you feeding him? I mean, he's let loose some old grave-yard funk. I'll bet he's back there farting so hard his back is cracking." Elaine laughed at the truthfulness of her comment as she cranked down her window.

"He can sit tight for a minute," Cynthia said. "It won't hurt him. We'll be back at your house in a few minutes."

"Whew. I don't know if I can make it. What's got him smelling like that?"

"Well, it's certainly not hot links or rib tips." Cynthia tried to make a joke but Elaine didn't find her humor to be all that funny at the moment.

"You've got that right, because whatever he's letting loose is strong enough to wake the dead."

"Mom, stop talking about my baby like that." Cynthia got serious with her.

Elaine turned to look at her grandson. "Yeah, I'm talking about you, mister," Elaine teased her grandson as he continued to scrunch his tiny chocolate nose and grunt.

Cynthia fired up the motor and began heading toward Elaine's home. Elaine switched the car stereo to AM and fumbled with dial until she found her favorite radio station, which played music that made her feel young. James Brown was singing his hit song "Make It Funky." Cynthia and Elaine both laughed.

When Cynthia arrived back at her mother's apartment she immediately took Anthony into the bathroom and she bathed him. Once she got him out of the tub, she took him into Elaine's bedroom and placed him comfortably on the bed.

"That's my baby," Cynthia spoke to her son as she sprinkled baby powder on his naked body. She loved rubbing his brown chubby belly. He seemed to get a kick out of it, and he certainly enjoyed all of the attention that she was giving him. Cynthia went about placing a fresh diaper and some dry clothes on him.

"Now, isn't that better?" Cynthia said as he rested on his back. She inhaled his fresh baby scent and savored the moment. She loved the fragrant scent of baby power on his skin. She put her face close to his so that he could reach up and touch her. Anthony caught her by surprise by reaching up and clutching a clump of her hair. Cynthia let out a shriek as he tugged at her hair, which startled him and made him cry. She picked him up, got a bottle of milk and carried him into the living room, where she began pacing the floor with him in order to calm him.

"Have you fed him?" Elaine asked as she entered the living room, having just checked her mailbox.

"I'm trying to feed him now, but he won't take his bottle," Cynthia said over Anthony's loud crying.

"I think he's just fighting sleep. You should lay him down and just let him holler himself to sleep instead of holding him."

"I can't do that. I can't stand it when he screams like someone is killing him," Cynthia admitted.

"Well, honey, you're just spoiling him by holding on to him. He has to learn that he isn't going to be held all of the time."

"As long as I'm with him, he'll be held. That's the problem with children today. They don't get enough love or attention."

"Fine. Suit yourself. I've raised my children. If you don't want to take my advice, you don't have to. I'm going back into my bedroom to watch television." Elaine pivoted and left Cynthia and Anthony alone.

"What's wrong with Mama's baby?" Cynthia asked Anthony, but all he did was wail louder. Cynthia stood up with him and began pacing the floor back and forth between the window and the fake fireplace on the opposite wall.

Several minutes later, Anthony had finally grown weary of wailing and drifted off into a light sleep in Cynthia's arms. For the moment, she was hesitant about putting him to bed, fearing he'd wake back up. Cynthia decided to pace the floor with him a little longer to assure herself that he was truly asleep.

Now that Anthony's crying had subsided, she began to think about her life and how she'd arrived at where she was. She'd been married for two years, and soon she'd be turning twenty-one. Her life was tolerable at best and nothing like she'd imagined it would be when she'd married Butch. They'd only been married a short time, and already she was feeling abandoned. Butch, who was three years older than her, had developed a habit of coming home whenever he saw fit and Cynthia had an issue with that. She wanted to consult Elaine about it, but wasn't ready to hear her mother's criticism about her having rushed into marriage. Cynthia was also dying to prove to her mother that she was a strong woman who knew exactly what she wanted in life. Although she had to admit, having Anthony so soon wasn't part of her plan.

Cynthia opened the door to Elaine's bedroom and found that, like Anthony, Elaine had dropped off to sleep. The way Elaine had fallen asleep so quickly concerned Cynthia. Her mother's declining health frightened her and although Elaine's doctor was confident that she'd be okay if she made changes in her lifestyle, Cynthia knew that getting Elaine to follow through wouldn't be easy. She placed Anthony next to her and immediately noticed how hard Elaine was breathing. It was as if she was having trouble getting air. Cynthia shook her to wake her up for a moment.

"Mom. Are you okay?"

"Yeah, I'm fine. I'm just tired. Let me sleep for a minute," she said as she adjusted her wig.

"Okay. I've placed Anthony next to you," Cynthia said. Elaine nodded to acknowledge the presence of her grandson. Cynthia left the room and walked down a corridor past the living room and into the kitchen. Elaine's apartment was hot from the radiators, especially in the kitchen. Cynthia opened the back door to cool it a bit.

"It's a good thing she doesn't pay heating costs," she said aloud. Cynthia pulled a glass down from the dish rack sitting on the countertop adjacent to the sink. She turned on the faucet and waited for the water to turn cold. She filled up her glass, drank her water and then closed and locked the back door. She was about to walk back into her mother's bedroom to watch television while Elaine and Anthony slept, but stopped at the archway between the living room and the kitchen. She looked at the dinette set and how her mother kept it set and ready for dinner.

Behind her and over to the left was the doorway to her old bedroom. She walked over to it and opened the door. Elaine had said on numerous occasions that she was going to convert the room into a knitting room but never got around to it.

Cynthia's room hadn't changed all that much since she'd moved out two years ago. Although she considered herself to be grown and married, whenever she entered her old bedroom she felt like a kid again. For some reason, her small bedroom felt more like home than the apartment she shared with her husband.

Jeez, if I could only turn back the hands of time, she whispered to herself.

Cynthia sat down on the edge of her old bed and thought about her wedding reception, which had been held at her mother's apartment. She remembered how she thought that she'd finally escaped from her mother and her stern rules. On her wedding day, she'd felt grown-up and ready to take on the world with her husband.

Cynthia laid down flat on her back, closed her eyes, and thought back to her wedding reception.

Cynthia and Butch couldn't afford to have their wedding reception at a banquet hall, so Cynthia had convinced her mother to host the reception at her home. She couldn't believe how many people had crammed into the small dining room area of her mother's modest three-bedroom apartment. Even though the dining room was cozy, it had become the nucleus of the celebration. Friends and family were sitting and standing around the dinette table, drinking alcohol and smoking cigarettes. The smoke was thick and heavy, but no one seemed to mind because the mood was so festive.

Hanna, her favorite cousin and best friend, who was two years older than her, switched the music from the funky sounds of Rick James to gospel music, which made everyone in the room yell at her.

"Hanna, if your crazy ass touches the music again, you'd better dig your own grave," Elaine shouted at Hanna.

"Y'all need to get saved up in here," Hanna announced as she took a big gulp from a glass filled with alcohol. She loved to party with alcohol or some other stimulant while listening to gospel music. Cynthia had always wanted to ask her what that was all about, but never got around to it.

Hanna was six foot one and had a slender frame, a light complexion and a very large black mole on the left side of her upper lip. She was very self-conscious about it, and hated when people stared at her.

Elaine went over and switched the music back to "Bustin' Out" by Rick James.

"Leave the damn music alone," Elaine said as she took a hard gulp of the liquor and then began talking loudly. "That's my song," Elaine proclaimed as she contorted her face into an odd expression and began grooving to the rhythm of the music.

"All of you are wrong. You need to find some spirituality," Hanna said.

"Open up one of those windows over there by the radiator," Elaine instructed Hanna, who was mixing her Puerto Rican rum with Coca-Cola. With all of the bodies crammed so tightly together, the room had become unbearably warm. As soon as the window was forced open, the blustery and chilly February wind blew inside.

"I didn't say raise it all the way up," Elaine shouted. "I meant it should be cracked so a little fresh air can get in here. Let the window down some." She continued to give out orders as she approached the window to make sure her wishes were met.

Cynthia had known all of the people in attendance most of her life, and she was grateful that they'd come to wish her and Butch love, happiness and good health. She scanned the room looking for her husband, but remembered that earlier she'd seen Uncle Jo Jo, Hanna's father and her favorite uncle, and her other uncles surround Butch and then escort him out the back door to have a man-to-man talk with him about being a newlywed and how to treat their beloved niece. Cynthia had warned Butch that they might do this and hoped he wouldn't take their comments and intimidation tactics too seriously.

"Why are you leaning up against the wall like that in your wedding dress?" her mother asked. "I know you're only supposed to wear it once but there is no need to get the thing all dirty. These apartment walls aren't the cleanest. I've been trying to get cockeyed Larry the Landlord to pay for a fresh paint job but his cockeyed ass has been ignoring my request. I tell you, every time I look at that fool too hard I get dizzy. I can't tell if he's looking at me or at something else." Elaine laughed.

"Thing?" Cynthia was a little offended. "It's not a thing, Mom. It's my wedding dress."

"Well, start treating it like your wedding dress," Elaine countered.

"At this stage in your life, I would have preferred to see you in a cap and gown. This could have easily been a college graduation party."

Elaine had been drinking and the alcohol was making her boldly say things that Cynthia didn't particularly care to hear right now.

Cynthia took a deep breath and tried not to allow Elaine's criticism and mind games to ruin her moment of happiness.

"Mom, don't start, please."

"I'm not starting anything. I'm just speaking my mind. I can do that. I pay the cost to be the boss around here." Elaine took another sip of her drink. "I wanted you to finish school out so that you could have a better life than the one I gave you."

Cynthia studied Elaine's eyes. She knew that her mother was attempting to select her words carefully so that they wouldn't end up getting into a spat in front of everyone on her wedding day.

"I wanted you to have a good job so that you could

buy your own home," Elaine said. "I just don't see why you're rushing into marriage. You're not pregnant or anything. You're just rushing in the wrong direction for no reason at all."

"I am grown. I'm nineteen," Cynthia said, sensing the need to defend her decision as well as her love for Butch.

"And you got married to the likes of Butch Clark, the most mannish boy in the neighborhood. You may not be pregnant now, but you won't have to wait long before that happens."

"Mom, can't you just be happy for me? Huh? For once in my life, will you be happy for me and not ruin this moment," Cynthia pleaded. Elaine caught her daughter's gaze and held it for a long moment that seemed like an eternity. She finally exhaled and embraced her daughter.

"I'm sorry," Elaine whispered. "I'm just not ready for you to leave. You're so beautiful," Elaine said as she touched her daughter's hair. "You're such a striking young woman. You've got high cheekbones, pretty smooth light brown skin and gorgeous straight black hair. I've always admired your beautiful long hair. You know, your hair turned out like this because we have Indian blood in our family."

"Yes, Mom, I know. You've told me that on countless occasions."

"Well it's true and you should be proud of that."

"I am, Mom, but—"

"But nothing," Elaine cut her off. "I wish I had long pretty black hair like yours." Elaine smiled at her. "Come with me for a minute. We need to talk privately."

Cynthia cringed at the thought, because talking to her mother when Elaine had had a little too much alcohol would only end up in an argument.

"Okay, but I don't know where we're going to find some privacy with all of these people in here," Cynthia said as she turned and grabbed an open bottle of champagne sitting on the kitchen countertop.

"In my bedroom," Elaine said. "No one had better be in my bedroom or they're going to have to deal with me."

The two women made their way through the crowd of guests, down the corridor and into Elaine's bedroom. Although Cynthia had been in her mother's bedroom countless times, for some reason it seemed different this time. She glanced at a few photos of her and Victor when they were younger wedged into the frame of the dresser mirror.

"Sit down," Elaine said as she kneeled and searched under the bed. She came up with a small cash box that she kept hidden there. She retrieved the key to the box from another hiding place in her closet.

"There are things about being grown and married that you haven't experienced yet," Elaine said.

"Mom, not this speech again. I'm a grown woman, and I know Butch is my soul mate. He's the love my life. And I know that together we'll overcome any roadblock that life puts in our path."

"Cynthia, I don't want to spoil your day. Believe me I don't, but as your mother, there are some things that I have to say. I want you to listen. I'm only telling you these things and expressing my feelings because I love you. I'm not trying to be hurtful. I'm just trying to be truthful. I'm worried. You've lost your cashier's job, but you still went ahead with this wedding. You should have waited until things were a little more stable."

"Mom, I don't think I can take this right now," Cynthia said, unable to handle this type of criticism. Cynthia knew that she should have waited to get married after the cutbacks at her job, but she couldn't take living with Elaine anymore and she thought marriage was the only option for her to get out of her house.

"No, Cynthia. You have to listen to this. It's part of what being grown is all about."

Cynthia remained silent, honored her mother's request and listened to her.

"When I got with your father, I was just like you," Elaine said. "I was young, stunningly beautiful and eager to be grown and out on my own with my husband. My mother told me that my marriage was an accident just looking for someplace to happen. I resented her for that at the time but years later, after your father and I separated, I began to think about some of the things she would tell me. At the time, I thought she was just being mean, but now I understand that she was just telling it like it was." Elaine stopped and organized her thoughts. "She told me that people have children and raise them until they're eighteen and then think their job is done. 'But I'm here to tell you,' she said to me, 'you're never done raising your children. The older the child, the more adult the problem, and every day will not be a sunny one.'"

"Grandma said that to you?"

"Yeah, she did. What I'm driving at here is this. I'm concerned. Butch is twenty-three and you're nineteen. I know you've been sneaking around with him ever since you were seventeen. That bothered me, but I'm not going to go down that road again right now. I'm not wishing for problems in your marriage, and I want you to be happy. But shit happens and sometimes loving someone just isn't enough. Over time, a man and a woman can reach a point where they walk on each other's love without so much as taking off their shoes. Men have a way of wanting to have complete control over their women. Sometimes a man gains control by trying to make the woman feel insecure or inadequate. A man may, over time, start to think that you're not as smart, sharp or as clever as he is. He may start identifying all of your faults and voicing his dislike of them. A man may find a variety of ways to keep you exactly where he wants you. He may even get it in his head that he has a right to beat up on you."

"Stop! Stop it right now. That's not going to happen with Butch and me, no way, no how. We love each other way too much for anything like that to happen."

"Cynthia, love can sometimes cloud your vision and judgment about a person. Sometimes you may not see the reality of a situation until it's too late."

"Mom, my marriage isn't even a day old yet and already you're trying to destroy it. Why are you saying these things? Why are you doing this?"

"I'm not trying to destroy your marriage. I'm just trying to get everything that I need to tell you out."

"You know, I'd expect this type of uncertainty and doubt to come from one of my girlfriends, not my own mother." Cynthia paused. "Butch and I promised each other to always have good communication. I'll do anything for him and he'll do the same for me. If that's not the cornerstone of what love and a healthy marriage are based upon, then I don't know what is. Mom, what you're talking about just doesn't apply to Butch and me. Can't you see that? Don't you see that I've found the perfect man and husband? We're young and love each other. We're never going to part. We're going to grow old and still love each other just as much fifty years from now."

"Wow!" Elaine said not believing how blind, idealistic and stubborn her daughter was. "He's really got your head way up in the clouds. You've always had a strong mind, Cynthia. You've always done things your way, and you really can't stand it when someone tries to point out an error in your judgment."

"So what are you saying? Marrying Butch was a mistake? Are you trying to do the same thing to me that Grandma did to you? Huh? Is that what this is all about?" Cynthia felt her anger and irritation swelling up in her heart. "You know, I'm not going to allow you to spoil this day for me. I'm just not. I'm not going to give you the power to do that. This is my day and I'm going to be happy, whether you like it or not."

"Okay. All right." Elaine tossed up her hands in defeat.

"There is no use in trying to provide you with any wisdom about life and how people change over time. I'm not trying to spoil anything for you."

"Then why are we talking about this on my wedding day? We could've had this conversation long before this," Cynthia said.

Elaine huffed before she spoke. "I didn't know exactly how to bring it up without sending you rushing out the door before I was ready to let you go," Elaine huffed. "However, it appears as if things are perfect in your world. You must have had an in-depth conversation with Old Man Life and he must have promised you one hell of an existence on this planet."

Elaine's voice grew loud and Cynthia knew that she was about to have a classic Elaine moment. She knew Elaine couldn't help her tone of voice; that was just the way she was. She always got loud when she couldn't get her point across effectively.

Elaine paused before speaking again. Cynthia, to her surprise, remained calm.

"I want you and Butch to make it. I really do. But if for any reason you need to come back home, the door is always open."

Cynthia lassoed her feelings of frustration for the moment and waited for Elaine to finish before she rejoined the celebration. At that moment, she just wanted to find Butch and be with him. Elaine opened the box that was sitting on her lap. She removed all of the money from inside it.

"Here, take this." She placed the folded money in Cynthia's hand. "It's fifteen hundred dollars. I want you to get yourself a personal bank account, place this money in it, and leave it there. Don't tell anyone about it, either. Not even Butch. Because if push comes to shove and you need to get away, this money is to be used to make an exit."

"Mom, I'm not going to take your money. Not for something like that. I also don't want to start off my marriage by hiding things from Butch. We don't have that type of relationship. It's not going to fail. We're honest with each other and that's just the way it is."

Cynthia tried to decipher the stunned look in her mother's eyes.

"Cynthia, you don't have a job, child. You're depending on Butch's income to provide for you. You're leaving yourself open to be mistreated because he will have all of the power. Take the money so that you'll have something put away for yourself." Elaine closed the box, signaling that under no circumstances would she take the money back.

"Mom—"

"No!" Elaine cut her off. "Don't say another word. If there is one thing I do know, a woman can always use some extra money."

Cynthia was about to explain how Butch's job at the auto parts store provided them with more than enough income but was interrupted by someone knocking on the bedroom door.

"Come in," Elaine said.

Victor, Cynthia's older brother opened the door. "There

you are. Come on out here, girl. I got a nice little wedding gift I picked up for you and Butch."

"Where did you get it from?" Elaine's tone was sharp and suspicious. She'd been having troubles with Victor getting mixed up with the wrong crowd. The police had already picked him up for looting during a civil unrest incident.

"Don't start, Mom, okay? Not today. I got her a nice gift because she deserves it."

Cynthia smiled at her brother and told him to turn his baseball cap around because he looked more like a hardened thug than her big brother. Victor was a tall and brawny man who, when he wanted to, could look and be very mean. He and Elaine were so much alike that it was hard for them to get along. However, in Cynthia's eyes he was harmless.

"Come on out here," Victor urged. "Where's Butch at?"

"He's somewhere with Uncle Jo Jo and our other uncles getting grilled," Cynthia explained.

"Jeez, those old dudes are always up in somebody's face trying to get into their business. I'll go get him," Victor said, walking back down the corridor and into the dining room where everyone was gathered.

"You know I've got my hands full with him don't you?" Elaine said, feeling edgy about her son and his fascination with having a reputation as a badass on the streets.

"It's just a phase, Mom. As he matures he'll change. I've already been giving him a hard time about me being the first to move out," Cynthia assured her as she caught her reflection in a mirror hanging on the wall. "Don't you think I look beautiful in this wedding grown?"

"You look stunning. You have the perfect shape for such a formfitting wedding dress. Enjoy it now while you can. Your shapely curves will only last for so long."

"Well, if I can help it, I'm going to keep myself together," Cynthia said.

"We'll see how you manage that after you've had a baby or two," Elaine said, chuckling. "The Howard women have been known to gain a little extra weight in the ass once they've had a child."

"Well, hopefully that will not happen to me. I'm going to save and preserve this dress. Maybe one day, if I have a little girl, she'll be able to wear it on her wedding day."

"Perhaps," Elaine answered as if she were distracted. Cynthia stopped admiring herself and glanced over at her mother.

"What's wrong now?" Cynthia had grown weary of dealing with her mother.

"It's Victor. That boy is on the wrong path. I can feel it and I don't know what I can do about it. Victor has got my blood pressure so damn high that my medicine doesn't seem to work as fast as it used to," Elaine admitted and then abruptly stopped talking, looking as if she wished that she could take her words back.

"Mom, Victor is going to be fine. He's just going through a thing. He'll outgrow it."

"He may break my heart, just like you."

Cynthia was silent. She refused to allow her mother's comment to rattle her nerves.

"I just hope he grows out of it before he ends up in the back of a squad car," Elaine continued.

"Victor isn't going to get caught up like that. He may be dumb, but he isn't that stupid."

"Well, he was stupid enough to get caught by the police for looting," Elaine reminded her.

"You know what? Let's not have this conversation right now." Cynthia didn't want to get her mother wound up any more than she already was.

"I'm sorry. I shouldn't be bringing up these types of things on your special day." Elaine smiled at her daughter. "I'm happy for you," she said. "I know that you'll be just fine."

"Thank you, Mom." Cynthia hugged her mother. "I really needed to hear that from you."

The two women embraced each other tightly for a long moment and didn't hear Victor and Butch approach.

"Can your son-in-law get one of those hugs?" Butch asked. Elaine allowed Butch to embrace her.

"All right, enough of all of that," Victor said. "I want you two love birds to follow me downstairs to my friend's car. Your present is with him. Butch, we'll need to put it in your car."

"I'm not about to go out in that cold air." Cynthia glared at Victor as if he'd lost his mind. "I have a wedding dress on."

"Come on, Cent," Victor said, calling her by her nickname. "Just toss on your coat and come on downstairs to the curb with me. I just want you to see it."

"What is it and where did you get it from?" Elaine asked suspiciously.

"Mom." Cynthia cut Elaine off before she and Victor engaged in a shouting match. "Victor, I'm only going to take a look and then I'm coming right back up, okay?"

"Cool. That's all I'm asking."

"Well, I'm going to go get me a drink," said Elaine and walked back down the corridor to rejoin the celebration.

Cynthia grabbed her coat and followed her brother and husband downstairs. They walked out of the illuminated entryway of the three-story apartment building and over to the curb, where a man was sitting in a pickup truck. In the back of the truck was a large object, all covered up. Victor raced ahead of them and leaped onto the back of the truck.

"Come on over here," Victor instructed as he pulled back the several layers of covering. "Tada!" Victor bellowed with a smile.

"It's a floor model television," Cynthia said, a puzzled look on her face.

"Yeah," Victor said excitedly.

"Where did you get it from?" Butch asked.

"And where is the box for it?" inquired Cynthia.

"Damn, what is this? Twenty questions? I thought you guys would be happy to have a nice television set like this. It works and everything. I checked it myself."

"Victor, please tell me you didn't rip off some store. I'm not—"

"Girl, relax, damn it. No I didn't steal it. How in the hell would I carry this big sucker out of a store?"

"Victor, this is a nice gift and all, but man, I have my doubts about taking it," Butch said.

"Okay, all right. I'm going to be straight up with you." Victor jumped down from the back of the truck. "I know some people who had some stuff that they had to get rid of quickly. They stopped by the pool hall and asked if anyone was interested in buying a television set. I'd just won a few hundred dollars shooting pool, so I decided to check it out. The television was in the box. I told them I'd buy it if I could bring it in the pool hall, plug it up and make sure it worked. They agreed. We took it inside, I took it out of the box, plugged it in, saw that it worked and paid them. It's been sitting in a storage room down at the pool hall. That's J.B. in the driver's seat. You can ask him if you don't believe me."

"I think I will," Cynthia said. She knocked on the window of the truck's door and J.B. rolled down the window.

"I told that boy I wasn't lifting that television," J.B. said before Cynthia asked her question.

"J.B., where did my brother get this television from?"

"Some dudes came by the pool hall a week or so ago and sold it to him." J.B. didn't offer any additional information and before Cynthia could ask more questions, he rolled up the window.

"See?" Victor said. "Come on, Cent. It's a gift, okay? Don't make me have to haul this television in the house. You know the minute Mama sees it, she's going to have a damn fit. Then she's going to complain about her blood pressure and how I'm trying to kill her."

"Okay, Victor. You win. Thank you for the gift."

"Yeah, man. Good looking out," said Butch.

"Now we only got one problem."

"It's always something with you, Victor," Cynthia said.

"It's not a problem like that. We need to get this bad boy over to your place, and J.B. isn't about to help me lift it up off this truck."

"Well, I'm certainly not about to lift it." Cynthia looked at Victor as if he'd gone mad.

"Don't worry about it, baby," Butch said. "Victor, sit tight for a minute. I'll run around back and get my car. You and J.B. can follow me to our new apartment a few blocks west of here, and you and I will get it upstairs."

"Cool," said Victor, agreeing with Butch's plan.

"No," said Cynthia. "I have plans for you later on tonight and I can't risk you hurting your back lifting some damn television. I'll go talk to Uncle Jo Jo and have him take it over to the house. Wait down here, Victor. I'll send him out."

"Hey, whatever you say, Cent."

"Come on, Butch." Cynthia pulled his arm so that he'd follow her back inside.

Cynthia was startled out of her journey down memory lane by the sound of the back door slamming shut. By the time she sat up in bed, Victor was hastily making his way into the room.

"Damn, girl! You scared the hell out of me," Victor said as he maneuvered a large box into the room. Victor was now twenty-three and had put a little more muscle onto his already brawny frame. His hair was slicked down close to his skull with pomade grease and styled with waves.

"What's in the box?" Cynthia asked.

"Just some stuff from my locker at the pool hall," Victor answered vaguely as he placed the box in a closet and shut the door.

"What kind of stuff?"

"Personal stuff," Victor answered defensively. "What's up with all of the questions?"

"You just seem like you're hiding something, that's all. And you seem nervous."

"I don't have anything to hide and I'm not nervous," Victor answered. "What are you doing up in here anyway?"

"Just lying down and thinking."

"About what?" Victor asked.

"Just life in general. Stuff like that."

"Yeah, I know what you mean. I be thinking about life sometimes, too."

"I be?" Cynthia was cringing at her brother's poor use of English.

"Don't start with me, Cent. Mama always be on my back about stuff. I don't need you riding me, too."

Cynthia exhaled and let her questions about what he was hiding in the box go. "You know Mom was real upset about you not coming to the hospital to see about her."

Victor smirked. "I knew she'd be all right. She's too damn pigheaded to die."

"You shouldn't say things like that, Victor. She's your mother and if something happens to her, you'll regret it."

"Shit, I doubt it," he said, smirking again. Cynthia didn't like his attitude.

"She has to be the meanest woman this side of hell," Victor stated with absolute certainty.

"You know what? I'm going to give you a pass right now and change the conversation because you're saying stuff that you really don't mean."

"I'm a grown man. I know what I'm saying and I mean what I say." Victor glared at her daring her to challenge him.

"How are the GED courses going?" Cynthia asked, changing the subject.

"Sitting around in a room with a bunch of stupid so-and-sos isn't for me," Victor answered as he walked out of the room and back toward the kitchen.

"What do you mean, learning isn't for you?" Cynthia demanded, following him.

"Just what I said." Victor shut the back door and then sat down at the small white kitchen table.

Cynthia rested her behind against the countertop and folded her arms across her chest. She noticed that Victor was refusing to look her in the eye.

"And?" Cynthia pressed.

"And what?"

"Victor, you were supposed to get your GED six

months ago but you didn't because of poor grades. You promised Mom that you'd try harder. Mom is excepting you to graduate with a GED this June. She's been talking to me about it and has been trying to figure out how she could get some extra hours at work to help pay for some of your college courses so that you can get a degree and get out on your own. By the way, have you filled out any of the financial aid information that she gave to you?"

"No, I haven't."

"Victor, you can't wait until the last minute to submit your paperwork. There is only so much money available and the sooner you get your paperwork in, the better. Dang, boy, you've got to get on this."

"I dropped out."

"You what!" Cynthia raised her voice so loudly she feared she'd woken up her mother and son.

"Shh, damn. Are you trying to let the five o'clock news team know about it? I don't feel like her ornery ass coming back here to fight with me."

"Victor, you can't just drop out, and stop calling her ornery," Cynthia said, defending her mother.

"Yes, I can," he countered. "I don't have to do that if I don't want to. I'm old enough to make my own decisions. Besides, right now I have bigger needs."

"Needs like what?"

"Money, Cent. I'm so tired of dealing with Mom and her money problems. Every month, we fall short. I just don't see how she goes to work every day and is broke all of the time. If it's not the electric bill sucking up her money, it's the rent or her medicine. Once she gets done paying bills, we barely have enough money for food. And then when I eat, she rides my back about eating all of the food. I got tired of going hungry up in this place so I did what I had to do. Sometimes she doesn't know whether to spend money on food or her medicine. Shit, I'm not going out like that."

"Okay, for argument's sake, let's say by some miracle you do make it. What about Mom?"

"What about her?"

"Are you going to help her?"

"Hell no! If I'm busting my ass hustling for the money, it's all mine."

"How can you be that empty, Victor? She's your mother." Cynthia glared at her brother as if he were a complete stranger.

"Hey, that's just the way it is," Victor answered.

Cynthia decided to try a more understanding approach. "Victor, listen to me. I know it isn't easy having to struggle for everything, but dropping out of the GED classes isn't the answer."

"It is the answer, Cent. Every time I ask her for a little money, the first thing out of her big mouth is, 'Go get a job. I don't have time to take care of you. You were supposed to be long gone by now.' She acts as if we live in the suburbs where I can go to the local strip mall and get myself a nice little part-time job. Well, it ain't like that. I'm also tired of her foot being in the middle of my back. Sometimes I wish she'd look around and realize there isn't anything around here for me but broken glass and concrete."

"Victor, sometimes you just have to stick with something to be successful," Cynthia said.

"The damn foreigners can come over here and get all kinds of money to start up a business, but a brother like me who's been living here all his life can't do a damn thing." Victor paused to gain control of his anger. "I can make money out there doing my thing. I'm going to do like you did and run the hell away from her. I'm tired of her chewing on my ass every time I walk up in the house. She acts as if I'm the cause of all of her problems."

"Victor, you're not the cause of her problems. She's being hard on you because she wants you to listen to her and follow her advice. And for the record, I didn't abandon you and Mom. I fell in love and got married. There is a difference."

"Yeah, right. This is me you're talking to, Cent. And for the record, it's too hard to take advice from someone who is on the same level. It'd be different if she was making a lot of money and was willing to show me how to do the same."

Cynthia was now even more concerned about her mother. "Victor, you can't hurt her like this. You know that she's sick and can't deal with stress."

Cynthia wanted to place a little guilt on his shoulders. "Her blood pressure is going to go through the roof when she hears this."

She paused and then exhaled. She knew that talking to

Victor about hurting their mother's feelings was a lost cause. "So what have you been doing all day?"

"I've been doing what I do," Victor answered vaguely.

"And what's that?" Cynthia asked, fed up with his cocky attitude.

"Handling business," he said, nodding his head to the right side for emphasis. "I'm making it."

"Victor, you've done some pretty stupid things in your life, but I have to say this is the dumbest one yet. You're not thinking straight. You're going to screw up your life." Cynthia felt better now that she'd said what she really meant.

"I can't be too damn stupid," Victor snarled defiantly as he removed a wad of money from his front pants pocket.

"If being dumb makes me cash money like this, then call me stupid," he said, raising his voice at her.

Cynthia ignored the wad of money, which appeared to be nothing more than a bunch of one-dollar bills rolled up in a rubber band. "Victor, you're being an ass as well as being dumb."

"No dumber than you getting married to a motherfucker with a problem." Victor's words were as sharp as a surgeon's knife and they stunned Cynthia. She was surprised by how cold his heart had gotten and how deep his anger was.

"Problem? What are you talking about?" Cynthia suddenly felt paranoid.

"Oh, you don't know about it yet?" Victor chuckled. "And you're the one standing here calling me dumb.

Cent, you're so worried about what's going on over here when you need to be worried about your own damn house." Victor glared at her for a moment, then laughed condescendingly.

"You need to open your eyes," Victor whispered and left the room.

Cynthia wasn't about to allow Victor to make her paranoid with vague accusations. Granted, she and Butch had been fighting a lot about money, but all couples did that. At least that's what she told herself.

"No, Victor," she muttered as she watched him enter his bedroom and shut the door. "My man and I are just fine. We're struggling a little bit right now, but I know in my heart things are going to change and get better."

Another part of Cynthia's heart suddenly began to question whether she actually believed what she'd just told herself. She felt herself begin to panic as she wondered if Butch was doing something behind her back and trying to cover it up.

CHAPTER 3

The following Saturday, Cynthia was busy making sure that the small one-bedroom apartment she shared with her husband and son was spotless. It was Butch's birthday and Cynthia wanted to make sure that everything around the apartment was perfect. She'd planned to spend the entire day preparing their home and cooking for him. That was her way of showing how much she loved and cherished him. She also hoped that her efforts to make his day special wouldn't go unnoticed.

Lately, Butch had been argumentative and unjustifiably critical of the way she handled payment of the bills. Specifically, Butch was upset that they never seemed to have extra money to do anything special for himself. This was a selfish trait of his that she'd hoped he'd outgrow once they had their son, but Butch, in some ways, seemed to be competing with his own son for her affection and attention.

He also didn't understand that being a stay-at-home mother was a job all in itself. He'd gotten the notion that she only sat around all day watching television while he went to work to try to make the ends meet.

Their one-bedroom apartment was cozy, but some of their furniture was mismatched pieces, which Cynthia was upset about. Lately, they had to get rid of some pieces that got damaged from the house parties that Butch was so fond of hosting. It wasn't uncommon to find a dining room chair with a cigarette burn, a broken lamp or even a doorknob hole punched in a wall because someone was careless when opening the door. Cynthia finally put her foot down when a glass cocktail table got smashed.

"Baby, I really don't like a bunch of people up in my house all the time."

"But I do," Butch argued. "I like having people around. I like having parties."

"I'm not saying that we shouldn't go to parties. I just don't understand why we're the ones who have to host them all of the time."

"Because," Butch answered.

"Because what?" Cynthia didn't comprehend his unclear answer.

"Look, I've been partying with the crew long before you came on the scene. How am I going to look if I suddenly tell everyone that they can't come over because you said so?"

Cynthia didn't like his condescending tone of voice, and she felt that he thought she was dumb. In some ways, she'd allowed him to make her believe that she wasn't as knowledgeable as he was.

"You can tell them that we got tired of all of our furniture getting damaged. You can also tell them that one of them could of at least offered to pay for the stuff they broke," Cynthia snapped.

"I'm not going to tell my friends that," Butch said, his eyes full of rage.

"Butch, this is our place now. Not just yours." Cynthia glared at him and wondered why he didn't see that his so-called friends were costing him more money than they were worth.

"I don't like you right now." Butch's words were filled with anger, and they hurt Cynthia. Cynthia could tell from the look in his eyes that she was forcing him to grow up, which he wasn't ready to do just yet. Eventually, after she started acting ugly with houseguests during one of his impromptu parties, the rowdy guests got the message and their visits became less frequent, which suited her just fine. Over time, the parties stopped altogether and Cynthia redecorated their apartment as best as she could on their limited budget. She was pleased with her living room, where they had a long black leather sofa that sat three people. It was situated in front of three windows that were old and in need of replacing. She hoped it would block some of the cold winter wind that seemed to penetrate the room at will.

The modest-sized television was the focal point in the room. Situated between the sofa and the television was a makeshift cocktail table. Cynthia had taken a few of the boxes she'd moved into Butch's apartment with and sealed them up tightly. She then placed some decorative fabric over the boxes so that guests would think that the "table" was just covered. It worked perfectly for the time being, although she had to scold Butch on occasion about placing drinks on it.

Cynthia's dining room didn't have a formal dinette set because that had also gotten destroyed during one of Butch's grand gatherings. Two of Butch's buddies got into a fight during a poker game and fell on the table, breaking the legs beyond repair. Cynthia got even angrier about it when Butch didn't insist on making them pay for the damage. That was one of the dumbest things he'd ever done, in her opinion. For the most part her dining room was just open and unused space.

She dealt with not having one at present because she wasn't working—again. Shortly after she'd gotten married, she landed a job doing clerical work at a neighborhood medical center but stopped working once she had Anthony. Once Anthony arrived, it became cheaper for her to remain at home instead of paying a hefty sum of money on decent day care and other expenses. The plan she and Butch mapped out was for her to remain home until Anthony was two years old. They'd have to do without a few luxuries, but Cynthia didn't mind, especially since she no longer had to share her home with all of Butch's cronies

Cynthia pivoted to the left and headed down a short corridor. The bathroom was on the right side, and the bedroom was on the left. She entered the bathroom, which was the room she hated the most. The pedestal sink needed replacing and the landlord, for some reason she couldn't understand, had painted the bathtub. Now, after less than two years, the paint had begun to chip and peel.

"He's going to have to replace this tub soon," Cynthia said aloud, glaring down at the tub as if it were an uninvited houseguest. She'd purchased two boxes of candles and began to place them on the ledges of the windowsill in the bathroom. She wanted the bathroom to have a nice romantic glow so that when she and Butch took a bath together, the otherwise gloomy room would have a different feel to it. Cynthia was also holding out hope that their lovemaking today would be better than it had been recently. Although Cynthia hated to admit it, she wasn't satisfied with the way Butch made love to her. Even though they had a child, something wasn't exactly right in that department and she blamed herself for her inability to be completely satisfied.

Cynthia didn't bother lighting the candles yet; she'd decided to do that later. She exited the bathroom and entered the kitchen, which, in her opinion, wasn't much better than the bathroom.

"I can't wait for us to save enough money to buy our own home," Cynthia said aloud. The cabinets were covered with wood paneling, which wasn't very attractive. The countertop had seen better days, as well, but she accepted her living situation for what it was—temporary. She believed in Butch and knew in her heart that he'd do great things for her and Anthony. It was only a matter of time before he started an auto repair service. Once he did that and got some financial backing, their lives would start moving in the right direction.

Cynthia began preparing dinner. Once everything was in either a pot or marinating, she went into the bedroom in order to get off of her feet for a moment. Cynthia's bedroom wasn't particularly exciting, just a queen-size bed in need of a headboard, a few white baskets filled with laundry, two lamps, two closet doors and a small television on a nightstand. She relaxed on the bed and in spite of the fact that the life she'd envisioned wasn't all that she'd hoped it would be, she was still happy that she was independent.

As Cynthia relaxed, she thought about her forbidden relationship with Butch. She thought about how they'd formally met during a citywide Fourth of July weekend concert and carnival at Garfield Park. The festival was sponsored by the mayor's office of special events and a popular radio station. She remembered the perfect summer day well because she and her cousin Hanna were cheering on a local singer who'd taken off his shirt and was thrusting his hips very suggestively.

"Damn, he's fine," Hanna said as she leaned close to Cynthia so that she could hear her words clearly over the loud music. "I'll bet you any amount of money that he's the son of a preacher."

"I hope not, especially if he's dancing around like that," Cynthia said, laughing. "But then again, you never know."

"He looks like he's packing, too," Hanna said, referring to what appeared to be an erection growing inside of his jeans. The sight of the large bulge straining against his jeans made Hanna scream out "Hey, baby!" as loud as she could. In fact, she was so loud that the performer responded to her during his song.

"Girl, he's going to be my husband. I'm going to marry him and we're going to live in a big house, go to church on Sundays and have at least three kids," Hanna said as she stared at the man with lustful eyes.

"Don't you think you should at least meet the man first?" Cynthia said, laughing at Hanna's fantasy. Hanna didn't respond back she just rolled her eyes at Cynthia. Once the singer was done, the two women began walking toward the concession stand for a cold drink.

"Do you think that fine-ass singer would like a cool drink?" Hanna asked Cynthia.

"I don't know. You should just leave him alone because you know half the women out here probably want him," Cynthia said.

"He may not want them. He may want some of my tall and fine and chocolate ass." Hanna did a little dance move to show how she'd work him over with her sensual movements.

"You are crazy." Cynthia said, laughing.

As Cynthia and Hanna made their way through the crowd of partygoers, Cynthia felt someone lightly tug on her arm. At first, she was startled and jerked her arm away, but when she looked into Butch's beautiful and harmless eyes, she relaxed. Cynthia knew Butch from around her neighborhood. Besides being incredibly handsome, he'd developed a reputation as a real charmer among women young and old. In fact, she'd overheard several women in their thirties talk about how they'd show him a wild time if he were closer to their age. Cynthia always laughed to herself when she heard those types of discussions from women who were too old to lust after Butch. At least, they were in her eyes. Whenever Cynthia saw him at the neighborhood grocery, she always became nervous. Time after time, she wanted to find the courage to introduce herself by saying, "Hey, I'm the girl who lives down the street from you would you please notice me." Cynthia figured that approach would only make her look like a foolish and desperate young girl who knew nothing about men. Still, despite his reputation and all of the butterflies prancing around in her belly, she'd had a secret crush on him for a long time.

"What's your name?" he asked right away. "I've seen you around."

"Why?" asked Cynthia wanting to sound as if men approached her all the time wanting to know her name.

"Because I've just met the sexiest woman out here," he said with absolute certainty. Cynthia swallowed hard. Her butterflies were dancing around with wild abandon now. She couldn't believe that Butch had actually called her sexy.

"Well, this fine young girl is still in high school. But I might be more of your speed," Hanna interjected. At that moment, Cynthia wanted to scratch Hanna's eyes out. She couldn't believe that Hanna had busted her out like that. She gave Hanna an ugly look that she didn't pick up on.

"He's not interested in you, Hanna," Cynthia mumbled, hoping that Hanna would catch her drift. Cynthia was thankful that Butch didn't pay Hanna much attention. In fact, he never even took his eyes off of Cynthia. He just slowly brushed his sweet tongue across his chocolate lips and continued.

"Like I said, I just met the finest woman out here. I know I've seen you around. You have an older brother, right?"

"Yeah, his name is Victor."

"And your name is?"

Cynthia was still trying to get over the fact that Butch was speaking to her. She found herself studying the sound of his voice.

"Cynthia," she answered, suddenly feeling special.

"Girl, leave this grown man alone. He is out of your league," Hanna interrupted. "Besides, a real diva never tells a man her real name. You're so inexperienced," she said, chopping Cynthia's confidence level down. "Now, what a man like him needs is a woman who can handle him."

Hanna stood directly in front of Butch and captured his gaze. She did a little shimmy dance for him to see what type of reaction she'd get.

"Do you catch my drift?" Hanna asked him.

"Yeah, I catch your drift," Butch answered. "But I'd still like to speak with Cynthia, if that's all right with you."

Hanna didn't move out of his way or say anything additional. She just studied him as if he were supposed to continue speaking to her.

"Who's the pit bull you're walking around here with?" Butch asked Cynthia.

"What did you just say?" Hanna's voice rose about twelve octaves. Cynthia sensed that Hanna was about to make a real loud and ugly scene.

"Nothing, Hanna." Cynthia quickly moved Hanna off to the side because she didn't want her cousin to ruin the moment. "Go over there and get yourself a drink. I'll be over in a minute."

"Why do you even want to be bothered with him, anyway? He doesn't even know what a real woman looks like when one is right in front of him."

Cynthia knew that Hanna's feelings were hurt, but she didn't care about Hanna or her feelings at that moment.

"Just go and get your damn drink," Cynthia said through gritted teeth. She made a mental note to confront Hanna about her attitude and her failed attempt at trying to steal a man away from her.

"Fine," Hanna conceded. Then she turned to Butch. "You have no idea of what you're missing," she yelled and walked away.

"Don't pay her any attention. She's just really man crazy," Cynthia said. "So, how old are you, Butch?"

"I'm twenty-one. And you?"

"I'm seventeen, but I'll be eighteen in a few months,"

Cynthia said quickly, fearing her age might make him turn and run.

"I'm not that much older than you," Butch said with a smile and Cynthia felt much more at ease because her age wasn't deterring him.

"So, tell me why you wanted to speak to me again?" Cynthia couldn't help smiling. She thought she appeared goofy to him, but no matter how hard she tried she couldn't remove the smile from her face.

"I like your smile," Butch said.

Cynthia felt her heart skip a beat.

"Look, I don't want to say too much right here because of all the noise and stuff," Butch said. "But I'm giving a little party at my house tonight. I'd like it if you dropped by."

"Are you for real?" Cynthia's voice came across louder than she wanted it to.

"Yeah. I'd like you to come by if you can get out."

Cynthia knew that she had to be home at a certain time but didn't want to seem like such a little girl to him.

"Yeah. I'll be there. I need to find something to wear," she said.

"Just come as you are. You look so good in those shorts. They complement your long legs."

Butch's flirting sent butterflies prancing around in Cynthia's belly again.

"These old shorts?" Cynthia chuckled excitedly. *I'm going to wear something so hot that you won't be able to take your eyes off of me,* Cynthia thought to herself.

"Let me give you my address." Butch searched his pocket for a pen.

"That's okay," Cynthia answered. "I know exactly where you live."

"Well, okay." Butch smiled at her again. "Look, I'm going to go meet up with some friends of mine, but I'm really looking forward to seeing you tonight."

"Same here." Cynthia let her eyes speak for her. She knew how to communicate her intentions through them and wanted to make sure that Butch read her thoughts correctly.

"Girl, you shouldn't look at me like that. I might get ideas."

"What kind of ideas?" Cynthia prompted.

Butch leaned in toward her and spoke purposefully in her ear.

"When you come over tonight I'll share my ideas with you."

Cynthia could have melted right on the spot. The way that his words tickled her ears and the way his warm breath gave her goose bumps made her want to shout out his name.

"Okay," Cynthia said. "We'll continue this conversation later on tonight." She stared at him for a long moment and then watched as he walked away from her.

When Cynthia met back up with Hanna, she was far too excited about being invited to the party to want to remain at the festival. She was having a difficult time containing her excitement about the party.

"Girl, he invited me to a party tonight," Cynthia told Hanna who seemed upset when she heard it.

"He only invited you?" Hanna asked sarcastically.

"Yeah, but I'm sure he wouldn't mind if you came along. The more the merrier, right?" Cynthia said, trying to smooth over Hanna's hurt feelings.

"Good." Hanna's sour attitude changed. "I've heard that his house parties are live. Besides, when I walk up in there he's going to—" Hanna trapped her words. "Never mind, we'll have a good time."

"Never mind what?" Cynthia asked.

"Never mind," Hanna said again. "Listen, we've got to get out of here. I've got to find something to wear, as well as do something with this hair of mine." Hanna paused in thought. "I know that I can get out of the house but what about you? Your mother isn't going to allow you to go and hang out at some house party. You're only seventeen."

"I'm almost eighteen," Cynthia corrected Hanna. "I'm going to have to sneak out."

"Plus, you have to do something about Victor and his big mouth. You know he'll get a kick out of getting you in trouble."

"I know, he's not going to think twice about busting me out in front of Mom. I'll have to pay him."

"Pay him?" Hanna seemed disgusted by the idea.

"Girl, if I don't pay him, he'll snitch."

"Fine. If it were me, I'd just threaten to beat his ass. But you're not like me at all, so I don't expect you to roll like that."

"Whatever, Hanna."

Cynthia hated it when Hanna made her feel as if she weren't as good or as smart as her. She was going to speak to Hanna about belittling her, but then a new realization hit her.

"I don't have a thing to wear," Cynthia cried. "I mean, I just thought about it. I need to buy something to wear. I don't want to walk up in his house looking like some high school groupie."

"I know that's right," Hanna said. "Look, I have my dad's car for most of the day. Why don't we leave here and head over to the mall. How much cash do you have on you?"

"I have one hundred dollars, but I have more at home," Cynthia said.

"Good, we should be able to hook you up with something at the mall. If you don't have enough money for the outfit you want, I'll cover it, but you have to pay me back when I drop you off at home."

"Okay, you know that's not even an issue," Cynthia said, feeling energized.

The two of them headed toward Austin Boulevard where Hanna had parked Uncle Jo Jo's car. Once they reached it Hanna unlocked the passenger door and then walked around to the driver's side. When they were both inside the car, Hanna cranked it up and pulled off.

"So, have you had sex yet?" Hanna asked as she drove toward the expressway.

"Girl, please, I know how to handle it," Cynthia

boasted, even though she'd never handled anything other than her sexual fantasies.

"Good, because you can't go to this party acting like you're all square."

"Don't worry. I'm not going to embarrass you or myself for that matter," Cynthia assured her.

"Okay then, tell me what a dick feels like." Hanna was pressing the issue, something Cynthia hadn't anticipated.

"I'm not about to sit here and tell you what one feels like. That's kind of freakish, don't you think?"

"Oh Lord, you are square. Don't you know that's what women talk about? One of the first things we want to know about a man is what he's working with. Your mama has really kept you sheltered."

Hanna's comment hurt Cynthia's feelings. Cynthia didn't respond, just remained silent. She wished she had a little more experience with men.

"Okay, then. What does one look like?" Hanna wasn't about to let Cynthia off easily.

"Girl, what's up with all of the sex questions?" Cynthia didn't understand what Hanna wanted.

"Look, if you're trying to be a big girl, there is a lot that comes along with the territory. I'm just trying to school you a little bit. I know how stern and overprotective your mother is when it comes to you. So there are certain things that I know you may not have been exposed to. So what I'm trying to do his educate a sister real quick."

"Hanna, I can handle myself."

"How many house parties have you been to without your mother or other family members?"

Cynthia had to admit that, technically, she'd never been to a real house party.

"Yeah, that's what I thought," Hanna said. "Okay. Here are few things to keep in mind while you're there. People will be doing all types of things. Since this is your first house party, don't get high with anyone other than me. Dudes will try to slip you something in order to make it easier to get between your legs."

"Girl, I'm not dumb. I told you. I can handle myself." Cynthia was being both overconfident and stubborn.

"Boy, you are truly just like your mother," Hanna said, chuckling.

"And what's that supposed to mean?"

"It means that when you set out to do something, no one is going to stop you."

"Like I said, Hanna, I'm my own woman and I know how to handle myself."

"All right. Go on with your bad self. But if you get jammed up, just know that I'll be there for you."

"I'm not going to get jammed up, so when you get there you can go ahead and have a good time. I don't need you to be my babysitter."

"Well, now that we've gotten that clear, let's go over a few sex things just to make sure. Big dicks are nice, but if a dude pulls out his johnson and it stretches down to his kneecaps, he needs medical help and you're not a doctor. Uncircumcised dicks, in my opinion, are the most hideous things on the planet. And if a dude isn't keeping his hygiene together in that area, that can be a real problem."

"Problem?" Cynthia was confused by what Hanna meant.

"Cleanliness, girl. Not every man is clean and some men will come to a party smelling funky as hell. Stay away from men like that." Cynthia could only blink rapidly at the thought of someone coming to a party smelling funky. Still, she tried to give the appearance of knowing exactly what Hanna was talking about.

"Anything else?" Cynthia asked.

"Yeah. Don't be surprised if you find all of the men trailing behind me trying to get some this good Hanna loving," Hanna said, laughing. "Seriously, though, I just want you to have a good time and get back home in one piece. You're my girl and I have to look out for you. You know I've always thought of you as my baby sister."

"I know, Hanna." Cynthia smiled, feeling good about having someone with Hanna's knowledge looking out for her.

"I can't wait to get to the mall so that we can buy our outfits and arrive looking like the two hottest women up in the place."

Cynthia chuckled because Hanna was very tall and always had difficulty finding clothes that fit just right. To her, Hanna had always seemed to have an awkward shape. She didn't have a lot of ass and she was rather thin, but to hear Hanna tell it, she was the finest woman to ever walk God's green earth.

"What's so funny?" Hanna asked.

"Nothing, Hanna. I'm just glad I have a big sister like you," Cynthia said as they continued on toward the mall.

Cynthia knew that her mother would have a fit if she learned that she'd planned on attending a house party hosted by Butch Clark. So to avoid the irritation of dealing with her mother's quick and decisive "Hell to the no! You can't go!" Cynthia decided not to mention it. Her desire to attend the party overcame her fear of her mother's fury. She knew Elaine would fall asleep like clockwork and go to bed early on Saturday so that she could get up in time to watch her 7:00 a.m. church service on television.

Cynthia's only real concern was her loudmouthed brother Victor. She knocked on his door and waited for him to say that it was okay for her to come in. When she opened his bedroom door, she gently shut it behind her.

Victor was lying on his bed with the television remote in his hand. His room had an odor that was a mixture of smelly gym shoes and marijuana smoke. The walls of his room had posters of various women in bathing suits in compromising positions.

"I'm going to sneak out to a party tonight down the street at Butch Clark's, so don't go running to tell Mom," Cynthia said to Victor.

"I heard about his party tonight. I was going to go myself but I got this new lady I'm dealing with," Victor said. "What time are you leaving?"

"When Mom falls asleep. You mean to tell me that you're not going to snitch on me?" Cynthia asked.

"No. Not this time. Go on and have a good time. But if you get caught, you're on your own because you know that Mom is going to try and blame me for allowing you to sneak out."

"Don't worry. She'll never find out," Cynthia assured him.

"Good. You make sure that you're careful while you're over there and come in through the back door. That way, Mom won't hear you. Trust me on that one," Victor said with a chuckle.

"Thanks for the tip," Cynthia said and then left Victor's bedroom.

Later that evening, after a nice long shower, Cynthia went into her bedroom and began removing the outfit she'd purchased from the shopping bags sitting on her bed. She'd bought a formfitting black miniskirt, along with some sexy fishnet panty hose to accent her thick and shapely legs, a gray blouse that accentuated her breasts, a pair of black pumps that weren't too uncomfortable to dance in and some simple earrings. Once she was fully dressed, she placed a few extra pins in her hair to make sure that it stayed put. Just as she was about to sneak out the door, Hanna phoned.

"Hello," Cynthia whispered into the phone.

"Are you ready yet?" Hanna asked.

"Damn, girl, what are you trying to do, get me busted?

You know that I'm sneaking out of the house tonight. Why would you call here and possibly wake up my mother?"

"Calm down, girl. I was trying to let you know that I'm running late. Damn."

"Well, I got the message. I'll see you there," Cynthia said in a loud whisper.

"I can tell your ass is nervous," Hanna said with a laugh.

"Don't laugh at me, Hanna. I hate when you do that."

"Here is a tip for you, Miss Smartass. When sneaking out to a party that you're not supposed to be going to, unplug the damn phone. That way, no one can get in contact with your mama on the same night of the party to bust you."

"Oh. That's a good idea," Cynthia admitted.

"Lord, you're such an amateur," Hanna said and then hung up.

Cynthia was finally out of the house and happy that everything was going so smoothly. As she approached Butch's apartment building, she noticed a large gathering of people waiting to be enter the building. She could hear music and a loud ruckus emanating from his second floor apartment. When she focused her attention in the direction of the sound, she saw that his place appeared to be packed with partygoers. *Oh, yeah. This is going to be one jammin'-ass party.*

Cynthia entered the vestibule of the building, feeling both nervous and energized. In a strange kind of way, she was glad that Hanna's perpetually late behind hadn't arrived yet because she didn't want Hanna talking down to her. As Cynthia walked up the stairs, the music became louder and guests who were mingling in the hallway stalled her momentarily.

"Excuse me," she said as she eased past two men who were drinking longneck beers.

"Damn, baby," said one of the men. "I'm the man you're looking for." The attention he gave Cynthia made her turn and smile at him. She teased him with her eyes for just a moment so that he understood how much she appreciated him noticing her efforts to look spectacular.

Cynthia made her way toward the living room, which was where the music was emanating from. The female rap group Salt-N-Pepa were bellowing out the lyrics to a song called "Push It." It was entirely too crowded for Cynthia to distinguish anything but a mass of people moving to the rhythm of the music. She backed away from the crowd of dancers and headed for the back porch to get some air. Butch's apartment had gotten stuffy from all the people and gyrating.

"It's funky up in here," Cynthia said aloud as she continued to maneuver her way toward the back porch.

Just as she was about to step out onto the porch, she felt someone tug her arm.

"Leaving so soon?"

Cynthia smiled because she recognized Butch's voice right away. She turned and locked gazes with him.

"No," she answered, feeling a funny nervous sensation in the pit of her belly.

"Wow. You look fantastic tonight."

Cynthia studied him as his eyes recklessly ran all over her body. Cynthia knew that he was undressing her with his eyes but she didn't mind at all. She smiled sexily and spoke to him with her eyes. She wanted to make certain he understood that she wasn't some young girl who had no clue. She wanted him to know that she was ready for whatever the night had in store.

"Would you like something to drink?" Butch asked.

For a moment, Cynthia thought about declining the offer, but she didn't want to seem square as Hanna had suggested. Cynthia had never drunk before. This would be her very first time.

"Yes," she replied, trying to sound confident.

"What do you want? I can pretty much have anything made up for you."

"I'll have whatever you're drinking," she said.

"All right," Butch said, smiling at her. She smiled back again, letting him know that she was attracted to him. She watched him as he walked away to get their drinks. She studied his swagger, his build and his clothing. She was fascinated by everything about him. In fact, she couldn't find a single flaw in him. A short time later, he returned with their drinks.

"Here you go," Butch said as he handed her the drink.

"Wow. There are a lot of people in here. Aren't you afraid of the police coming in to break it up?"

Butch laughed. "That's not going to happen. Do you see that man over there, the one mixing the drinks?"

"Yes. I sort of see him," Cynthia said because she could only see the side of his face. He sort of looked like the man who spoke to her in the hallway, but she wasn't sure.

"That's J.B. He's a cop."

"Really," Cynthia said, surprised.

"I'm Butch Clark, baby. I know everybody and everybody knows me," Butch boasted.

Cynthia took a gulp of her drink. The sting of alcohol surprised her and caught her off guard. "Whoa! He made it a little strong."

"Sip it," Butch suggested. "Don't guzzle it."

"Okay. What's in it, though?" Cynthia asked not caring a thing about how strong the drink was anymore. "Wow," she said as the alcohol opened up her sinuses.

"You took that first gulp real hard," Butch playfully scolded her. "J.B. was probably a little heavy on the rum."

"Yeah, I think he was," Cynthia said as she exhaled away the sting. "I taste something sweet in it."

"Yeah, I believe he put cherry mix in it," Butch said.

"Whoa," Cynthia said as she took another sip of her drink.

"Are you okay?" Butch asked.

"I'm cool, I can handle it." Cynthia quickly answered. Her biggest fear was that Butch would see her as a young high school girl instead of a woman.

"I noticed," Butch said.

Cynthia took a few more sips of her drink and a short time later she found herself laughing and feeling giddier than she'd ever felt before. It seemed as if everything that Butch said was either laugh-out-loud funny or sexy in one way or another. Her senses were also buzzing, and she was aching to kiss Butch's sweet brown lips.

"Butch," Cynthia said to him as she pressed her back against a wall in his kitchen. She pulled him in close to her and whispered, "What do you think of me?" She looked him directly in the eye, as if his answer would determine the fate of her life.

"Man, I look at you and think to myself, 'What a beautiful woman.' You're funny, too. In a sexy sort way. I like your smile and your sexy eyes."

"Do you really think that my eyes are sexy?" she asked just so that she could hear him repeat the words.

"Yes. I think you have sexiest eyes I've ever seen," Butch answered, and Cynthia felt herself melt on the inside.

"I'm standing here thinking to myself that there is no way you're so young."

"Is my age a problem for you?" Cynthia really didn't want to know the answer. She was only trying to reassure him that she was much more mature than her years.

"It's a mind-over-matter thing I suppose," Butch replied, and she could sense that he was hesitant.

"Look, baby," Cynthia cooed as she pulled him even closer to her, wanting to feel his body against hers. "I don't mind my age, so why should it matter?"

There was a long pause, and Cynthia was aching all

over. She wanted him. She wanted him to make her feel like a woman. She lowered her eyelids, licked her lips, sending him a clear message that it was time for him to kiss her.

When Butch's lips touched hers, her knees buckled. She was mesmerized by the fact that she was with a man and not some young boy from school. And not just any man—she was with Butch Clark.

At that moment, Cynthia didn't hear the loud music or the buzz of multiple conversations. She could only taste and smell the sweet scent of their kiss. She wanted the moment to last longer, so she placed her arms on his shoulders and kissed him again.

She felt his pride for the first time through their clothing. His pride was stiff, and she wanted to free it from its prison of clothing, as well as touch it and make it like her. She felt his hands glide down to her arms and to her waist. His hips ground against hers, allowing her to feel his solidness more easily. His hands found their way below her hips and to her ass. Cynthia didn't know that her ass could be such an erogenous zone. When he cupped and squeezed it, she exhaled and broke away from the kiss.

"Wooo, you are doing things to me," Cynthia admitted.

"Damn, Cynthia, you have me on the edge," Butch said.

"You have me on the edge, too," Cynthia replied. "What are we going to do about that?"

"Let's take this party on up to my bedroom," Butch

said as he pulled her along by the hand. When they entered his bedroom, the only thing on her mind was finally getting an opportunity to make out with a guy and not have to worry about his mama coming home.

"I have a lock for the door so no one from the party can barge in on us," Butch said as Cynthia sat down at the foot of the bed. Cynthia bounced up and down a few times on the bed to see if it made squeaking noises. To her delight, it didn't.

"Damn, you look so pretty," Butch complimented her again. He made sure that the door was locked and then dimmed the lights. Cynthia felt her body tingling all over as she watched Butch take off his clothes. He began with his shirt and once it was off, all she wanted to do was place kisses all over his smooth chocolate skin.

"Wait a minute," Cynthia said as she stood up and approached him. "Take off your shoes and I'll remove the rest."

"I like a woman who knows what she wants," Butch said.

"Well, I'm all woman," Cynthia said.

"I can see that. You're certainly more mature than I'd anticipated."

"That's not a bad thing, is it?" Cynthia asked nervously.

"Hell no, baby. It's a real good thing."

"I want you to know that I just don't go around doing this kind of thing," Cynthia said, suddenly fearing he'd gotten the wrong impression of her.

"That thought never even crossed my mind."

Butch smiled and Cynthia once again felt her body ache for him. She unbuckled his pants, squatted down so that her face was in front of his pride and pulled down his slacks.

"Damn, your dick is as big as my head," Cynthia said with a sense of uncertainty and excitement. This was it; she was about to see a live man naked for the very first time. She'd seen photos of naked men before and once when she was at a movie theater, some young boys decided to flash the audience as a practical joke, but this would truly be her very first time.

She placed nervous kisses on his belly and ran her tongue around the rim of his belly button. She squeezed his pride through his underwear and became turned on by the coos of encouragement that escaped his lips. She finally removed his underwear and saw it. It was a beautiful shade of caramel-brown and very thick. Thicker than she'd imagined one would be. He was circumcised, and the head of his manhood was moist at the tip.

"What are you going to do? Just look at it?" Butch asked. Cynthia couldn't tell if he was being humorous or if it was a sign of frustration. At that moment, Cynthia realized that perhaps she'd taken on more than she'd bargained for. She suddenly realized that she had no idea of how to please a man. She'd viewed an adult film once when she was thirteen, but she hadn't watched it to learn techniques, she had just been curious about sex. She'd also had sex education in school, but that just made her laugh as the teacher talked about it. She didn't know the proper way to touch his penis, caress it, suck it or anything. At the moment, she was only fascinated by its appearance and she doubted that her body could take in something so large. She reached up to touch it, but her nerves were on edge and her hand trembled.

"You're nervous aren't you?" Butch said and Cynthia hated that he noticed.

"It's just the alcohol," Cynthia lied as she tugged on his pride as if she were trying to tear it off of his body.

"Whoa." Butch flinched.

"I'm sorry," Cynthia quickly apologized. She feared that she'd ruined the moment and that Butch would give up on her.

"This is your first time isn't it?" he asked. Cynthia's silence served as her answer. She couldn't bring herself to lie by saying no.

"Wow," Butch said as he moved away from her.

"Can you teach me?" Cynthia pleaded with him. "I may not be like other girls you've known, but I learn really quickly." She didn't want it to end, and she wasn't ready for him to be done with her.

"Yeah, I can teach you." Butch smiled. Cynthia tried to decode the meaning of his awkward grin but gave up when he began unbuttoning her blouse.

"You're so young and so ready," Butch said as he removed her blouse and bra. Her breasts were now exposed and begging to be touched. He guided her to the bed and she lay down on her back. Butch removed her skirt, panty hose and underwear.

"Damn, you're so young and ready," Butch repeated.

"Yes, I am," she admitted.

"Look at how hard you have me," Butch said. Cynthia took another look at his pride and saw that it appeared to be even more erect than before. At that moment, she tensed because she couldn't imagine how he was going to get all of him inside her.

"Scoot up on the bed," Butch said. She followed his direction but was suddenly giving everything more thought.

It's okay, girl. You can do this.

Cynthia closed her eyes. She thought for sure that Butch would want to kiss her womanhood. She'd heard about how good that felt and thought that if he did, she'd be a bit more relaxed.

However, Butch didn't even consider stimulating her more. He removed a condom from a small table drawer next to the bed and put it on. Once the condom was in place, Butch attempted to insert himself into her. It felt nothing like she thought it would.

"Damn, you're so tight," he said as he tried to force more of himself inside her. She felt an uncomfortable amount of pressure between her legs and then pain.

"That hurts. Am I doing something wrong?" Cynthia asked, a bit embarrassed by the difficulty they were having.

"Open your legs more," he whispered. She did as he asked but she found that she was tensing up from being uncomfortable. This wasn't going the way she'd hoped it would. She wanted him to stop, but out of fear of being disliked she didn't say a word.

Something has to be wrong with me because this doesn't feel good at all.

Butch finally got the rhythm he was searching for.

"You like it, don't you?" Butch whispered in her ear.

"Yes," Cynthia lied. She'd never experienced pain like this before.

"Come on, give it to me," Butch said. "Move your hips. Give it to me."

Cynthia rotated her hips one time and the next thing she knew, Butch grunted, howled and then collapsed on top of her. Cynthia had to shift her weight a bit because she felt as if she were being crushed. Once she adjusted and got comfortable again she thought, *Was that it?*

Cynthia was startled out of her daydream by the scent of her food burning.

"Shit," she hissed as she quickly left her bedroom and rushed into the kitchen to salvage the special dinner she was preparing for Butch.

CHAPTER 4

Cynthia heard the sound of the front door opening and was thankful that she was able to salvage the special dinner she'd prepared for Butch. She called out his name as she walked toward the front door.

"Butch, is that you?"

"Yeah," he answered as he closed the front door behind him. Butch was wearing his white dress shirt with his company's logo embroidered on the pocket. He also had on navy-blue work pants, which had ground-in dirt stains on the thighs.

"How did your pants get so dirty?" Cynthia asked as she silently thought about how she was going to get them clean again.

"I was in the work area with the guys. I must have leaned up against something and didn't realize it."

"Well go and take them off. I've placed your robe, pajamas and house slippers on the bed so that you can change into them. But before you do that, go wash your hands so that we can eat dinner."

"Dinner?" Butch said, as if he were surprised.

"Yes, baby. I made a surprise birthday dinner for you. Plus, we have the apartment all to ourselves. My mother is watching Anthony for me tonight."

"You can just leave my dinner on the stove because I'm not staying. I'm going out," Butch said as he walked past her toward the bedroom.

"What do you mean you're going out? Butch, I know you heard me. Don't ignore me. You know how much I hate it when you do that," Cynthia said as she pursued Butch into the bedroom.

"I'm going out tonight for some fun," Butch said as he undressed.

"What about me and the food and the special evening I'd planned for us?"

"Cent, I'd be right here in the house tonight having a party if you hadn't ran everyone off. You do remember doing that, don't you?"

"Butch, those people were destroying what little furniture that we had. It was ridiculous the amount of broken items that I'd find after one of your parties."

"Regardless, I'm going out tonight to celebrate my birthday." Butch pulled down an old shoebox from the top shelf in the closet.

"Fine," Cynthia huffed. She wanted to be with him, so she began to think about what she was going to wear. "I can put the food up and find something to put on real quick."

"You're not coming with me to this party."

"Excuse me?" Cynthia had an ugly expression on her face.

"Don't give me that look, Cynthia." Butch's tone of voice had suddenly changed. He began speaking to her as if she were beneath him. "I don't need you around me tonight."

"You don't need me around you?" Cynthia repeated the words to make sure she'd heard him correctly. "What's that supposed to mean?"

"It means that I don't want to spend tonight with you. I want to do something without you. What part of that don't you understand?"

Butch opened the old shoebox, moved a few items around but didn't find what he'd been searching for. "What the hell happened to the money I put in here?"

He frowned, then glared at Cynthia with murderous eyes.

"I took the extra money you had in there to do a little something special for you tonight, but I guess you don't care about my efforts," she said.

"Goddammit, Cynthia! I had plans for that money," Butch barked at her in a way she'd never heard before. He suddenly seemed agitated to the point that he wanted to harm her. Cynthia stood her ground and defended her actions.

"Butch, there wasn't that much money in there. Besides, I used most of it to buy Anthony some new clothes. He is growing, you know," Cynthia said. Butch often behaved as if Anthony didn't exist. "I used the remainder of the money to buy food in order to cook your favorite meal."

Even though her argument was rock-solid, Butch continued his tirade.

"Did you ever stop and think that I might have hid the money there to do something special for myself, huh? And why in hell are you going through my things?" Butch shouted at her.

"Don't yell at me, Butch!" Cynthia warned him. She hated it when he raised his voice to her because she felt belittled by it.

"Cent, some times you do the dumbest damn things." Butch literally shoved her out of his way and stormed out of the room.

"Who are you calling dumb?" Cynthia said, trailing behind him.

"I only see one other person in here," Butch said as he headed toward the door. His mean-spirited words went straight to her heart and bruised her feelings.

"Where are going? You haven't even bathed or changed your clothes," Cynthia was shouting at him. Butch stopped at the front door, then turned to face her.

"My life was filled with fun before I met you. Now it's not. I'm getting the hell away from you," Butch said as he opened door.

"Why?" Cynthia felt her tears welling up. "Why are you acting like this, Butch? What did I do?" Butch didn't answer her. He flung open the door and began walking down the stairs. Cynthia entered the hallway and watched him as he descended the stairs.

"Butch!" she called, but he didn't acknowledge her.

"I'm sorry," she said but he continued on his way. Cynthia went back inside the apartment and shut the door. Her feelings were battered and her mind was racing. She sat down on the sofa, placed her face in her hands and tried not to cry.

After a while, Cynthia's mind began playing tricks on her by suggesting that perhaps there was another woman involved.

Maybe that's what my brother Victor meant when he said to watch my back.

"But Butch and I made a vow to love each other," Cynthia said aloud. "This can't be happening. I can't let this happen. I'm not going to allow some other woman to steal my husband away from me."

Cynthia got angry. "I'll bet he's met some woman down at the job and she's got him all confused." She was talking to herself again. "No, Butch. We have a vow and you're not going to turn me into a single mom. No, sir. When you come back in here from wherever your ass is at, we're going to confront this head-on."

After Cynthia had decided what her next course of action would be, she was eager for Butch to return home so that they could resolve the argument and fix their marriage so that the other woman would leave them alone.

By nine o'clock that evening, Butch still hadn't returned. Cynthia became nervous and decided to phone a few of his friends to see if they knew his whereabouts.

"No, I haven't seen Butch all week," said Keith, who was a good friend of his.

"Is everything okay? You don't sound too good."

"Yes, I'm fine. Thanks for asking," Cynthia said and then concluded her phone conversation with him.

Cynthia called every friend of Butch's that she could think of and all of them claimed that they hadn't seen him. That made Cynthia believe their problems were due to another woman. She went from being emotionally hurt to being outright furious. A massive headache overcame her, so she decided to lie down. Before she realized it, she'd fallen asleep.

Cynthia was startled awake by the sound of the telephone ringing. She glanced at a digital clock on the nightstand. It was one-thirty in the morning.

"Hello," Cynthia answered.

"Hey, baby, it's me." Butch was sounding much more cordial, and Cynthia was instantly suspicious of his mood swing.

"So, are you still with that bitch you're screwing?"

"Come on, Cent. You know you're the only woman for me."

"Yeah, right." Cynthia felt her anger beginning to balloon all over again.

"Baby, I'm in a jam," Butch said, "and I need your help."

"Oh, now you need my help? What did she do, put your ass out after she realized that you wouldn't put your face between her thighs and eat—"

"I'm in jail, Cent. Can you come and bail me out?"

"Jail!" Cynthia immediately sat up in bed. "What do you mean, you're in jail?" she asked, just to make sure she'd heard him correctly.

"I'm at the police station over on Fifty-First and Wentworth streets. Bring one thousand dollars with you."

"One thousand dollars!" Cynthia began to panic, she didn't have that type of money.

"Baby, make a few phone calls in order to get me out of here. Just do it quickly. I don't want to be in here."

"Butch—"

"Baby, I don't have time to answer questions right now. Just come and get me out of here. They only gave me three minutes to make this call and my time is up."

Before Cynthia could say another word, the phone call was disconnected.

Having to bail Butch out of jail was the last thing she was expecting to have to deal with. Now she had to figure out how she was going to approach her mother about lending her the money.

CHAPTER 5

Cynthia drummed her knuckles hard and fast against Elaine's wooden front door. She was wound up, and her nerves were on edge. She waited a moment, but no one answered the door.

"Damn it! Now I called her and told that this was an emergency. Why isn't she answering the damn door?" Cynthia hissed. She began to knock hard and fast on the door again.

"Who is it?" a husky voice asked.

"Boy, it's me. Open the door," Cynthia said to Victor. Victor began unlatching the door.

"Damn, girl, you're knocking on the door like you're the damn police," Victor complained as he allowed her to enter the apartment. He was wearing his Chicago Bears T-shirt and matching sweat pants. He looked as if he'd just woken up.

"Well, this is important," Cynthia said. "Sorry that I woke you up. Where's Mom?"

"In bed asleep, where else? You should leave her there

because she and I had a real nasty argument tonight," Victor said.

"Does she know that you've dropped out of the GED program yet?"

"Yeah, she's aware of it now. I'm surprised she didn't call you to vent about how I've disappointed her."

"Whatever. I can't deal with you and your drama right now. I've got my own," Cynthia said and shifted her focus toward her mother's bedroom door.

"Y'all never have time for anyone except for yourselves. Y'all never think about me or what I'm going through."

"Victor, it's not about you right now," Cynthia declared. "I can't believe she fell back asleep!"

Cynthia marched over to her mother's bedroom door, knocked a few times and then entered. The scent of baby powder was wafting through the air, and for a brief moment it soothed her ragged nerves. Elaine was snoring loudly and Cynthia cringed at the fact that she had to wake her from her sleep.

This is life or death, she reasoned. Her husband was in jail and she needed to get him out at any cost.

She flipped on the light and saw that her son Anthony was in the bed with her mother. Elaine was sleeping in an odd position to make sure that Anthony didn't fall out of the bed or that she didn't roll over on him.

"Damn," Cynthia whispered aloud as she paced back and forth for a moment.

"I don't want to wake up Anthony," she mumbled,

then walked over to Elaine, touched her shoulder and shook it gently. "Mom!" she said in a loud whisper. "Wake up."

Cynthia had to repeat herself several times before Elaine stirred in her sleep. Elaine awoke slowly and focused her eyes on Cynthia. It took her a second to realize that Cynthia was staring at her.

Cynthia noticed how red the whites of her eyes were, as well as the swelling around her eyelids. These were indicators that she'd had an intense shouting match with Victor about dropping out of the GED program.

"He's doing fine. You ready to take him home now?" Elaine asked. "You could've waited until the morning instead of coming over here to get him this late at night. It's cold outside and he might catch a cold in this chilly air."

Elaine paused and then began discussing Victor. "Did you know that boy hasn't been going to the GED classes? He dropped out. I damn near broke my foot off in his—"

"Mom, I didn't come to pick up Anthony or to talk about Victor and his madness. I called you earlier. Don't you remember?"

Elaine yawned for a long moment. "No. You must have been talking to me in my sleep. I was so tired after fighting with your brother. I don't remember you calling."

"I have an emergency," Cynthia said. For a brief moment, she thought about not bringing her drama into her mother's world, but she didn't have a choice. "Butch is in jail and I need to borrow one thousand dollars to get him out."

"What?" Elaine's voice went from soft and dreamy to harsh and loud enough to wake the dead. "What the hell is he doing in jail?"

"I don't know. He called me and asked me to come and bail him out."

"Wait a minute." Elaine sat up in bed, slipped her feet into her brown house slippers and then left the room. "Come on in here. I don't want to wake the baby up."

Cynthia followed Elaine into the dining room and took a seat at the table.

"Now what's going on, Cent?" Elaine asked.

"I don't know." Cynthia paused as she organized her thoughts. "I did everything right. I cleaned the house, I cooked dinner for him and was planning to spend the evening with him. When he came home, he was moody and didn't want to be with me. He said that he wanted to go to a party. I was upset that my plans for a quiet evening weren't what he had in mind, but I decided to go with the flow. I told him that I'd go to a party with him but he didn't want me around him. Well, one thing led to another and we got into a fight about that and some money that he'd saved up, which I took to buy food and some new clothes for Anthony."

"Why was he upset about you taking money to do something for him and his son? That doesn't make any sense," Elaine said as she scratched her head vigorously with her fingertips. "Sounds like he's got someone on the side, if you ask me." Cynthia could tell by the expression on her face and the tone of her voice that Elaine was already convinced that Butch had another woman.

"Mom, I don't have all of the facts yet," Cynthia said, not wanting to get into a debate with her mother.

"You should've never married him. I knew from jump street that he didn't have any intentions of doing right by you."

Cynthia felt her blood pressure rising because she couldn't cut off Elaine or change her low opinion of her husband.

"Low-down bastard." Elaine was about to head into all-out criticism about Butch and his alleged affair.

"I just need to get my man out of jail. Can you help me?" Cynthia asked, trying as hard as she could to not raise her voice or get into a shouting match with her mother. She needed her and any extra money she had.

"Why should I?" Elaine wasn't about to budge. "I work too damn hard for my money to use it to bail a son-in-law that I don't like out of jail."

"Okay. I know that you don't like him, Elaine," Cynthia said angrily. "Do it for Anthony. Do it for your grandson."

"I do a lot for Anthony already. Hell, from what I can tell, I think I do more for his son than he does. Now what kind of man is he if he doesn't like taking care of his children?"

"Mom, Butch does what he can. Our money is just real tight and we can't spend a lot of money on expensive items. Besides, we're saving up so that he can get his business off the ground. Once that happens and he starts making more money, things will be much different."

"Cynthia, you need to wake up. That man has no intention of starting up a business. Besides, you need money or collateral to start a business, and you and Butch don't have either."

"Mom, we're going to get a loan from the bank, okay? Butch knows what he's doing."

"Tell me. How is he going to get a loan from the bank when he doesn't even have a checking account and believes that banks play with his money too much?"

Cynthia was about to argue the point but stopped herself. Elaine had just struck a raw nerve, and for the first time Cynthia really began to pick her words carefully.

"Look, we're getting off of the subject here. Butch and I need to work some things out, granted. I'll give you that one. But right now is not the time to deal with that issue. He needs my help."

"What about his friends? Can you borrow the money from them?"

Cynthia exhaled deeply and hung her head for a moment. She realized that Elaine wasn't about to allow herself to get as worked up over Butch as she was.

"I called a few of his friends. None of them could help out," Cynthia confessed.

"Wait. After all of the parties and good times he's sponsored, you mean to tell me that not a single one of his friends can come up with any kind of cash to help bail him out?"

"Yes, that's correct," Cynthia answered. Her emotions

were yo-yoing between anxiety and frustration "Not a single one of his freeloading friends thinks enough of him to help him out in this time of crisis."

"That should tell you something," Elaine said as she stood up and went into the kitchen. Cynthia sat at the dining room table, unable to think of another way to raise the money.

"Mom!" Cynthia called out. "I really need the money. If Butch stays in jail too long, he might lose his job. If he loses his job, we'll be evicted. You've got to help me."

"I don't have to do a damn thing except stay black, pay taxes and die. He'll probably get out in a few days. Call his job for him and tell them that he's sick."

"Why are you doing this to me?"

"Doing what to you? I haven't done a damn thing to you. You're the one in my house in the early morning hours asking me for a large sum of money to get a man out of jail that I don't even like. Shit, if I didn't get your father out when he got in trouble, what makes you think I'm going to put my hard-earned money down on Butch. Boy, you and Victor, both of you are pushing me into my grave. And you know that I've got a bad heart and can't deal with stress like this."

There it was—the guilt trip Cynthia didn't want to deal with. Cynthia had tried her best to place guilt on her mother's shoulders, but she was not nearly as good at it as Elaine was.

"I expect madness from Victor but not you, Cynthia. You're supposed to be better than this. You're not supposed to be in a situation like this, baby. See, had you went on and finished school, you'd be doing so much more for yourself."

Elaine came back into the dining room chewing on a chocolate doughnut she'd picked up in the kitchen.

"You should let him sit in jail and think about the mess he's gotten himself into and what he's putting you through. They can't hold him more than forty-eight hours without him seeing a judge."

"I can't do that, Mom."

Cynthia wanted to criticize Elaine by pointing out that if she'd stuck by her father in his time of need, they might still be together. But Cynthia didn't have the nerve to go there with her mother.

"Fine. I'll figure out another way to get the money."

"How?" Elaine asked, chewing her doughnut.

"I don't know. Maybe I'll sell some ass out on the street corner," Cynthia said as she stood up to leave. Elaine chuckled—it was not the reaction Cynthia had been hoping for.

"What's so funny?" Cynthia asked.

"You wouldn't last two seconds as a prostitute."

"What do you mean? I've got good looks. Men would want me."

"Baby, it's not that men wouldn't want you. You've got the looks, there is no denying that. But the other prostitutes would kick your ass for coming around taking money out of their pocket."

Cynthia was shocked and hurt that Elaine didn't seem

to think that her situation carried any legitimacy. She felt tears welling up and she had to fight to keep them from spilling over.

When Elaine got in a mood such as this, she could be insensitive. Cynthia didn't understand why every time Elaine got upset, she felt obligated to make her mother feel better, but when it came to Cynthia's feelings, Elaine had the option of either caring or not giving a damn.

Cynthia went into her mother's bedroom to gather up Anthony's belongings so that they could go home. As she was packing his bag, Victor came up behind her and rested his shoulder against the door frame.

"I hear you need some money," Victor said.

"Yeah, but that's okay. I'll find a way to get it," Cynthia said, trying to sound confident.

"I'll give you the money to get him out. But you're going to owe me." Victor paused. "You're going to owe me big-time."

"Are you serious? Do you have the money?" Cynthia asked, only caring about getting Butch released.

"Yeah, I got it. But you're going to have to pay every dime of it back."

Cynthia stopped stuffing Anthony's belongings into a bag and approached her brother. "I promise you that Butch and I will return every dime of your money."

Victor paused for a moment, then spoke. "Do you know why he's locked up?"

"No. I just want to get him out."

Victor exhaled and frowned. "How do I know his ass isn't going to jump bail?"

"Because I said so. I'll make sure that he appears in court on the date and time that the judge assigns. Once we go to court, they'll return the bail money and I'll make sure you get every dime of it back."

Victor didn't say anything, he just glared off into space.

"Look, Victor. I told you I'd make sure he'd go to court and you'd get your money back. What do you want me to do? Beg you for it? Is that what you want? Do you want to see me beg you for the money to get Butch out of jail?"

Victor was still silent.

"Please, Victor."

Cynthia swallowed her pride and begged her brother for the money.

CHAPTER 6

By the time Cynthia arrived at the police station, her nerves felt as if they'd gone through a paper shredder. She was so disoriented that she had difficulty processing the instructions that the desk sergeant had given her in order to bail Butch out. She felt as if she'd suddenly lost her hearing and had to rely solely on her limited ability to read lips.

The only thing that Cynthia fully understood was that she had to get him out of there. Butch was her life, and she lived and breathed for him. She honestly had no idea of what she'd do without him.

She finally comprehended the instructions she had been given and went to another side of the police station to wait her turn in line with others there to bail loved ones out of jail. When she was finally asked to come forward, she explained who the bail money was for and asked what Butch had been taken into custody for.

"Hang on. I'll have the arresting officer speak to you," said the officer behind the counter. Cynthia found a seat and waited.

A few moments later, a female officer approached her. "Are you here for Mr. Butch Clark?"

"Yes," Cynthia answered, barely getting the word out of her mouth.

The woman officer sat down next to her. "I'm Officer Lisa Granger."

"Why—I mean, what was he taken into custody for?" Cynthia's eyes kept blinking and she couldn't stop her leg from bouncing up and down like a jackhammer.

"Are you okay?" Officer Granger asked.

"This is all new to me," Cynthia explained. "I've never been in a police station before or had to deal with something like this."

"And who is Mr. Clark to you?" Officer Granger asked.

"My husband," Cynthia answered.

"Oh, I see."

"Look, Officer Granger I just—I don't know what to think."

"Your husband was arrested for purchasing drugs from me. I'm a narcotics agent who was working undercover."

"No, that's impossible. My husband doesn't do drugs. I mean, he drinks but he doesn't do the hard drugs."

"Drug abusers are very good at hiding their habit," Officer Granger explained. "How long have you been married?"

"Two years."

"Children?" she asked.

"Yes. A son," Cynthia answered as she searched her mind for clues that she should have recognized.

"I'm sorry you had to find out this way," Officer Granger said as she stood up.

"I don't understand," Cynthia continued. "He was just going out to celebrate his birthday with a few of his guy friends. Did they put him up to doing this? Maybe he was getting it for one of his friends."

"He was with another woman when he tried to purchase the heroin," Officer Granger said.

Cynthia felt as if she'd been kicked in the head by a mule. "Who was he with? What's her name?"

"I don't know," Officer Granger answered. "I'm sorry you had to find out this way. You seem like a reasonable woman. I hope everything works out. I'm no expert but if you feel your marriage is salvageable, your husband should seek help for his addiction."

Officer Granger didn't have anything to add, so she left Cynthia to contemplate what to do next.

When Butch finally emerged from the detaining area, Cynthia saw him as a completely different man. It was as if someone else was inside of his body.

"Come on, let's get out of here," Butch said as he grabbed her arm just above the elbow and escorted her out.

"I had to take the bus over here," Cynthia said. "Where is the car?"

"It's been impounded," Butch answered angrily. They exited the police station and walked across the street to a bus stop just in time to catch the next bus. Once they sat down, Cynthia began asking questions.

"What happened?"

"We'll talk about it when we get home," Butch said bitterly.

"Did they give you a court date?"

"Didn't I tell you that we'd talk about this once we got home! Isn't that what I just said?" Butch shouted, making Cynthia all the more uneasy. She wanted to snap back at him for his ungratefulness, but she didn't. Her feelings were so torn that she started to cry. She controlled her emotions as best as she could, but other passengers noticed how upset she was. Butch didn't attempt to comfort or reassure her, he only told her to stop.

"You're embarrassing me with all of that sniffling. Get yourself together," he whispered. Cynthia didn't say another word during the remainder of the ride home.

Once they entered the apartment, Butch went straight to the bedroom without saying a word. Cynthia, who now had better command of her emotions, followed him because she wanted answers to her questions.

"So what happened tonight, Butch? What's this all about?"

Butch was searching the dresser drawer for something but he stopped briefly, glared at her and said, "You wouldn't understand."

His words kicked her in the stomach.

"Butch, I'm your wife. I need to know and understand what's going on."

"Okay, little girl. What do you want to know?"

"Little girl?" Cynthia was offended. She paused for a moment and collected herself. "Butch, are you a drug abuser?"

"Who isn't?" Butch responded. Cynthia felt the air rush out of her lungs. She felt weak-kneed but managed to stay standing.

"How long have you been doing this?"

"Long before you came along." Butch's answer was cold and heartless.

"What about our plans? What about starting a business?"

"What about them?" Butch asked as he moved to search the closet.

"Were they just lies?" Cynthia asked.

"No. I really did want to do that some day. But not right now."

"What do you mean 'some day'?" Cynthia wanted clarification. All of this information was new to her and she felt as if she were meeting Butch for the first time.

"Look, girl, get off of my back. I don't feel like answering a bunch of damn questions right now," Butch said as he began searching beneath the bed.

"No. You're going to answer my damn questions!" Cynthia shouted at him but her raising her voice meant very little to him. He had no fear of her.

"Cynthia, sit down and shut up before I hurt you." The look in Butch's eyes was murderous but Cynthia didn't care. She wanted answers.

"No!" she barked. Butch stood up and faced her. Cynthia looked at him with judgmental eyes.

"Who was the bitch you were with when you bought the drugs?"

"I was with a woman who understood my needs."

"Understood your needs? Butch, you're not making any sense. What needs? We are a happily married couple. We made plans to build a better life together. How could you bring another woman into our life?"

"Listen!" Butch approached her and grabbed the fabric of her shirt just below her chin. "You made plans. I didn't. I only said that one day I'd like to open up a shop. I never really planned the shit out. It was just a dream, if you want to know the truth. I thought with you being younger, you'd be trainable and learn how to follow my lead. But you're not. You just run off at the damn mouth all the time."

"Butch, you're hurting me." Cynthia began crying. His words were driving swords through her heart.

"No. You need to listen to this."

"I'll leave you alone, Butch," Cynthia said through her tears. "But you need to get some help, baby. You're not in your right mind. Let me help you. We can make it through this together."

"What! Get help? I'm not ready to be done using drugs yet." There was pure madness in Butch's eyes, a type of madness she'd only read about or seen on television. She suddenly feared for her safety.

"Let me go," she said as she tried to break free of his clutch.

"No," Butch answered defiantly.

"Let me go, Butch!" Cynthia began to struggle harder, but Butch had her tightly in his grasp.

"Help!" Cynthia yelled out, hoping that someone would hear her.

"Shut up!" Butch snarled at her

"Help!" she shouted out again but he punched her in the mouth to silence her. Cynthia fought him and scratched up his face to get free. During the struggle, her shirt was ripped from her body and she ended up falling to the floor.

"Leave, Butch! Go back to that bitch you were going to get high with!" Cynthia screamed through her tears.

Butch's chest was heaving. "You found my stash didn't you? That's why I can't find it, isn't that right?"

"What are you talking about? Just leave."

Cynthia tried to get to her feet but he rushed over to her and placed his body on her to keep her down on the floor.

"My drugs, Cent. You tossed away my drugs, didn't you?"

"Butch, I swear to you I don't know what you're talking about."

"Yes, you do. You think I'm dumb. You think that I don't know what you've done."

"Let me up, Butch," Cynthia pleaded. "I'll leave."

"Where is my stuff, damn it?"

"I don't know, Butch. I didn't even know you had drugs in the house." Cynthia couldn't stop crying. "Please just let me up so that I can leave. I'll go stay with my mother and Anthony."

At that moment she saw something else in his eyes. She saw a crazed man.

"You look sexy begging me," Butch said as he continued to restrain her.

"What? Butch. Let me go." Cynthia struggled to get free again but she was outmatched by his strength.

"Please. Just let me go."

"No." Butch was now breathing heavily. "I want some."

"No!"

"Well then, I'm going to take it," Butch said. Cynthia was horrified that Butch, the man she'd loved, had turned into an evil monster ready to rape her. She held her legs closed as tightly as she could to prevent him from getting what he wanted.

"Didn't I tell you that I wanted some!" Butch slapped her face repeatedly until she gave in.

When Butch had finished, she was too afraid to push him off of her for fear of being hit again. After a long while, Butch finally got up. He continued to search the closet and finally found what he was looking for. He then went into the bathroom and locked himself inside.

"You're not even going to fucking apologize?" Cynthia asked, but he didn't answer her.

Cynthia finally found the will and courage to move. She grabbed what she could, and shoved it into a duffel bag. She put on some fresh clothes and rushed out of the apartment. By the time she made it back to Elaine's apartment, it was seven-thirty in the morning. She drummed on Elaine's front door as hard as she could.

"I'm coming," Cynthia heard her mother yell. She could tell by the pitch of Elaine's voice that she wasn't happy about her sleep being broken up twice in such a short period of time. When Elaine opened the door, she gasped in horror.

"Oh my God!" Elaine shouted. "Victor, call an ambulance."

Elaine quickly pulled Cynthia inside and escorted her into the bedroom, where they sat down side by side. Elaine draped her arm around Cynthia's shoulder and pulled her close to her.

"Baby, who did this to you?" Elaine asked, even though she already knew the answer.

"I just want to sleep," Cynthia said as she gently laid herself on the bed, then curled up and shut her eyes.

"Victor!" was the last thing Cynthia remembered hearing Elaine shout.

CHAPTER 7

When Cynthia awoke two paramedics were towering above her, putting on latex gloves. The sight of the two medical professionals startled Cynthia.

"What's going on?" Cynthia was about to sit up in bed.

"No. You need to lie down and let them look at you," Elaine said forcefully.

"I'm okay," Cynthia said. "All of this isn't necessary." Cynthia felt embarrassed by all of the attention she was getting.

"No, baby. You need some medical attention. Do you know what you look like?"

"No," Cynthia admitted. As she held Elaine's gaze, she saw that her mother had been crying. Her eyes were puffy, glassy and red.

"What happened?" asked one of the paramedics. Cynthia looked at the young man, but couldn't form a coherent sentence. She just couldn't explain all that had happened. After a long moment, she tried to speak but only ended up sobbing.

"I think her husband did this to her," Elaine said softly.

"I understand," said the paramedic and began tending her injuries. Once they were finished, they began packing up.

"She doesn't need to go to the hospital unless she wants to."

"No hospital," Cynthia said, finally able to speak.

"The police should be contacted so that a report of the abuse can be on record. You don't want this to happen again. At a minimum, you should at least have a judge issue a restraining order."

"No. This wasn't abuse. It was just a bad argument." Cynthia wanted to soften the severity of her situation. The last thing she wanted was to be viewed as a battered woman.

"I'm going to leave you with some information about domestic violence. This is a place where you can find help when you're ready."

Elaine took the pamphlet for Cynthia and thanked the paramedics.

"She should also see her regular doctor, too," said the second paramedic as he walked out the bedroom door. Once they were gone, Cynthia laid back down, shut her eyes and went back to sleep.

Cynthia rested all day and night. When she awoke the following morning, she wanted to believe that what happened to her had never occurred. Her face was still tender from where Butch had punched her. The very thought of what he'd done caused her to cry. She curled up in the bed and tried to think about what she'd do next.

But she couldn't focus or develop any type of plan; she was still in shock from the horrible experience.

After lying awake in bed for more than an hour, Cynthia finally found the courage to get up and face the day. She located the overnight bag she'd arrived with then left her mother's bedroom. Taking small, hesitant steps, she walked down the narrow corridor, entered the bathroom and bolted the door behind her. She flipped on the light switch, moved over to the basin in front of the medicine cabinet mirror and placed her palms face down on it.

Cynthia hung her head and took a few deep breaths before she examined the damage Butch had inflicted upon her. Once she was ready, she craned her neck upward, opened her eyes and was horrified by the reflection staring back at her. The right side of her face had turned black from bruising. Her lip was swollen and her right eye was puffy almost to the point that it appeared to be permanently shut. She wanted to cry again but she held back her tears. Her nose began to run, and she quickly wiped it.

"Damn bastard!" Cynthia cursed him for what he'd done. Her emotions were shifting between self-pity and anger. She turned on the shower, undressed and then stepped inside the tub. She washed her body frantically, wanting to remove his scent. She scrubbed her skin so hard that she swore she'd taken off a few thin layers of it. When she'd finished, she stepped out and removed some clean clothes from her bag and put them on. She looked at her reflection once again and was filled with sadness.

"Damn, I wish that I had some makeup or something to cover my face up."

At that moment, there was a soft knock on the bathroom door.

"Cent." It was Elaine. "Are you okay in there?"

Cynthia exhaled as she thought about what "okay" really meant. If the question meant was she alive, the answer was yes. If it meant how she was doing mentally, the answer would be no, she wasn't okay.

"Cent?" Elaine called to her again. "Answer me."

Cynthia swallowed hard. "I'm fine. I'll be out in a moment."

"Okay. Do you want something to eat? I just went grocery shopping and have plenty of food." Cynthia knew that Elaine wanted to make her feel better by offering to cook a meal.

"I'm not hungry right now."

"You've got to eat something."

"Then I'll snack on something when I come out," Cynthia said softly. She just wanted to be left alone for a little while longer.

"Well, how long are you going to be in there?"

"Mom, just give me a moment, okay?"

"Okay. I'll be out here waiting for you."

"Augh!" Cynthia exhaled.

I really don't feel like talking about it, Mom.

The last thing she wanted to deal with right now was

her mother's harsh brand of reality. Cynthia sat down on the edge of the bathtub and placed her swollen face in the palms of her hands. She tried to think, but she just couldn't. Her mind was numb.

Cynthia was at a crossroads. She could break down and lose what little of her wits she had left, or she could somehow find the courage to deal with this and stay with Butch, or she could start over on her own.

At that moment, she heard Anthony begin to cry. She looked up and glared at the bathroom door. He was crying so loudly and although she knew that he was probably just feeling cranky, she felt compelled to get up and see to him.

After calming Anthony's howls, Cynthia picked him up and joined Elaine at the kitchen table.

"I'm not going to be a burden to you. You have your hands full dealing with Victor. You don't need me adding any more drama to your life than I already have. I'll go back home eventually," Cynthia said as she slumped her head down.

"Hold your head up," Elaine ordered. "You're safe here with me. Don't ever think that you don't have a choice in a situation like this. As long as I'm around, you'll always have a place to stay. Now, I don't like getting involved in your marriage but if you want me to, I'll call up Uncle Jo Jo and my other two brothers and they'll make Butch understand why he shouldn't be hitting on you."

"God no. Let's not drag them into this."

"Are you sure? This wouldn't be the first time they've had to handle something like this."

"What do you mean?" Cynthia was suddenly interested in what her mother was trying to hide.

Elaine paused to choose the right words. "Your father and I were going through problems, and he thought that he had the right to use me as his punching bag."

Cynthia caught her mother's gaze.

"Yes, it's true," Elaine said, seeing Cynthia's perplexed expression. "That's why we didn't last. Oh, I stayed there and tried to cope. I tried to cover up the abuse with makeup, or if that didn't work I made up stories about what had happened to me just so that people wouldn't interfere."

Elaine paused again and Cynthia could see that she was sorting through all of the information that she was telling her.

"I became a prisoner in my own home. I lived in fear of him and I didn't know how to escape. He seemed to be everywhere. I felt that there was no place on this earth that I could hide from him."

"Dad never seemed like that type of person to me," Cynthia said.

"Well, he was. And he'll probably never hit another woman, especially after what happened to him when I'd finally had enough."

"What happened? What'd you do?"

"This one particular night he'd come home mad as hell about something. I don't even remember what it was. All

I do remember was that he beat my ass. I mean, he did some damage to me."

"Where was I?" Cynthia asked because she couldn't recall the incident.

"You were no more than two years old at the time and Victor was at your grandmother's this particular night." Elaine paused before continuing. "I can take a lot but after that night I'd had enough of lying to people about the abuse. So I called up my brothers. They all came over in the middle of the night when your father was asleep. When they saw me, they made me take you out of the house. I went and stayed with Uncle Jo Jo that night. I remember it so clearly. I went into Hanna's room and placed you in the bed with her. Anyway, when Uncle Jo Jo came back home, he told me that everything was taken care of. I didn't know exactly what he'd meant so I asked for more details. Uncle Jo Jo looked me square in the eyes and without so much as blinking told me how they woke him up and whipped his ass. After that, your father never even so much as raised his voice to me. I thought things would be better, but in the end I just didn't love him the way that I once had. Our relationship had changed. We eventually went our separate ways, but I never loved another man the same after that."

Cynthia continued to study her mother's eyes. She felt as if she'd grown up a little.

"So, if you want, arrangements can be made to get a clear message to Butch. Hell, if your brother keeps trying my nerves, he's going to get a message, as well, sent special delivery." Elaine chuckled at the thought.

"No," Cynthia said, trying to laugh then stopped because it hurt to do so. "I'll handle this."

"Okay," Elaine said. "I'm going to stay out of it. But know this. If he feels that he can beat on you and get away with it, he's not going to stop." There was a long moment of silence, then Elaine embraced her and Anthony.

Later that morning, Cynthia was relaxing on the sofa in the living room with Anthony who was cooing and buzzing with energy. Cynthia had been spending more time with him as a way to get her mind off the negative situation and to plan her next move. Behind all the cooing noises that Anthony was making, Cynthia heard the phone ringing.

"I got it," she heard Elaine yell out. A moment later, Elaine was standing in front of her with the phone.

"It's for you," she said, handing her the phone.

"Let me take the baby," Elaine said. Cynthia handed Anthony to her. "Remember what I told you," Elaine said and then left the room.

"Hello," Cynthia said.

"Hey, baby." Butch was much calmer now. Cynthia decided to be silent for the moment. "I, um, wanted to call you to say how sorry I am about what happened. You know that's not me, and I just want you to come on home."

"No," Cynthia answered, surprised at how strong she sounded.

"Come on now, Cent. I made a mistake and I'm trying to say that I'm sorry. You know that I need you. Why are you being like this?"

"Why? Butch, are you crazy? Have you lost your damn mind? You kicked my ass and raped me, remember?"

"Don't say that. You know damn well that I didn't rape you."

"Yes, you did!"

"No, I didn't."

"Whatever, Butch."

"Cent, when are you coming home? I'll come and get you."

"You don't have to come and get me. I don't need you to do that."

"Well, when do you plan on coming home?"

"When do you plan on telling me about the other woman you were with?"

"What woman?" Butch's voice rose several octaves.

"You know what, Butch? I don't have time for this," Cynthia said, her anger rising. "I'm not sure that I love you anymore. You're not a man." Cynthia paused. "You're not the man that I thought you were, or the type of man that I thought you'd mature to be."

"I'm my own man. I don't need you to tell me what type of man I need to be," Butch snapped.

"Butch, you don't even know how to please me. Sex with you is horrible. You're so damn selfish," Cynthia said, suddenly feeling the urge to get rid of a lot of emotional baggage. "You treat me as if I don't know anything, sometimes you belittle me and you don't spend enough time with your son."

"I spend plenty of time with Anthony. What are you talking about?"

"No you don't, Butch," Cynthia yelled. "You act as if he doesn't even exist. You treat me like that sometimes, too."

"Look, you need to come home so that we can talk about this in private. I don't like the idea of your mama all up in our business."

"Well, if you were a man who could handle business, I wouldn't be over here with my mother."

"You know what, Cent? Forget it. Just forget it. Don't come back. I don't need you."

"And I don't need you. You need to take your drug-addicted ass somewhere to get some help."

"I'm not addicted! And if you say that to me again, I swear I'll beat your ass again."

"I hate you, Butch!" Cynthia yelled as she slammed down the receiver. She sat in silence for a moment as the reality of her situation sunk in.

"What do you mean, you hate Butch?"

Cynthia was startled by Victor's voice. He must have caught the tail end of her conversation with Butch.

"Stay out of this, Victor," Cynthia warned him. She was so angry that she felt like murdering Butch or anyone who reminded her of him, including her brother.

"No, I'm in this, Cent. I've got my money all up in your business." Victor raised his voice. "I want my money back, Cent."

"I've got bigger concerns than your money right now!" Cynthia snapped.

"I'd better get my money back, Cent, or I'm going to kick your ass!" Victor answered.

"Victor!" Elaine walked into room. "Get your empty-feeling ass out of here! Go on! The girl has been through enough. She doesn't need you making false threats!"

"Mama, that's not right. I gave her one thousand dollars to get that fool out of jail. She promised I'd get it back and I want my damn money."

"Victor, just leave! Leave her alone." Elaine began to tug his arm.

"Can't you see that I've gotten my ass kicked, Victor? Huh? Don't you even care that your baby sister has been beaten up?"

"Cent. I told you that fool had a problem. All I care about is getting my damn money back," Victor said once again. "He's going to show up for court, right?"

Cynthia didn't respond, she glared at him.

"Cent, you promised me that he'd make it to court. I need my money!"

"You'll get your damn money, all right," Elaine said. "Even if I have to give it back to you. I'll make sure you get your money. Now leave." Elaine began to push him out of the room. Satisfied with the answer he'd gotten, Victor turned and left.

"Damn, that boy is so insensitive," Elaine complained as she sat down next to Cynthia. "He shouldn't have said all of that to you. That was wrong."

"I don't know what to do," Cynthia whispered. "I don't want to cry because I'm too angry, but then again I want to cry just to let out my pain."

"Then cry," Elaine said. "Crying will be the first step toward healing this wound," she whispered as she embraced Cynthia.

CHAPTER 8

Cynthia had sensed that her marriage was over after Butch had beaten her, but she wasn't quite ready to accept it. It was difficult for her to just let it all go when she'd invested so much in her marriage. After more conversations about how sorry he was for what he'd done and how he wanted his family back, Cynthia developed a hope that her distressed marriage had a chance to survive. After three weeks of listening to more promises from Butch about how he was going to get his life together and put more effort into their marriage, she returned home with a renewed feeling that they'd somehow make it and not struggle and fight with one another so much. Cynthia willed herself to believe this to be true. She wanted and needed it to be true. She had to prove that she hadn't rushed into a marriage that was doomed from its beginning.

However, her hopes were crushed when, just one week after she'd returned home, she and Butch engaged in another vicious argument about his whereabouts and why he didn't phone home if he knew he was going to be late.

"You were out with that bitch you were getting high

with last month, weren't you?" Cynthia's suspicions about Butch's mistresses couldn't be contained, and the slightest change in his daily routine heightened her feelings of insecurity.

"I told you that I had some business to handle," Butch barked.

"What business, Butch? How come you're keeping secrets from me? You promised you'd never keep secrets from me."

"I am not keeping secrets from you!" Butch howled.

"Yes, you are!" Cynthia accused him. "I know that you're keeping something from me. I can feel it. You must be slipping around doing drugs again. I thought that we agreed that you'd get some help. You promised me, Butch, that you'd start getting help for your addiction."

"Damn it, Cynthia! I don't have a fucking addiction. And if you say that to me once more, I swear I'm going to knock your head through a wall."

"You do, Butch. You do have an addiction."

Suddenly, Butch slugged her and knocked her to the bedroom floor. "Now look at what you made me do! Are you happy now? Huh? You made me do that, Cynthia. I didn't want to but you made me. You and that mouth of yours made me do it. If you had just shut up, this wouldn't have happened."

The hard blow to her head made the room spin. As Cynthia tried to stand up, the room spun even faster. Butch attempted to help her, but Cynthia fought him off.

"Leave me alone!" she screamed.

"Baby, I'm sorry. You just keep pushing me. I've told you a hundred times not to push me."

"Just leave me alone, Butch," Cynthia said a bit more softly as she managed to make it to the edge of the bed. Butch wrapped his arm around her.

"I didn't hit you that hard, did I?" he asked, even though he knew that he'd hit her hard. "Just rest a minute. The dizziness will go away."

Butch was speaking softly now in an effort to show her that he was done with hitting on her for the moment.

Cynthia was so shocked and angered by this second attack that she wanted to kill Butch. But something strange happened. The room stopped spinning and suddenly she thought about a melody that made her chuckle.

"What's so funny?"

Cynthia gazed at Butch, who was completely perplexed by her laughter. Cynthia conjured up the most evil smile that she could.

"Nothing, baby," she answered in a voice she didn't recognize. It was as if someone completely different had taken over her being. The words to a melody from soul singer Al Green kept looping in the back of her mind,

"Love and happiness," Cynthia bellowed out.

"What are you talking about woman? You're not making any sense."

"The power of love!" Cynthia shouted out another verse to the melody in her head. She stood up, touched the side of her face that Butch had punched and began laughing again.

"You've gone crazy," Butch said. Cynthia caught his gaze in hers.

"You're right Butch. I've lost my mind." Cynthia continued to smile at him. To her amazement, she was surprisingly calm.

"Stop smiling at me like that!" Butch demanded.

"Whatever you say, Butch." Cynthia removed the wicked smile from her face. "You should get some rest. I'm going to go clean up."

"What are you going to do after that? Try to cut me in my sleep or something?" Butch asked suspiciously.

"Now why would I cut the man that I love so dearly? I'd never do that to you, Butch," she said. "You're the man, and you've put me in my place."

Butch smiled at her response. "See, now if you'd act like this more often, we wouldn't have all of these problems."

"You are so right, Butch. I'm the reason, the only reason for all of our problems." Cynthia knew that her answer would appease Butch. Her plan seemed to be working because Butch calmed down.

She waited until Butch fell into a deep sleep. She then got out of the bed and quietly gathered up as many of her and Anthony's belongings as she could. She placed everything in a suitcase and placed it at the front door.

She gathered up Butch's clothes and placed them in a nice pile. Cynthia opened up the back door and removed the lid from the black barbecue grill. She packed all of his clothes into the belly of grill, poured a healthy amount of lighter fluid on them and then set his clothes on fire.

She walked back into the house and shut the door. She quickly scooped up her son and walked out of the front door.

Cynthia hustled up the block and stopped at a pay phone. She called the fire department and reported a fire at her address, just in case the blaze got out of hand. Once that was done, she hailed a cab and went over to Elaine's house, where she asked her to call Uncle Jo Jo and the rest of her uncles. She wanted to give them her set of door keys so that they could pay Butch a visit in the middle of the night and deliver a message to him.

Six weeks after Butch had attacked her the second time, Cynthia was sitting in her old bedroom reflecting on her marriage and concluded that it had, indeed, been troubled from the start. Although it hurt her deeply that the marriage hadn't worked out, she found the strength that she needed to continue on as a single mother.

With a clear mind, she contacted an attorney and filed a petition for divorce with the court. She had Elaine to thank for giving her the eleven hundred dollars to get the process started.

Cynthia made plans to find employment and locate affordable day care for Anthony. She'd also made arrangements with Butch to pick up her belongings at a time when he wouldn't be home.

"I don't want any of the furniture," she said to him during a phone conversation. "Just a few things that I left behind."

"You're kidding me, right?" Butch's voice sounded strained.

"No, Butch, I'm not," Cynthia said defiantly.

"You'd better watch your back," Butch threatened. "That wasn't right for you to set all of my damn clothes on fire and send your crazy-ass Uncle Jo Jo and his brothers over here. You're lucky that I'm not pressing charges against your ass!"

"No! You're lucky I didn't set your ass on fire. And I don't know a thing about Uncle Jo Jo coming over to see you," Cynthia lied. She was glad that she'd given her uncles the keys to her apartment so that they could sneak in on him while he was asleep and kick his ass.

"You just wait until I get healthy again. I'm not going to take this shit lying down, Cynthia. I had to be hospitalized for two days."

"Two days?" Cynthia had no idea of what Uncle Jo Jo and her uncles had done to him. She only knew that when she spoke to Uncle Jo Jo, he said that he'd make sure that Butch got the message.

"Yeah. Those fools tried to kill me."

"Well, they did tell you when we got married that if you ever broke my heart they'd be paying you a visit."

"So you admit sending them over here?"

"I didn't do a damn thing," Cynthia answered defiantly.

"That's okay. You don't have to say you did it. I know you did. Just watch your back, girl." Cynthia didn't take Butch or his threats seriously.

"Look, I'm coming over there this Friday to pick up the rest of my things. Please make sure that you're not home."

"No. I'm going to be here to make sure you only take stuff that belongs to you."

"Fine. I'll have my uncle Jo Jo come with me just to make sure you don't get it in your head that it's okay to beat up on me."

"Why you bringing him? You can't fight on your own?"

"Butch," Cynthia sighed, tired of talking to him. "Just make sure that you're not home when I come over." She hung up the phone.

God, what did I ever see in that fool? Cynthia asked herself.

CHAPTER 9

At times, it was hard for Cynthia to stop crying about her failed marriage. She had her good days as well as her bad ones. On the good days, she was happy to be free and looked forward to starting over. But on the bad days, she thought about the years spent with Butch and what they represented, which was nothing more than her failed attempt at taming a playboy. She began to think that perhaps she had pushed the issue of marriage too hard before really considering what nurturing a relationship meant.

In spite of it all, Cynthia was very optimistic about her future. She only had herself and Anthony to worry about. Soon she'd be receiving income from child support and wanted to put the money to good use by helping her mother with some of the bills. After all, she and Anthony were two extra mouths that needed to be fed. Cynthia was also considering going to night school to work toward finishing her college degree. That was something that Elaine supported fully.

"I wouldn't mind watching Anthony for you while you went to school," Elaine mentioned to her one evening when she was braiding Cynthia's hair. The two of them had been sitting in the living room talking. Elaine was sitting on the sofa and Cynthia was seated on the floor between Elaine's thighs.

"I could get a job, as well," Cynthia said, feeling as if she could turn her life around with the help and support of her mother. "I'd have to find a babysitter, though. Hopefully I can find one that charges reasonable rates."

"You know, there is this lady that I work with who has a sister who owns a day care center. When I see her I'll ask her to give me some information about it. She may offer you a discount since her sister knows me."

"That might be worth looking into, Mom. If they're licensed and have a clean facility I'd be willing to send Anthony to them," Cynthia said.

Over the weeks, she and Elaine had put aside their differences. Cynthia finally started listening to her wisdom and knowledge, using them to help guide her. She felt herself changing into a different woman and was grateful because it was allowing her to discover a strength she never knew she had.

"And let me tell you another thing you can do," Elaine said. "Build up your credit history. You should always make sure that you have good strong credit. Don't be like me and mess it up to a point where you can't straighten it out without filing for bankruptcy. Make sure that when you talk to your divorce lawyer that you don't end up having to pay for Butch's debt."

"Butch never did have good credit, Mom. You knew that before I was willing to admit it," Cynthia said.

"Well, if he was keeping his drug habit a secret, you just never know what other surprises he might have that will catch you off guard. Just make sure that you explain your concerns to that lawyer you hired."

"I'll keep that in mind," Cynthia said as she mulled over the possibility of Butch having outstanding debt that she was unaware of. Cynthia hoped that she hadn't been so blind as to not notice something like that.

Victor was a pain in the ass. He was hardheaded, stubborn and believed that the world revolved around him. It was difficult to speak to him about his unacceptable behavior because he immediately became standoffish.

Victor had become completely fascinated by street culture and all of his plans, from what Cynthia could tell, centered on making money quickly and then quickly spending it on tasteless items. He didn't have any plans to save any of his earnings or to better himself or his situation. He only wanted to live for the moment, with little or no thought about the future.

The constant bickering between him and Elaine had Cynthia concerned about the effect it was having on Elaine's health. Cynthia tried to remain out of their arguments as much as she could, but out of concern for her mother she felt that it was her duty to get involved and negotiate a truce between them. Cynthia decided to go down to the pool hall where Victor liked to hang out to talk to him.

"Let me tell you something about Ms. Elaine Howard. She's the driver who likes to get worked up over nothing. But she's the one driving me crazy. It's not the other way around. I try to avoid her ass," Victor said as he leaned on the pool table, took aim with his cue and tried to sink the solid four ball into a corner pocket. He missed.

"It's a good thing I'm just in here fiddling around by myself. Because had I been playing for money, I'd be losing right about now," he admitted.

"Well, can you at least try to be nice?" Cynthia pleaded with him.

"I don't have to do a damn thing except stay black, die and pay my taxes," Victor answered pompously.

"You sound just like Mom. Perhaps that's the problem. Both of you are just too much alike."

"Let me tell you something, Cent. Don't ever compare me to that woman for as long as you continue to live. I am nothing like her, do you understand me? I am nothing like her." Victor had flames in his eyes. "She put you up to this didn't she? No, you don't have to answer that. Because I know she did. She put you up to coming down here to the only place that I can think clearly to ruin my happiness."

"Victor, she doesn't even know I'm down here. Why are you so angry with her?"

"You're lying." Victor released a sinister laugh. "Elaine put you up to coming down here. She's up to something, isn't she? What is she trying to do? Come on, Cent, tell me. I know her. She's up to something, I can feel it."

"Victor, what is wrong with you? You're talking like a crazy man. I came on my own. I thought I'd be able to negotiate a truce between you two."

"A truce, huh? Well, you tell her that all she has to do is stay out of my way and we'll get along just fine. You go back and you tell her that." Victor took another shot.

"How old are you now, Victor?"

"You know that I'm about to turn twenty-four. Why are you asking a dumb question?"

"Because don't you think it's time for you to leave home and get your own place?"

"I'm not ready to leave yet," Victor said, raising his voice. "I'll leave when I get good and ready, all right." Victor glared at her. "What? Are you trying to put me out so that you guys will have more space? Is that it?"

"No, that's not it. I just thought you were at a point in your life that you wanted your own place and space."

"No. I have enough space where I'm at right now. Living at home is working out for me. All you have to do is to tell her to leave me alone and we'll do just fine."

"You know that she's sick, right?"

"She's been sick for years. If I know Elaine, she's blaming all of her health problems on me. That's what I am to her, nothing but a damn problem."

"Victor you're not a problem to her. It's just fighting with her isn't helping." Cynthia was trying to get Victor to see that his behavior was killing their mother.

"Look, I'll be cool just as long as she's cool, all right? I'm not some little boy that she can bully. Do you know that she tried to get me to help pay the rent the other night? Can you believe that shit? I've been living with her all of my life, now suddenly she feels that I should pay her rent."

Cynthia was dumbstruck by Victor's attitude toward helping their mother. To her, his position was unimaginable. Victor took aim at another ball and sank it into one of the pockets of the pool table.

"You mean to tell me that you don't help her out at all, Victor?"

"Yes. That's exactly what I'm telling you," he answered sarcastically. "I'm out here struggling, trying to get and maintain the little bit that I do have. There isn't enough money in my bank vault to help out Elaine."

"Victor, she's our mother. You're supposed to help."

"Says who?" Victor glared at her. "Where is it written, huh? Tell me, because I want to know. Or is it an unwritten law that my mother should be a godly figure in my life and therefore I should give her whatever she asks for? What are you? Crazy?" Victor chuckled. "I don't think so."

"Wow. You're way out there, Victor. I mean way out there." Cynthia's anger toward her brother was mounting by the second. "Before I say something really nasty, I'm going to leave."

"You can say what the hell you want to. It's not going to change a thing," Victor said as he took aim at another ball. "You can tell Elaine that if she stays out of my way, I'll stay out of hers."

Cynthia didn't like Victor very much at that moment. As she turned to exit the pool hall, she glanced back at him and wondered what had happened to the lovable big brother she used to have.

The truce between Elaine and Victor didn't last long. By Friday evening, the two of them were once again at each other's throats. The spark that ignited the flames came in the form of phone calls Elaine had received from strangers wanting to know when certain merchandise would be available. The phone calls caused Elaine's anger and blood pressure to skyrocket and the moment Victor entered the apartment from spending yet another afternoon at the pool hall, Elaine began barking at him about his whereabouts and the strange calls. The confrontation between her and Victor left Elaine winded, drained and weak. After the shouting sessions, Elaine confided in Cynthia about how she felt.

"I'm tired, Cynthia. I'm tired of dealing with him. I've been on my knees asking the Lord to help me with him. I don't know where I went wrong with him. I don't know why he has so much anger and animosity in him. Maybe I should have stayed with your father. Maybe he needed a man to help show him the way. I just don't know."

Elaine was in tears. Cynthia tried to calm her mother down by rubbing her feet with cocoa butter as she relived the intense moments of the argument.

"That boy has grown up and has lost his mind all at the same time." Elaine's face was contorted into an anguished expression.

"Try to relax," Cynthia said as she continued to massage her feet. She noticed how dry and callused Elaine's skin was and that she needed a pedicure.

"I didn't think I could raise such a disrespectful child," Elaine said. Cynthia listened but was concerned about Elaine's labored breathing. "Did you hear how he was talking back to me? My baby has got the devil in him."

"Yes, I heard him, Mom. Victor just needs his ass whipped, that's all. You should call Uncle Jo Jo and have him deliver a message to Victor. Maybe they can talk some sense into him."

"No. Victor is my problem, not theirs. He's going to get his act together or I'm going to put him out on the street for good. I mean that, Cynthia. All I've ever tried to do was give him a halfway decent life and a shot at a good future. I never wanted to be the type of woman who raised a man who didn't know how to be one. Where did I go wrong with him?" Elaine asked tearfully.

"Mom, you didn't go wrong. He's just caught up and doesn't even know it."

"I'm trying to reach him, Cynthia. I'm trying so hard to reach him but I'm just not getting through. He's already been caught and put in jail for looting. Even after being in jail, he still thinks he can do the same things that landed him there."

"Mom, stop thinking about it for a while, okay? I just want you to relax while I rub your feet. I know it's hard not to talk about it or think about it, but I want you to do that for me. I want you to get some rest."

"I can't rest with my blood pressure raised up so high," Elaine said as she exhaled. Cynthia was quiet because she didn't know what else to say. Elaine was agitated and struggled to calm down. After a long moment of silence Elaine spoke again.

"Okay, I'll try to get some rest," she said, "but I doubt if it will help.

Later that night after Elaine had fallen into a very deep sleep, Cynthia left the room and went over by the bay window to wait for Victor. She'd placed a chair in front of the living room window so that she'd spot him walking into the building. She waited patiently and watched the activity on the neighborhood street because, as pathetic as it was, she had nothing better to do. She watched as neighbors came and went, and even got excited as she watched a couple quarrel in the middle of the street. Although their voices were muffled, Cynthia determined the argument was about an ex-lover that the woman had been caught sneaking around with.

"It's a damn shame that the entire neighborhood has to know all of their business," Cynthia mumbled. After a while, Cynthia grew bored with watching people and decided to go to her room. She passed the time by watching late-night television.

It was well past midnight when Cynthia heard Victor entering the apartment.

She came out of her bedroom and watched him as he came down the corridor toward her as if he were the king of the world.

"Victor?" she greeted him.

"What are you doing still up?" he asked "Anthony keeping you up again?"

"No, thankfully he's sleeping. I'm waiting on you," Cynthia said. "We need to talk."

"We can talk in the morning. Right now, I need to catch some sleep."

"No, Victor," Cynthia said to him as he was about to enter his bedroom. "This can't wait."

"Aw, come on, Cent. Don't you start in on me, not right now. I don't need any drama from you," Victor whined.

"Why are you so defensive? Every time someone says something to you, you get all wound up. You need to take a chill pill," Cynthia said as she followed him into his bedroom. Victor didn't pay her comment much attention, he just crashed face-first down on the mattress.

"I need to know what's going on with you," Cynthia said, standing with her arms folded across her chest.

"What do you mean, what's going on with me. I'm cool. Is there a problem?"

"You're upsetting Mom again. You have strangers calling this house looking to buy stolen stuff and she's worried to death about you getting caught up in the prison system. Now you need to slow down and straighten up."

"You know what?" Victor turned over and sat up.

Judging by the blaze in his eyes, Cynthia had scraped a raw wound and what Victor was about to say wasn't going to be pretty. "I wish that she was dead."

"Victor! Don't you ever say that again. That's a real evil thing to wish on your own mother."

"It's true, Cent. I wish that woman would just die. I'm tired of her riding me all of the time."

"What is it between you and her? Why do you hate her so much? Do you even know?"

"She started hating me first," Victor answered childishly. Cynthia stared at him, perplexed.

"I've got problems, okay? I've got serious shit that I'm dealing with and I don't need you or her riding my back right now."

"Serious shit like what?" On the one hand, Cynthia had become frustrated with him, but on the other she was trying to understand him. Victor paused and Cynthia studied his facial expressions as he thought about what he wanted to share.

"You know that she never wanted me, right? She told me that if she'd had the money, I'd be dead. She would have had an abortion. Now what kind of crazy shit is that to tell your son? She treats me differently, too. You're her favorite and she makes sure that I know it. She told me that when I was born, it ruined her life. She said that she had plans to make a better life for herself, but then I came along and changed everything."

"Victor, that's not true and you know it. Mom is being hard on you because you're not living up to your potential. Have you really taken a hard look at the lifestyle you're leading? You're throwing rocks at the penitentiary and daring someone to come out and catch you for it."

"Hey, I'm just doing what I have to in order to make it. It's not easy out there!"

"Make it where, Victor?" Cynthia asked. When Victor didn't answer her, she knew he didn't have any idea what he wanted.

"Do you have any idea where you're headed?" Cynthia asked. "You're just caught up, confused and lost."

"No. I'm not lost at all." Victor captured her gaze, and she saw a slice of evil in his eyes that frightened her. "I'm not going to stop doing my thing out there in the streets. There is money to be made out there, and I'm just the man who knows how to take it. You women don't understand that I'm going to do what I've got to do. Y'all can gang up on me all you want, but it doesn't matter. Y'all can't control me."

"Victor, you're scaring me." Cynthia's voice trembled.

"No, I'm not," Victor replied.

"Yes, you are. And I'm afraid for you because you just don't see that eventually something horrible is going to happen."

Victor smirked, then laughed. "Last time I checked, you were the one who had something horrible happen. You let the fool beat your ass, then you went and bailed him out so that he could beat it again. What kind of stupid shit is that, Cynthia?"

Victor's words hurt her in a way that she didn't think was possible. She felt belittled, dumb and worthless. It was as if he'd punched her in the gut without even touching her.

"You didn't have to say that to me, Victor." Cynthia felt her tears rising up.

"Well, it is what it is now, isn't it?" Victor was just as cold and mean as Butch.

"What have I done to you to make you treat me like this?" Cynthia asked through her tears.

Victor paused and regained his composure. "Nothing. I'm just very irritated, Cent. Irritated about how Butch treated you, about always wanting things that I can't afford and Elaine barking at me all of the time. Sometimes I think that she's forgotten how to be nice to me. Sometimes I don't think she loves me at all. Every time I see her, she's in my ass about something. Sometimes I just wish she'd say, 'Victor, I know it's hard but I love you no matter what you have to do in order to make it.'"

For the first time, Cynthia could tell that her brother was being honest about his feelings.

"Ever since I can remember, she'd always tell me how she couldn't wait for me to grow up and get out on my own. She's always had her foot in my back. She's been pushing me out the door ever since I can remember. She doesn't want me. She's the reason I dropped out of high school, Cent. She's the reason that I didn't complete the GED program."

"What are you talking about? I don't understand."

"Remember how well I was doing in high school?"

"Yeah, I remember. You are so smart, Victor. You were an honor student and if I remember correctly you were even invited to apply for a full scholarship to Northeastern Illinois University."

"Yeah, and the minute Elaine found that out that I had a chance at a full ride, she started up again by saying that she couldn't wait for me to get out of the house. She kept talking about all of the things she'd be able to do once I was gone. That shit made me feel unwanted, Cent. It made me feel like she'd been waiting all of her life just to get rid of me. Just like she wanted to do when she found out she was pregnant with me."

"Victor, I think you've got it twisted. I don't think she meant it like that."

"Yes, she did. I know she did. When I dropped out of school, she wasn't worried about my education. She was pissed off that I wouldn't be leaving like she wanted me to. I'm showing her ass, though. You can't get rid of me. I'm going to stay right here to remind her every day that she has a son that she can't turn her back on."

Cynthia was at a loss for words. Victor's honesty and pain were both twisted and deeply emotional.

"I'm proving to her that no matter how much she wanted me to disappear, I am right here, in her face every goddamn day! She needs to notice me, Cent. She needs to notice me the way she notices you. When you moved back up in here, she was happy as hell that you came back. If I left and had to come back, she wouldn't feel the same and you know it. She'd probably turn her back on me."

Cynthia swallowed hard because she wanted to choose her words carefully. She sensed that her brother was torn up emotionally and was battling a demon that had been with him for a long time.

"Have you talked to Mom about this?"

"She doesn't listen to me the way she listens to you," Victor snapped. The blaze of hate in his eyes made Cynthia flinch. She exhaled before speaking again.

"Do you want me to talk to her for you?" she asked.

"It doesn't matter now, Cynthia. I'm a twenty-four-year-old high school dropout who lives in the hood. She's stuck with me and I'm stuck with her. She likes making me feel miserable, so I make her feel miserable in return. That's just the way it is. Now get the hell out of my room. I need to get some rest. I have to get up in an hour or so to go meet some people."

"Meet some people about what?"

"Some important people who know how to make money like me. I'm going to have a ton of cash in my pocket real soon. And as soon as I get it, I'm going to toss it in Elaine's face and then tell her she can't have a single penny of it."

Victor's animosity toward their mother was cruel and ugly. Cynthia really didn't know what to say. She only knew that in her heart she felt something terrible might befall him. She thought that if he taunted Elaine in the manner that he said he would, her mother might end up killing her only son.

CHAPTER 10

"Hanna, if it weren't for bad luck I wouldn't have any at all," Cynthia said. She was visiting Hanna, in whom she was confiding her most recent dilemma. Cynthia was sitting in a white wicker chair that Hanna had inside of her bedroom. Hanna was sitting Indian-style on her bed while hugging a pillow.

"You're in a real fucked position right now," Hanna said as she leaned to the left, stretched out her arm and opened her dresser drawer. She removed marijuana she'd stashed there and offered some to Cynthia.

"How am I supposed to smoke weed in my condition?"

"Oh, I forgot," Hanna said. "You don't mind if I smoke, do you?"

"No," Cynthia said, exhaling loudly.

"Open up a window so that the smoke doesn't give me a headache," Cynthia said. Hanna got out of the bed and cracked her window. She then pressed Play on her cassette recorder and the voice of Al Green singing gospel music filled the room.

"Yeah, that's my song there. Everyone needs some church in their life," Hanna proclaimed

"Girl, you are crazy. How can you smoke weed and listen to gospel music at the same time?" Cynthia asked.

"Hey, some of the biggest church goers are no strangers to smoking some weed. Hell, many of them smoke more than I do. We all have our issues. I'm not letting my issues stand between me and God. Now what's wrong with that?" Hanna said as she sat back down on the bed and fired up her smoke.

"Hey, if it floats your boat and makes you happy, who I am to judge you. So what am I supposed to do?"

"Get rid of it," Hanna said casually. "Call up Butch, tell him that you're pregnant and that you want to get rid of it."

"Hanna, I can't do that. I'm not going to get an abortion." Cynthia glared at Hanna and began wondering why she was looking to her for advice in the first place. Hanna tilted her head up and released a steady stream of smoke.

"I'm just telling you what I'd do if I were you," Hanna said as she swayed to the sound of the church music. Cynthia cast her eyes disapprovingly as Hanna then stood up to stand near the open window. The stench of the smoke was too strong for her.

"Does Auntie know you're pregnant yet?" Hanna asked.

"No, my mom doesn't know yet. I'm trying to figure out a way to bring it up. I don't want to add to her problems. Victor is giving her enough grief already,"

Cynthia said. "I was making so many plans to start over and rebuild my life. Now, I just don't know what to do. I'm just at a total loss."

"I know one thing. You better not be thinking about going back to Butch," Hanna said.

"I know that I shouldn't be thinking about returning to him, but I am."

"Girl, no!" Cynthia was surprised by Hanna's tone of voice.

"But we're a family and family needs to stay together. Maybe if you had children you'd understand me better," Cynthia said. "I know it's crazy, but I miss him. I miss just being with him, I guess."

"Girl, I know one thing. If you go back to him, don't come crying to me when he beats your ass again," Hanna said as she took another hit and continued to groove to the music. Cynthia exhaled again as she tried to understand why her heart was sending so many mixed signals.

"You're done with Butch. And you should leave it at that."

"I know, but sometimes I feel as if I'm not ready for him to be done with me."

Cynthia turned and caught Hanna's gaze. It was a look that Cynthia didn't recognize, a look that was somewhere between anger and disbelief.

"What's that look for?" Cynthia asked.

"Shit, I thought I was fucked up in the brain but you're more fucked up than I am. You need to leave the man alone. Let him go. Shit, stop thinking about him so much."

"It's hard, Hanna. We have a child together." Cynthia felt her emotions getting the best of her. "And I'm pregnant again by him. I will see him every day through the eyes of my children. He'll always be with me."

"Stop saying that, damn. You sound like a damn scratched record, you just keep repeating yourself," Hanna said, then deeply inhaled.

"Are you sure you don't want any of this? You're only about seven weeks pregnant. A little hit isn't going to hurt."

"No, thank you, Hanna," Cynthia said. "I think I'm going to go. Tell Uncle Jo Jo that I said hello and that I'm sorry I missed him. But don't mention that I'm thinking about going back to Butch. He'd have a fit if he heard that after he delivered a special message to him for me."

"You know that's another reason you shouldn't go back to him. You had my daddy beat his ass. You know if you go back to him, he's going to want to get even with you about that."

"Yeah, I know. But I don't know what else to do."

"So what are you going to do about your situation? I mean, you don't have a job, you don't have medical insurance, you don't have an apartment, you're pregnant and in the middle of getting a divorce. On top of that, your brother is acting and talking crazy and has just enough evil in his heart to do some real fucked-up shit."

"I don't know what I'm going to do. One thing is for

sure, though. My situation can't get any worse than it already is. I'm going to go on back home and have my little pity party all by myself," Cynthia said.

"Well, let me know if you need anything or just need to get out for a drink."

"I can't drink." Cynthia again reminded Hanna that she was pregnant and had to restrain herself.

"Girl, a little alcohol isn't going to do any harm."

"Yes, it will. Besides, I'm thinking about calling up Butch for some sex. It's been a minute and a sister has needs." Cynthia laughed as she approached Hanna's bedroom door. "Besides, he can't get me pregnant twice."

"No!" Hanna shouted. "Leave him alone, Cynthia." Hanna stood in front of the door.

"What?" Cynthia was confused by Hanna's sudden aggression.

"I just think that if you see him again, he might beat on you and that wouldn't be good for you or the baby." An odd smile that seemed out of place spread across Hanna's face. "On top of that, having sex is overrated. Get yourself a toy. You can pleasure yourself without the drama or hassle of a man."

"Yeah, maybe you're right." Cynthia wrinkled her nose as she moved away from Hanna and walked to the front door. "That's some funky weed you're smoking. It's given me a headache that's out of this world. I'll call you later on."

"Okay. Just remember what I said. You should really just leave him alone. Let it go." Cynthia once again looked at Hanna and noticed that she seemed uneasy, but Cynthia didn't know why.

The following afternoon, Cynthia was giving Anthony a bath. She'd placed him in the bathtub and was down on her knees beside it. She was massaging the baby shampoo into his hair and working up a thick lather. Elaine was in the kitchen baking lasagna for dinner and the aroma of the baking pasta that was wafting through the apartment caused her stomach to growl. Anthony turned his head in the direction of the odd grumbling sound.

"That's Mama's stomach," Cynthia said to her son. "You've got a little brother or sister in there and they're rather hungry." Anthony glanced up at her with innocent eyes. He then began slapping the surface of the water while making sounds of his own.

Cynthia hadn't mentioned the pregnancy to her mother yet. Her plan was to wait until after she'd spoken with Butch about it. As much as she loathed him, his viewpoint regarding the pregnancy was still important to her. She needed to know that she had his support and that he would be around so that their children would know him. One thing she didn't want to do was deny him the right to see his children.

"Let's rinse this soap out of your hair," Cynthia said to Anthony. Cynthia turned on the water, checked the temperature, and then gently lowered his head under the steady stream of water. At that very moment, a loud crash startled her.

"It sounds as if someone has kicked in the front door," Cynthia said aloud as she tried to hurry up and finish bathing Anthony so that she could go and investigate the loud noise. "I know that Victor hasn't lost his mind like that," she said aloud as she continued to rinse the soapy shampoo out of her son's hair. She was being careful to make sure no soap ran into his eyes. She then heard Elaine yell at the top of her voice and then heard several other voices shout back at her to get down on the floor.

"Mom!" Cynthia called out to her. "What's going on out there?"

"Don't move!" someone commanded.

"Excuse me!" She turned her head and looked over her shoulder. She saw a police officer in full riot gear aiming a revolver at her.

"What the hell is going on?" Cynthia's pulse quickened as panic began to settle in.

"Let me see your hands!" the officer yelled.

"I can't. I'm holding a baby!" Cynthia informed him.

"Don't move," he said. She watched him carefully as he inched closer to her.

"See?" she said in a panic-stricken voice. "I'm holding my son."

"Get off of me!" Cynthia heard Elaine's shrill cry and was concerned about her safety.

"What are they doing to my mother?"

"Finish up," said the officer.

"Why are you here? What in the hell is going on?" Cynthia screamed at the officer. Anthony began go wail and Cynthia's nerves felt as if a bolt of electricity had struck them.

"It's secure in here," the officer said as another entered the bathroom.

"What's going on in here, Officer J.B.?" asked the second officer.

"She's giving the baby a bath," answered Officer J.B. Cynthia quickly pulled Anthony from the tub and wrapped him in a large drying towel. She held him tightly in an effort to calm him down.

"Will someone please tell me what's going on?"

"Follow me," said Officer J.B. Cynthia followed him into the front to the living room. Cynthia was shocked to see Elaine handcuffed and forced to sit down on the floor in front of the sofa.

"Why do you have my mother handcuffed?" Cynthia barked at Officer J.B.

"Hey, calm down, okay?" answered Officer J.B. as he reholstered his revolver. Cynthia was trying to make out his features so that when this was over, she could file a report complaining about how she and her mother were being treated.

"I can't believe that they've handcuffed me," Elaine complained. Cynthia stopped trying to study Officer J.B. and focused her attention on her mother.

"It's just for your own protection. You weren't cooperating so we had to restrain you," said another officer who was in the house. Cynthia counted six policemen altogether.

"This is my house," Elaine howled. "You have no right to break into my house like this."

Officer J.B. pulled out a search warrant and held it up. "Yes, we do. I have a warrant to search the premises for stolen merchandise and we also have a warrant for the arrest of Mr. Victor Howard. Do you know where we can find him?"

"Oh, Lord," Elaine said. "What has that boy done? Why is he doing this to me?" Elaine asked in a bizarre voice that Cynthia had never heard. Her words didn't seem to be coming out right.

"Mom." Cynthia placed her hand her on Elaine's knee. She noticed that her mother didn't seem to understand her. Cynthia studied her mother's gaze; Elaine had a very distant look in her eyes. It was as if her eyes were suddenly hollow. Cynthia waved her hand in front of her eyes, but Elaine didn't blink.

"Mom!" Cynthia sensed that something was very wrong with Elaine. In that instant, Elaine fell over to one side as if she'd lost all sense of balance.

"Mom!" Cynthia called to her yet again. She sat Anthony down and pulled Elaine back into an upright position. "Mom!" Cynthia noticed that Elaine's neck and mouth were twisted into a hideous expression.

"Is she okay?" asked Officer J.B.

"No!" Cynthia answered hysterically. "Take the handcuffs off of her! I think she's having a stroke."

CHAPTER 11

After Officer J.B. determined that Elaine, Cynthia and Anthony posed no threat, he removed Elaine's handcuffs.

"Don't just stand there looking. Call for an ambulance!" Cynthia screamed.

Officer J.B. finally radioed for an ambulance. Cynthia thought it took an eternity for help to arrive. Once the emergency medical personnel arrived, they began trying to revive Elaine. Cynthia felt helpless as she stood off to the side and watched Elaine receive medical attention. Once Elaine was stabilized, the paramedics took her out of the apartment so that she could be transported to the hospital.

"I need you to answer a few questions for me," said Officer J.B., who now seemed to be a bit more at ease.

"That's my mother," Cynthia snarled. She wasn't in any mood to answer any questions. "Am I under arrest?"

"No."

"Is my child under arrest?"

"No. I understand how upsetting this is, but we do have a warrant and the authority to search this home."

"Search all you want," Cynthia said as she moved

toward the sofa to scoop up Anthony. "I'm going to see about my mother. You can burn the fucking place down for all I care, but rest assured I'm going to file a complaint about all of this, Officer J.B. This isn't over." Cynthia glared contemptuously at him and then left.

When Cynthia arrived at the hospital, Elaine was rushed into the critical care unit. Cynthia filled out Elaine's medical history form and even gave the hospital staff the name and phone number of her primary care physician. Once the hospital staff had all of the required information, the admitting nurse directed Cynthia to the waiting area until a doctor could come out and give her an update on Elaine's condition. Cynthia then went over to a pay phone situated on the other side of the emergency room. She removed some coins from the bottom of her purse and called Hanna.

"Hello," Hanna answered.

"Hanna, thank God you're home. I need you to do me a huge favor."

"Girl, I don't have any money. I'm going to tell you that right off," Hanna said.

"Hanna, I don't need any money."

"Cool. What do you need, then?"

"I need you to get over to my mom's house and stay there until I can get back."

"Get back from where?"

Cynthia could hear the bewilderment in Hanna's voice.

"Hanna, it's a long story but the police raided the house about an hour ago."

"Raided whose house?"

"My mom's house."

"What the fuck did the police raid your mother's house for?" Hanna's voice rose several octaves.

"They were looking for Victor. He's done something, but I don't know what."

"Damn!" Hanna said. "I know Elaine acted a fool. I know she didn't like the police all up in her house."

"Hanna, Elaine has had a stroke."

"Oh, damn! Is she okay?"

"I don't know," Cynthia said as she struggled to hold back her tears and remain calm.

"What hospital is she in?"

"Jackson Park Hospital," Cynthia answered, then paused. "Hanna, the police kicked in the front door and I would like you to go over there and house-sit until Larry the landlord comes over to repair the door. I'm going to call him in a few minutes to let him know what has happened."

"Damn, girl. I'm sorry to hear that you're going through all of this. How is your mom doing?"

"I don't know. They're working on her now."

"Damn," Hanna said again.

"I'm going to call Butch," Cynthia said. "I just can't take being here by myself."

"Why do you want to call Butch?" Hanna asked.

"I just—" Cynthia paused. "I have Anthony here and I want him to come and take him home."

"Oh, I see. I'm going to head over to your place. I'll make sure that nothing happens to your stuff."

"Thank you, Hanna. I don't know what I'd do without you."

"Girl, just take care of Elaine. You know she's my favorite auntie. She's crazy as hell and if I know her, she'll probably be in there cursing out the doctor and telling him that he's doing things all wrong. You know how your mama is."

Cynthia chuckled for a moment as she imagined her mother dictating to the doctor how he or she should proceed with her medical care. However, the moment was a short-lived.

"I'll give you a call when I think you've made it over there," Cynthia said.

"Okay. I'm going to say a prayer for her, as well as let my daddy know. I'll talk to you later," Hanna said and then hung up.

Cynthia felt awkward about having Anthony with her through this trying time. He seemed content, but she knew that it would not last for very long. He'd need to be changed and she hadn't thought to grab her diaper bag when she left the house. She'd just picked him up and walked out. The only person she trusted him with was his dad. So she searched for some more change and phoned him at work.

"Hello, Butch?"

"No, this is Lonny. Butch doesn't work here anymore."

"Oh," Cynthia said surprised by that news. "I'll try him at home."

Cynthia was out of money, so she had to call collect. Thankfully, Butch picked up the phone.

"What do you want? And why are you calling here collect? I'm going to make you pay for this call." Butch was being evil with her but she just allowed his comment to roll off of her.

"Butch, I need you to come over to Jackson Park Hospital."

"Why?" he asked.

"I need you to pick up Anthony. My mom is very sick and I don't want him to be here with me right now. Can you please come and get him?"

"I don't know about that," he said and then was silent.

"What do you mean, you don't know about it?" Cynthia quickly became angry with him.

"How do I know that you're not setting me up or something? I'm still pissed off about you having your uncle Jo Jo come in here on me. So, hell no! I'm not coming."

"Butch, let that go," Cynthia said.

"What to do you mean, let it go? Woman, are you crazy? You had those men come in my house and—"

"Butch!" Cynthia shouted. "I don't want to go through this with you right now. All I'm asking is that you come pick up your son and take him back to my mom's house. You can leave him with Hanna. She's on her way over there now."

"What's Hanna doing over at your mother's house?"

"It's a long story. But could you please come and get him? I'll bring him outside to you. You don't even have to come in."

"Yeah, okay. I still don't have a car so it's going to take me a minute to get over there on the bus."

"That's fine. I'm not going anywhere. I'll keep an eye out for you. When I see you, I'll come out. I'll be waiting in the emergency room, so come around to that side of the hospital."

"Okay. I'll be there in an hour or so," Butch said and then hung up.

Cynthia sighed and then went to sit down. As her mind drifted, she began to wonder how and why Butch was no longer working and the impact it would have on her financially if she didn't receive child support for her children. She also thought about how she was going to break the news to him and cringed at the thought of the condemning and mean things he was surely going to say. Thankfully Butch kept his word and arrived an hour later to take Anthony with him. He didn't say much or ask how her mother was doing.

"I'll leave him with Hanna," he said, turned his back on her and walked away.

"Bastard," Cynthia muttered under breath. She loathed him for having so few feelings for her.

CHAPTER 12

"Elaine has had a brain attack," said Dr. Smith, updating Cynthia on her mother's condition. What she was learning didn't sound very promising.

"Brain attack?"

"A stroke. She's had a blowout of a blood vessel in her brain."

"Oh God!" Cynthia said, suddenly feeling very weak.

"The stroke has hit her pretty hard. The part of the brain that was impacted controls one side of her body and her sight."

"What does that mean?"

"The stroke has taken her eyesight and left her paralyzed. The other concern is her blood pressure, which we're having trouble getting under control. I've had to call in a specialist for that. It has been brought down slightly, but it is still dangerously high."

"What about her blood pressure medication?" Cynthia asked.

"It's no longer working but we're doing everything that we can to get it down," Dr. Smith replied.

"Can I see her?" Cynthia asked.

"Yes. I'll have the nurse come out and take you in to see her. She's in and out of consciousness. So just be aware of that."

When Cynthia followed the nurse into the intensive care unit, she tried hard not to look into the various treatment rooms. She feared that the sight of so many sick patients would upset her even more. The nurse stopped in front of Room B and said, "She's in here."

Cynthia whispered "thank you" to her and entered the room. She had never really experienced a hospital visit like this one. Her emotions were on edge but the moment she saw her mom, her composure snapped and she began crying. Plastic tubes seemed to be running everywhere—through Elaine's nostrils, arms, fingers and even her head. Cynthia swallowed hard and tried to regain command of her feelings. She entered a small bathroom located inside the room for some tissue to dry her eyes and nose.

Cynthia looked at Elaine once again and noticed how badly her head had swollen. She carefully touched Elaine's hand. It felt cold. Her eyes were closed and the sound of the respirator was the only noise.

"I'm here," she whispered. "I'm not going anywhere." Cynthia sat down in a chair near the bedside and stroked Elaine's hair.

"You're going to pull through this just fine," she said to Elaine. "I'm going to take care of you so I don't want you to worry about a thing." At that moment, she felt her mother's finger twitch.

"I'm here," Cynthia reassured her.

"I can't see you," Elaine said softly.

"It's okay. I'm right here with you."

"Turn on the lights so I can see you."

Cynthia wanted to break down and cry again but held herself together as best as she could.

"Just get some rest, okay?"

However, in typical Elaine fashion, her mother didn't listen to Cynthia's recommendation. Instead, she kept on speaking.

"It's a baby girl," Elaine said. "She's so beautiful."

"Whose baby girl, Mom? Who are you talking about?"

"She's so smart," Elaine continued. "She's smiling. She loves to smile. Where's Anthony at?"

"He's with Hanna. He's in good hands."

"Come here," Elaine said. Cynthia hesitated because a machine began beeping loudly.

"Come closer," Elaine whispered. Cynthia leaned in closer to her.

"You go and get your son. Don't worry about me. Just go get your baby."

"I'm not leaving you, Mom," Cynthia said. The monitor continued to beep louder and faster.

"Don't worry about Victor anymore, either."

Elaine paused and then squeezed Cynthia's hand. "Did Victor come to see me?" she asked.

"No. I don't know where he is," Cynthia said as her tears broke free. Her heart was torn and she couldn't control her emotions. At that moment, a nurse and several other medical staff rushed into the room.

"Would you please step out?" ordered one of the nurses.

"What's going on?" Cynthia asked in near hysterics. "What's happening to her?"

Cynthia saw Elaine's body jerk violently on the bed. Before she could see any more, a nurse drew back the curtain for privacy.

"Her blood pressure is on the rise again," she heard someone say as she left the room.

Cynthia went back into the waiting area feeling numb, her mind clouded like a ship lost in fog at sea.

She didn't recall how much time had gone by, but when she saw Dr. Smith and several other hospital personnel, she knew that they were coming to tell her that Elaine was gone.

CHAPTER 13

"May I see her?" Cynthia asked Dr. Smith and the other hospital staff who'd accompanied him to break the news to her.

"Absolutely," answered Dr. Smith. "Again, I'm so sorry for your loss."

Cynthia swallowed hard as she was escorted back into the critical care unit. She looked at her mother one last time and noticed an odd expression on her face. She almost seemed to be smiling. The expression was not one Cynthia expected to find and somehow it gave her a renewed sense of hope.

"You don't have to worry anymore," she whispered to her mother as she stroked her hair lovingly. "You don't have to worry about anything at all."

Cynthia wanted to say more but couldn't form the words. So she spoke to Elaine in her mind.

I love you, Mom. She thought to herself. *I miss you already and I don't want you to go. Life is not going to be the same without you. You look so peaceful. I wish I could be there with you.*

At that moment, Uncle Jo Jo and her other uncles came into the room and interrupted Cynthia's thoughts.

"She's gone," she whispered to them. "She was my heart."

Cynthia had never felt so hurt and alone in her life. Time and the world seemed to stop at that moment, nothing else mattered to her. She found herself at a mental crossroads. She could turn left and go down the road of depression and insanity, or turn right and somehow find the will and strength to continue on and fight for the better life that she and Elaine had discussed on many occasions. It was tempting to turn down the road of madness because it would be peaceful there, or at least that's what she believed.

Cynthia concluded that for the sake of her son and her unborn child, the right thing to do was to continue on against incredible odds.

Everything was stacked against her. She had no job, she was expecting, she lived practically free of charge with her mom, but that was about to change. She wondered how she'd pay the rent, find a babysitter and find a job. Cynthia also had to coordinate Elaine's funeral, prepare the apartment for visitors and find time to grieve, as well as confront Victor about the police raid that had taken the most important woman in the world away from her. Cynthia planned to make sure Victor understood the magnitude of what he'd done.

Five days had passed since Elaine's death and Cynthia

had been busy the entire time dealing with a funeral home and making sure Elaine's wishes were being met. She hadn't seen or heard from Victor and felt deep animosity building up toward him for not having help or support from him. The day before Elaine's funeral, she finally got a call from Victor.

"This is the operator. You have an incoming call from an inmate at Cook County Correctional Facility. Will you accept the charges?"

"Cook County Jail?" Cynthia was confused, then realized it was Victor. "Yes. I'll accept the charges."

"Cent, are you there?" Victor hurried his words and sounded desperate.

"Victor, are you in jail?" Cynthia asked even though she already knew the answer.

"They got me locked up, Cent. I need someone to come down here and raise some hell about having me locked up like this."

"Victor—"

"I'm not supposed to be in here, Cent. They got things all wrong. They said that they have me on videotape robbing an eighteen-wheel semitruck that was transporting flat-screen televisions. I told them I didn't know anything about no broke-down semitruck full of televisions."

"Victor—"

"I don't have much time, Cent. I told them to show me the videotape and they wouldn't. I need Mama to come on down here and raise hell about them having me locked up like this on false charges. I want you to talk to her for me. Let her know that I'm in trouble and that I need her. You're good at smoothing things over with her. So you are going to do that for me, right?"

"Victor, that's not going to happen," Cynthia said as she felt her heart grow cold toward her brother. She now knew why the police had raided the apartment and why Victor had disappeared.

"Come on, Cent. Don't do me like that. I helped you out when Butch was in jail. It's not right for you not to help me out."

"When did they arrest you, Victor?" Cynthia wanted to know how long he'd been hiding from the police.

"A few nights ago, I got picked up at the pool hall. Every time I called there, no one picked up the phone to accept my collect call charge."

"You're too much for words, Victor. On one hand you want to act as if you're a full-grown man who can hold his own, but on the other hand you want to act like some innocent young man who needs his mother to fight his battles and bail him out of trouble."

"Cent, I don't have time to get into it with you right now," Victor snapped. "Put Mama on the phone. I'll talk to her my damn self, shit."

Cynthia knew that if Elaine could speak with him, she'd really let him have it. For Cynthia it was much simpler. Victor had known the police were searching for him and probably knew all about the raid. But he had decided not to come home, probably because he knew that as soon as he showed his face, he'd be picked up.

"Cent, put Mama on the damn phone. I'm not playing with you. I've got to get out of here. These prosecutors in here are trying to say that they're going to try and give me some serious time."

"You can talk to Mama when you're on your knees at night. Mama is dead, Victor." Cynthia had finally got him to shut up long enough for her to get out what she had to say.

"You and all your bullshit killed her. She had a stroke and died four days ago. Her funeral is tomorrow. I hate you, Victor. I hate you for killing my mama!"

"What the hell do you mean, I killed her? I didn't kill her, Cent. Why you putting that shit off on me? I don't believe you just said that to me. I'm in here locked up, fighting for my life and you come telling me how I killed Mama."

"You did kill her! You killed Mama by worrying her to death. You knew that she had a medical problem, but you still continued to do stupid shit just to make her miserable. You even said that you wished that she were dead. Well now you have your damn wish. She's gone, Victor. Are you happy now? Huh? God, if I could jump through this phone, I'd kick your ass."

"Hey, I'm not the one who had to move back in because I was getting my ass kicked! I'm not the one that moved back in with an extra mouth to feed. You killed her, not me."

"How can you say that? How can you not see that you were the problem? I was helping her, Victor. I wasn't the one holding a childish grudge against her, you were. You were only trying to make her see that she couldn't get rid of you." Cynthia began crying. "Right before she died she was looking for you. Do you know how she felt, knowing that she was about to die and that her only son wasn't there? Do you even care? I hate you, Victor!"

There was a long moment of silence between them. Cynthia was waiting for a rebuttal but got none.

"Can you come down here and see about getting me out?" Victor asked more calmly. "They set my bail at ten thousand dollars."

Cynthia almost wanted to laugh at Victor's pathetic plea.

"I have to bury my mama, Victor. I take it you will not be there for the service?"

"You know damn well I'm not going to be there unless I get out."

"Well, since I don't have ten thousand dollars, I guess I'll see you when I see you." Cynthia's heart and words were as bitter as an artic wind.

"Cent, listen to me. I want you to go down to the pool hall and ask to speak to a guy named Johnny B. Tell him that I got jammed up and need a little help from him. Tell him I'm at the county jail and need a loan in order to get out. He'll take care of the rest."

"Victor, my priority right now is to bury Mama. Everything else will have to wait. Right now, I just don't have the time to be lurking around a pool hall trying to find some man named Johnny B. Besides, Hanna will be here any minute to take me back to the funeral home so that I can give them Mama's burial clothes and final corrections for the obituary. After that, I have to finish preparing the house for the guests who are going to stop by afterward. Helping you find some man named Johnny B will have to wait until next week."

"Fine, Cent. I'm never going to forget that you're the reason that I missed Mama's funeral," Victor said and hung up.

Four weeks after Elaine's funeral, Cynthia hadn't heard from Victor, nor had she gone down to the pool hall to search for his friend named Johnny B. She'd taken the death of Elaine very hard and just didn't feel like doing much of anything. Mentally, Cynthia was nothing like she used to be. Something inside of her had cracked and she didn't know how to deal with it. The family helped out with some financial support, but it wouldn't last long and Cynthia knew it.

She was in a really bad situation. Her pregnancy was progressing along and when she told Butch about it, he immediately denied that the child belonged to him, which really humiliated Cynthia because she was seriously considering moving back in with him. Even though he was unemployed, she rationalized that she'd work with him to help him get back on his feet so that he could provide for them.

"Woman, now I know you've lost your damn mind," Butch said to her when she met him at the attorney's office to finalize their divorce. "You got me down here about to sign divorce papers and talking about getting back together again. That is crazy."

"Fine, Butch. I'm sorry I even brought it up."

"You never were too damn smart. You were just a young girl with a hot ass. That's all. I'm sorry that I even got caught up with you."

"Go to hell, Butch. After all I've been through with you, I just don't believe you're going to talk to me like I'm nothing to you."

"You are nothing to me," he said with an evilness that made her stomach turn.

Cynthia sighed and remained silent for the remainder of the procedure. Once the papers were signed, she was glad to have her freedom back.

Just one week after her divorce was final, she was sitting at her mom's dining room table looking in the newspaper classified section for a job. She was searching for a job at a day care center, as a receptionist or as an office secretary. She thought that if she could land a job in that type of setting, she'd solve her problem. She'd have a job and at the same time a place where Anthony would be welcomed. As she was circling ads and making phone calls on the cordless phone, she heard a knock at the door. She thought it was Hanna, who was supposed to be dropping off some groceries sent over by her uncle Jo Jo. She walked over to the door and asked, "Who is it?"

"A friend," the voice said.

"Who are you looking for?" Cynthia asked suspiciously.

"Victor. I have something for him."

Cynthia placed the chain on the door and cautiously opened it. "What can I do for you?"

The man suddenly crashed through the door and was inside the apartment before Cynthia could react.

"Get the hell out of here!" Cynthia screamed.

"Shh. I'm Johnny B," he said quickly.

"I don't give a damn! He's locked up, if you haven't heard."

"I know about that. I'm here about the money your brother owes me."

"I don't know a thing about that," Cynthia said. She dialed 911 on the cordless phone she had in her hand. She backed away from him and put the phone to her ear. It was ringing. Johnny B swiftly moved toward her and snatched the phone from her.

"There is no need to call the police." He chuckled a little. "I am the police."

He showed her his badge, and Cynthia was puzzled.

"You don't remember me do you?" He smiled.

"Hell, no!"

"I'm Officer J.B. Does my name ring a bell now?"

CHAPTER 14

Johnny B frightened Cynthia. He had a persona about him that was toxic and mean-spirited. Johnny B was a caramel-brown man who towered over Cynthia's five-and-a-half-inch frame. By her estimation, he was at least six foot six and most people would think that he was a basketball or football player. He had a lean physique and an evil gleam in his eyes. Johnny B held on to the cordless phone and walked back toward the dining room and took a seat at the table. Cynthia didn't know what to do so she followed him, uncertain of why he was there.

"Sit," he commanded. If any other man had spoken to her in that manner, she wouldn't have followed the order. However, Johnny B looked as if he'd hit her so hard that she'd feel the pain of his blow for months. So instead of risking it, she dutifully sat down.

"What's this all about?" Cynthia asked nervously. She'd never felt so threatened before, not even by her ex-husband Butch.

"Let me start by telling you that no one crosses me and

gets away with it." He leaned toward her. "And I do mean no one."

He made sure that he captured her gaze. The look in his eyes was poisonous. "That's why I took your brother down. He didn't know his place and tried to get ambitious."

Cynthia felt a chill run through her. She was speechless and frightened.

"Victor is going to be put away for a while. It's been arranged. But that still leaves him owing me."

"Look, whatever was going on between you and my brother I had nothing to do with." Cynthia's voice cracked because she was so afraid. In her mind, talking to Johnny B was like talking to the devil himself. Johnny B didn't respond to what Cynthia had said. He just kept looking at her as if he were reading her every thought. She could see his emptiness in his eyes.

"I'm a reasonable man," he said, but Cynthia didn't believe him. "I could use a nice-looking woman like you. You're still very attractive, and you have a nice body. You look innocent, as well. That will help a lot."

Cynthia swallowed hard because she figured that he wanted her to sell her body in order to repay Victor's debt and there was no way she was about to do that. Never in her life had she ever met an individual as dangerous as Johnny B.

"I'm pregnant," she informed him. "My husband and I are excepting our second child."

"You let little Butch Clark knock you up again?" He laughed and that made Cynthia feel low. "I'm surprised he can still get it up after all of the abuse he's done to his body. I remember the first time I saw you. You'd come to one of his house parties. I was the bartender and he told me to make sure your drink was strong so that you wouldn't put up a fight."

Hearing this news made Cynthia's head spin. Nothing in her life was making sense anymore. Everything now seemed clouded. *Had Butch set her up long before she realized it?*

"You're looking at me as if you have no idea of what I'm talking about."

Cynthia remained silent.

"This is even better. You're naive, as well. No wonder you fell for Butch so easily."

"I'm not naive." Cynthia began trembling and she hated showing him how vulnerable she was. Something about her was changing, but she didn't know what it was.

"Let me get to the reason why I'm here. I plan to make you one of my sellers."

"Sellers of what?" Cynthia tried to sound standoffish, but once again her voice betrayed her by cracking.

"Drugs."

"I will do no such thing," Cynthia stated. "I have a baby and one on the way. I don't even know you and you don't even know me. I'll go to jail first before I do something crazy like that."

Johnny B sprung to his feet and before Cynthia could react, his fingers were clutched around her throat. He began choking her.

"If there is one thing that I can't stand it's when someone doesn't do what I tell them to do. That's been a pet peeve of mine for a long time. My first wife didn't like to listen to me. She let her mouth write a check that her ass couldn't cash. In the end I had to show her just how powerful I was. I am a powerful man, Cynthia. I can do whatever I want to you and no one will challenge me. I have all of the right people in the palm of my hand, and that includes the police department. You will do whatever I say or you'll end up six feet underground just like your mother. Do you understand me? Huh? Am I making myself perfectly clear?"

Cynthia couldn't answer. She tried to free herself from his grip but couldn't. She focused on his eyes, which were blazing with hatred. She was trying to understand what she had done to deserve this. She wanted to know why her safe little world was crumbling.

"Answer me, before I break your neck and dump you in a river and leave your son motherless."

The murderous glint Cynthia saw in his eyes made her believe every word he was saying. Johnny B wasn't bluffing.

"Yes!" she cried out. That was a turning point in her life. Cynthia knew that she'd just turned onto a road that was going to take her to places that were ugly.

"You're trapped. Remember that. I'm everywhere and I have people watching you. If you so much as sneeze too loudly I'm going to know about it." Johnny B finally let her go and Cynthia started coughing uncontrollably.

"Why are you doing this?" Cynthia asked.

"Because I want to," Johnny B answered. "In this part of the world, I do whatever I want to. Around here, I'm God and everyone knows it." Johnny B moved toward the front door.

"When I see you again, I'll tell you how I want things to go," Johnny B said. At that moment, Cynthia could only think about quickly packing up her belongings and running away.

"And don't even think about leaving. I have eyes everywhere," said Johnny B as he opened the door and walked out.

The following day, Cynthia went to the county jail to visit Victor. She wanted answers from him. She wanted to know why Johnny B was doing this to her. She wanted no part of the life that Victor was so fascinated with. When Cynthia saw Victor approaching, he looked harder. It was as if in the short amount of time he'd been locked up, he'd already experienced too much. His hair was braided and he seemed angry the moment he laid eyes on her. He sat down first and began speaking.

"Did you see Johnny B?" he asked.

"Yes."

"Well damn, did you tell him that I was locked up?" Victor was impatient. "I need him to pull some strings and get me the hell out of here."

"Victor, Johnny B is the one who had you locked up."

"What? What are you talking about?"

"Victor, you did something to piss him off." Cynthia began crying. It took several moments for her to regain her composure. "He's not going to help you out."

"Cynthia, they're talking about locking me up for a long time. I can't stay in here. Theses dudes up in here are crazy. They don't have good sense."

"What did you do, Victor? What did you do that was so bad that this man caused our mother to have a stroke and die?" Victor was silent for a moment. He focused on the floor beneath him so that he wouldn't have to look at Cynthia.

"You know that they record our conversations. I can't talk about that right now."

"Victor, the man has threatened me! He wants me to do things for him that I don't know shit about. I'm pregnant, Butch has left me, Mom is dead, and I don't have a job. I'm going to end up on welfare with an apartment in a housing project."

"I can't do anything about it locked up in here. Do you have some money so that I can get a lawyer?"

"Are you even listening to me?" Cynthia shouted. "Victor, I'm in a desperate situation."

Victor avoided eye contact with her, then leaned back in his chair. "Well I guess you have to do what you have to do." He swallowed hard.

Cynthia studied his eyes and concluded that he was thinking about his own predicament more than hers.

"What's that supposed to mean?" Cynthia asked.

"Just what I said. You have to do what you have to do."

"That's it? That's all you have to say to me? After all that's happened you're just going to blow it off as if that's just the way it is?"

"Cent, look, I can't help you. I don't know what you want or think that I can do."

"You could at least be sorry that your mother is gone," Cynthia growled angrily. Victor flinched.

"I do feel sorry that she's gone but I can't let that show or deal with that right now. I'm trying to survive in here and I'm doing what I need to do in order to stay alive. You can get killed up in here, in case you didn't realize that. Being detained like this isn't a cakewalk."

"Death may not be the worse thing for a lost soul like yours," Cynthia said bitterly. "You should have been concerned about being locked up when you were out there doing crazy shit. Goodbye, Victor."

She turned her back on her brother and left.

When Cynthia arrived back at Hanna's house, her eyes were red and swollen from trying to manage her anger at her brother. She was returning to Hanna's house to pick up her son. Hanna had agreed to watch him while she went to visit Victor.

"Are you okay? Did you have another breakdown about your mom?" Hanna asked as she allowed Cynthia to enter the apartment.

"No," Cynthia said. "Where is my baby at?"

"He went to sleep after I gave him a bottle."

"You didn't leave the bottle in his mouth, did you?"

"No. I didn't want my bed smelling like sour milk," Hanna answered.

Cynthia moved past Hanna into the kitchen and sat down. Her nerves were on edge and she couldn't seem to keep her mind from racing. Hanna, who had followed her, turned on a small radio that was on top of the kitchen table. She sat down beside Cynthia and once again asked what the problem was.

Cynthia sat for a long moment. She was trying to process everything that had happened in the past few weeks—the police raid, Elaine's death, Victor's incarceration and Johnny B forcing her to do things that she wanted no part of. Her mind was in a fog and she was trying to make sense of all of the craziness that was going on in her life.

"Damn, Cynthia, it can't be that bad," Hanna said, breaking the silence.

Cynthia couldn't figure out where to begin. She didn't know how to express her misery.

"Well, shit, I can't just sit here and talk to myself," Hanna said.

A familiar melody came through the speakers of the radio, and Cynthia noticed how Hanna instinctively found the rhythm and began grooving to the melody. Moving to a melody was so automatic for Hanna that Cynthia believed that Hanna didn't realize that she did it. She began to wonder if that was Hanna's way of dealing with uncomfortable situations.

"So what was Victor talking about? Getting out?"

Hanna laughed a little because she thought her humor would bring Cynthia out her zombielike state.

"You know, you're scaring me. You look like one of those creatures from *Dawn of the Dead*. You look pale," Hanna said.

"I—I..." Cynthia stuttered. "I saw Victor and I told him that some things have happened since I buried Mom."

"Things happened? What things?"

"Victor tried to double-cross a crooked police officer named Johnny B. And now Johnny B wants me to work for him."

"Johnny B!" Hanna's voice rose several octaves. "You've hit the jackpot, Cynthia. Don't you realize that?" Hanna said excitedly.

"Huh? What are you talking about?" Cynthia was thunderstruck by Hanna's reaction.

"Damn, Cynthia. Don't tell me you've never heard of him?"

"No, I haven't. I try to stay away from dangerous people like him."

"Well, go on and tell me what he said," Hanna urged. "I can't believe Johnny B wants you to work for him."

"You think it's a good thing to work for him?"

"Shit, yeah. I would. I'd risk it all for the chance to make the type of money that he makes. I heard that this one girl used to work for him and she was keeping like fifty thousand dollars in cash for him. Can you imagine that? Fifty grand in cash?"

"No," Cynthia said. "Why would she be excited about something like that? It's not even her money."

"I know, but just the thought of being around all of that money. I'm sure she worked some things out and got a little slice of it for herself, but that's beside the point."

"Johnny B threatened me, Hanna. He said that if I didn't work for him he'd kill me."

"Do you think he was serious?"

"Duh! Yes, he was serious."

"Damn," Hanna said and then paused in thought. "It's the chance of a lifetime either way you think about it. I hear that he has all of the connections. You wouldn't have to worry about the police because he is the police. All you'd have to do is what he says. Girl, you could make some money and then get out of the game. You wouldn't have to worry about paying taxes, or dealing with office politics, or any of that other stuff."

Hanna's viewpoint and knowledge of the underworld stunned Cynthia. She didn't expect Hanna be so outspoken about it.

"What? Why are you looking at me like that?" Hanna asked.

"You're fearless, and I'm just surprised by it," Cynthia answered.

"With a man like Johnny B on my side, I wouldn't worry about a thing," Hanna said. "I'd have all of the latest clothes, jewelry and money to burn."

"Yeah, but what if he wants more?'

"More like what?"

"What if he wants sex?"

"Hell, if the money is right, I'd let him get it anyway he wanted it. But I don't think that would be a big thing anyway, because from what I've heard the brother is lacking in that department."

"Hanna, how do you know so much about him?"

"I hear stuff. Besides, women talk and when they do, I listen. So, are you going to work for him?"

"Hell no, Hanna. The man caused my mother to have a damn stroke and put my brother in jail. What kind of idiot would I be if I went to work for him? I can't believe you just asked me that."

"Hey, I just thought you wanted to get paid quickly. You don't have a job, you have a son who has needs, you're pregnant and in a minute you're going to be getting eviction papers because you can't afford the rent at your mom's place. If it were me, I wouldn't look a gift horse in the mouth."

"Well, you forgot about one thing."

"What's that?"

"I can always go back to Butch if I really needed to."

"Girl, going back to Butch is even crazier than hooking up with Johnny B. You need to leave Butch alone."

"I need to leave Johnny B alone," Cynthia countered. "He wants me to sell drugs, Hanna. Can you believe that? I might go to jail. If he crossed my brother, he'll cross me."

"That's true but that's just a chance you'd have to take.

Look, there is money to made in the drug business. People are depressed and want to escape their reality by getting high. So what? You sell them a little something to help them get there."

"I'm not that type of person," Cynthia said. "I don't want to profit off of someone else's misery."

"So, what are you going to go do? Get on welfare and move into the projects? Hell, I heard that every night gunshots go off. You don't want to move up in there and have you or your son catch a stray bullet. Then you'll be all on the news going crazy."

"There has to be another way." Cynthia tried to think. "I could move in with you and Uncle Jo Jo. Or one of my other uncles."

"Ain't no room up in here for you. Me and Daddy barely get along now in this small two-bedroom, cold-water flat. Besides, Uncle Jo Jo and the other uncles are all living in Section Eight apartment buildings and you know that they monitor the number of people who live in them. You could mess them up and get them put out."

"Damn!" Cynthia said, feeling as if she had no way out of her situation and falling into a deep depression.

"Just work for the man for a minute and then get out of the game. He's not asking you to stand on the street corner to sell it, right?"

"No," Cynthia replied. She respected Hanna and placed a lot of value in her opinion.

"Then the way I see it, you have two choices. Either

you sign up for welfare and take your chances struggling to survive in some public-housing dump, or you can hook up with a man who is going to put some money in your pocket. It's just that simple."

CHAPTER 15

Cynthia had always envisioned a better life for herself. She'd always imagined that she'd have a nice home, a loving husband and that they'd have good jobs that supported the family. She imagined that she'd plan vacations where she and her family would spend memorable times and enjoy being with one another. She dreamed of having a home that had a wonderful kitchen where she'd enjoy preparing meals because she loved to cook. However, at this point in her life that was all just a foggy dream. Her reality was far from what she wanted it be.

The idea of partnering with Johnny B was seductive because it would fix her immediate need for money. However, Cynthia knew that she'd be lying in bed with the devil and her participation would have its price.

Cynthia weighed her options and decided that she would decline Johnny B and immediately begin searching for a job. She'd hoped to find a job at a day care facility or some other child-friendly environment. But as she began her quest down the path of righteousness, she discovered finding the job she needed was more difficult than she'd imagined.

Then, the inevitable occurred. Cynthia could no longer hold off or make excuses to Larry the landlord as to why she hadn't moved out or agreed to sign the lease that he'd left for her. Larry was as shady as they came. He was a burly man with a short haircut and a wandering left eye. Whenever Cynthia spoke to him, she found it difficult to make eye contact with him. Now Larry was at her door, demanding payment or she'd be out before nightfall.

"Now, I've been as nice to you as I can, Ms. Clark," Larry said. He attempted to step inside the apartment but Cynthia wouldn't allow it. "Now look here. I got bills to pay, as well, and I can't tell the mortgage people that I can't pay them because of you and your situation. I sympathize with what happened to your mom, but I've allowed you to live here free for some time now. In fact, I've already promised this apartment to a tenant who has paid me in cash."

"Larry, I've been searching for a job so that I can pay you. I just need a little more time." Cynthia thought he was bluffing about renting out the apartment while she was still occupying it. She felt like crying but held back her tears.

"Ms. Clark, crying isn't going to help me or you because crying doesn't pay the bills."

"Larry, just give me a little more time. I'm really trying but I'm pregnant and I've got my little boy that I'm trying to feed and clothe. I've applied for housing assistance, but it takes time for the paperwork to get processed," Cynthia lied. She'd already gotten some assistance money, but it wasn't enough to pay the rent so she used it to buy food and for her and Anthony.

"Legally, Ms. Clark, I can set you outdoors. You have not signed a lease with me so the police will look at you as a squatter. I want payment, one way or the other, and I want it now."

"I don't have it," Cynthia pleaded.

"Perhaps you can pay me in another way," Larry said.

Cynthia noticed a wicked expression on his face.

"I think I can hold off the new tenant for another month if you give me a little sample of yourself." Larry paused. "A pretty woman like you, your pussy has got to be as good as it looks."

Larry the Landlord smiled as he brushed his tongue across his lips. A cold chill rushed down Cynthia's spine.

"You're married and I've met your wife," Cynthia said.

"You think that I give a damn about her? Shit. You're not the first tenant who has had to put out some ass in order to remain indoors. It's cold out there, Cynthia," he reminded her. Cynthia was repulsed by his offer and was even more nauseated when she noticed how he began to perspire with lust.

"I probably got the best dick you've ever felt."

"I'd rather go and live with my family before I allow you to have your way with me."

"Then get out right now before I call the police and have you arrested. Hell, if your family was so concerned about you they would have made accommodations for you long ago. You're bluffing, Ms. Clark, and I know it. I know damn well that you don't have a place to go. Quite frankly, you don't have a pot to piss in or a window to toss it out of."

"Look, Larry, maybe I can sell you some of my mother's furniture. You should take a look at it. There is some really nice stuff in here."

"I don't want your mama's raggedy-ass furniture! Either you give me some pussy or get the hell out. It's just that simple."

Tears welled up in Cynthia's eyes as she imagined Larry the landlord mounting her. She swallowed hard because she was at her breaking point. Cynthia was about to consent to it—just this once—so that she wouldn't be put outdoors.

"Yeah, I thought you'd see things my way," Larry said, laughing with a hiss.

Just as he was about to enter the apartment, Johnny B appeared in the hallway.

"Larry!" Johnny B called out. "I know that you're not about to enjoy something that belongs to me?"

"Johnny B." Larry laughed nervously. "Hey, man, how have you been? I didn't know that you and Ms. Clark had dealings with each other."

It was suddenly clear to Cynthia that Johnny B was well-known and feared among the sleazy and the shady. It was evident by the fearful look in Larry's eyes. Cynthia watched as Larry squirmed like a worm on a fishing hook. Larry turned to face Johnny B.

"Listen," Johnny B spoke to Larry through gritted teeth. "I've paid you a lot of money so that I can set up my business at this location. Nobody, and I mean nobody, takes advantage of me."

"Johnny, man, I wasn't even thinking about messing with you or your setup. Look, this is all just a big misunderstanding."

Larry looked at her. "Ms. Clark, you can stay here as long as you need to. Don't you worry yourself about the rent. That's all taken care of," Larry said nervously and then rushed down the stairs without looking back.

"So does that mean that I owe you now?" Cynthia asked, afraid of his response.

"More than you realize," Johnny B said as he entered the apartment.

"Why are you doing this to me?" Cynthia asked. "I'm not the type of person who does this sort of thing. I don't sell drugs."

"That's exactly why I want you. No one would ever suspect a single mom of being a drug dealer, and that's exactly what you're going to be for me."

CHAPTER 16

Cynthia went into labor on New Year's Eve. She'd contacted Butch so that he'd be available to witness the birth of his child but he refused come.

"I don't even think that it's my baby," he said to her when she called him from the county hospital.

"Butch, that is so mean. You know that this is your baby. This is your rape baby."

"Mama's baby and daddy's maybe. Don't think you're going to get some money from me. I haven't been working," he said. "I'm not going to pay you a single dime."

Cynthia exploded at him for saying those hurtful things. If he were in the hospital room with her, she would have found a weapon and stabbed him to death. She called Hanna so that she could tell the rest of the family that she'd gone into labor.

"How much longer do you think before you have the baby?" Hanna asked.

"I don't know, but I'll be glad when they come and give me a damn epidural to stop the damn pain," Cynthia said, short of breath.

"I need a favor from you, Hanna. I need you to go and pick up Anthony for me. Johnny B brought me to the hospital, but I don't want to leave Anthony with him. I don't trust him like that. You can pick Anthony up from my mom's house."

"Girl, I've got plans tonight," Hanna said. "I can't watch him, either."

"What about your dad, Uncle Jo Jo?"

"He's out of town with his brothers. They all went down south together."

"I didn't know that. Why didn't someone tell me?"

"Well, you know that they're not in agreement with what you're doing, especially Uncle Jo Jo. He's hurt by it."

Cynthia became very silent. Hanna's frankness sliced through her heart. She suddenly felt as if she'd let everyone in her family down.

"Okay," Cynthia said, starting to cry. "I'll just ask Johnny B to watch him for me."

"Well, he should do that. After all, he knew your situation when he got involved with you."

Cynthia paused as a strong contraction hit her. "Are you fucking sure you can't cancel your goddamn plans and go pick up Anthony for me? What kind of fucking family member are you? Huh? If you were in my situation I'd do it for you. I mean what's so fucking important that you can't help me out in an emergency like this?"

"I've got a date with a man that I will not break," Hanna said. "I'll talk to you once you've calmed the hell down." Hanna hung up.

"You cold-hearted bitch!"

Cynthia felt abandoned and alone. It was the most miserable feeling she'd ever known. She also worried about her son being with Johnny B. She knew that he had a short fuse; if Anthony got restless, she feared that Johnny B might discipline him and be unable to stop himself.

"Are you done having that baby yet?" Johnny B said as he entered the room.

"I thought you went back home," Cynthia answered. Johnny B huffed and then began pacing the room.

"No, not yet. Is someone coming to get your son?"

"No. You'll have to watch him for me. Can you handle that until all of this is over with?"

"What do you want me to do?" Johnny asked. Cynthia was surprised that he was actually attempting to be human.

"I want you to sit out there in the waiting room with my son. Can you handle that?"

Johnny B stared at Cynthia for a long moment.

"Please!" Cynthia added.

"You're going to owe me big-time for this," Johnny B said.

Damn, Cynthia thought to herself. Why is my life so damn complicated?

Cynthia gave birth to a healthy seven-pound, eleven-ounce baby girl whom she named Angel. When the doctors placed the baby in her arms, she knew right away that she was special. Angel looked so much like Elaine that it was frightening. She held on to Angel, closed her eyes and prayed for guidance and help.

Johnny B had placed an iron gate across the frame of the front door so that no would-be thief would get the idea that he or she could rob him. He'd also convinced Larry the landlord to give up the apartment directly across the hall from Cynthia so that when the addicts came to buy, they could step across the hall and into the apartment to do what they needed to. It wasn't uncommon for tempers to flare and fights to break out among the junkies.

Cynthia was selling poison to people who looked like her. Whenever they came to the door, she just gave them what they wanted and took the money. She didn't like to look them in the eye because some of them were so young and so lost. She felt really low when she sold the poison to pregnant women, especially teenage girls. As much as she despised what she was doing, she continued because of the money. Cynthia collected sometimes as much as five thousand dollars a day for Johnny B. In exchange, she lived rent-free, and was given a reasonable stipend for herself and her children.

When she arrived back at the building after making a run to the quick mart for some Pampers, she became more depressed at the sight of the addicts loitering and asking for money to get high with. She entered the building and climbed the stairs up to her apartment door. When she knocked, one of Johnny B's fellow officers answered the door. He unlocked the gate and allowed her to come inside.

"Johnny is in the back."

Johnny B and all of his associates were detached from what they were doing.

"I'm glad your ass is back," Johnny said as he approached her. He studied her for a moment; for some reason, she hoped that he would be nice to her again the way he had been at the hospital.

"Go do what you need to do and then get out here so we can get down to business. I need you to help me count out some money."

"Johnny, I'm tired. Can I get some rest first?"

"What the fuck are you talking about? You've been in the hospital for three damn days resting. When you came back, I let you rest another additional day. My business doesn't stop because you're tired. Now get your ass in there, take care of the baby and come do what I told you before I put you and your damn kids out on the street!"

Cynthia believed every word he said and dutifully followed his orders.

It took seven weeks for Butch to stop bullshitting Cynthia and come by. She wanted him to meet his new daughter. She wanted him to be the man that she thought he could be. She wanted him to rescue her from the life she had been forced into. However, when he finally arrived, she wished that he'd never come at all. He looked horrible. His face was unshaven, his clothes were filthy and his breath was strong enough to make a person faint.

"I'm a new customer," Butch told her as he stood at

the gate. Cynthia ignored his comment and was about to let him inside so that he could meet his daughter.

"Her name is Angel," she told him as she fumbled with the lock.

"I told you. That's not my baby."

"Butch, stop being an ass and come inside to meet your daughter."

"Look, Cent, that's not my baby, okay?" Butch had a wild look in his eyes and Cynthia held off on opening the door. She'd seen that wild and crazed look in the eyes of far too many addicts. "Now, I didn't come to see no damn baby. I came by with my fiancée to buy me a little party candy. Word on the street is that this is the place to come to."

"Fiancée?" Cynthia didn't believe she'd heard him correctly.

"Yeah." Butch laughed. "I found my soul mate. She understands me much better than you ever did. Knows how to fuck me, too. She loves me. She loves everything about me."

"She must be one sorry bitch to want to deal with your ass!" Cynthia snapped.

"No sorrier than your ass!"

There was someone standing on the stairs behind Butch, but Cynthia couldn't see who it was.

"Is that her? Hiding behind you? Why is she hiding if she's so in love with you?" Cynthia asked. "What are you hiding for, whore? I'm done with him. He isn't going to do shit."

At that moment, the source of Cynthia's misery revealed herself. Cynthia felt as if she'd been hit by a double-barreled shotgun blast when she saw Hanna.

"What are you looking like that for?" asked Butch. "You look like you had no idea."

"How could you do this to me, Hanna?" Cynthia glared at her.

"I didn't do shit to you," Hanna answered defiantly. "You were done with him and I wanted him."

"Actually, let's just get it all out, okay," Butch said, rolling his eyes and looking wilder and crazier than Cynthia had ever imagined. "I've been doing Hanna for a long time." He paused, laughing. "In fact, the night I got arrested and you had to bail me out, I was out getting high with Hanna."

"You were screwing him behind my back?"

"You knew that I wanted Butch that day when we saw him at the park concert," Hanna complained. "But no, you had to take your hot ass over to his house and have him before I got there. You stole him from me."

"Hanna, I did no such thing. How could you do this to me? I'm your cousin! We're family. You ruined my marriage."

"Honey, your marriage had died before it even got started. I just buried the shit for you."

"Hanna," Cynthia sobbed. "I looked up to you. I believed in you. I'm telling Uncle Jo Jo on you."

"Look, don't start that crying shit!" Butch barked. "Just give us some shit to get high with so we can go."

Cynthia snapped inside. Her heart was suddenly filled with evil, but her anger gave her strength. Now she *wanted* to supply Butch and Hanna with drugs.

"I hope that both of you overdose on this shit and die. I've never felt so humiliated in my life," Cynthia said as she exchanged the drugs for money.

"You're dead to me, Hanna. I want you to rot in hell!" Cynthia snarled and then slammed the door.

CHAPTER 17

Cynthia had never felt so betrayed in all of her life. Hanna, her cousin and best friend, the one person who knew her well, had been stabbing her in the back.

"She's worse than Johnny B and Butch combined," Cynthia said aloud as she angrily paced back and forth across the living room floor.

"It all makes sense now." Cynthia continued to talk to herself. "That's why Hanna didn't want me to get back with Butch. She was doing him. As far as I know, she was probably telling him to kick my ass while he was at it."

Cynthia felt like murdering Hanna. She wanted both Hanna and Butch to suffer. Cynthia could hear Angel crying in the other room, but she ignored her for the moment as she contemplated all the evil things she wanted to do to get even with Hanna and Butch.

"Y'all are going to pay for doing me like this," Cynthia proclaimed. "I may not get even with you now, but I will get you when you least expect it."

Once Cynthia had decided to get even, she calmed down and went to tend to Angel.

* * *

Cynthia remained with Johnny B for three years. During that time, she gladly sold Butch and Hanna drugs and watched as they slowly rotted away. She had saved up a sizable sum of money to run away and start her life over, but she didn't. Her anger guided her and clouded her judgment during those years. She took wicked joy out of watching Butch and Hanna spiral downhill into the pit of hell.

Then one day, Hanna arrived at the door alone to buy drugs. She looked horrible. She was frail and her skin looked as if it were being cooked from the inside, but Cynthia showed no mercy.

"How you been, cousin?" Hanna asked in a child-like voice.

"What do want? The usual mind blowing shit?" Cynthia refused to acknowledge her as family.

"You know Uncle Jo Jo put me out. I haven't talked to him in over a year," Hanna said. "But that's okay, you know. Because me and Butch are making it." Cynthia hated her for mentioning Butch's name.

"Butch has been having it hard," Hanna admitted. "He's been sick. Doctors say that he has kidney problems. They're not working right or something. They want to put him on that…uh…uh… I forgot the name of the machine they want to put him on."

Cynthia knew that Hanna was trying to say that Butch needed to be on dialysis, but she didn't bother to help Hanna express herself. She just stared at her, stone-faced.

Inside, she was jumping up and down with glee because the two of them were rotting away.

"Doctors also told me that I'm pregnant," Hanna said as she stood shaking uncontrollably. "We're going to get it together and raise a family." Hanna tried to laugh. "Can you see me as a mother? All my kids would come out dancing," Hanna said as she tried to do a quick jig. Cynthia still refused to speak to her, but on the inside she was laughing.

"Look, I don't have any money and I know you're big-time now, but I was wondering if you could slip me a little something. You know, to help me calm my nerves." Cynthia was about to remind Hanna that she was pregnant, but then realized she didn't give a damn about Hanna anymore.

"Yeah," Cynthia said evilly. "I can do that for you." Cynthia gave Hanna the dope she'd been craving and then closed the door on her.

A few days later, Cynthia was in the parking lot of a grocery store which was a mile or two away from the apartment building. She'd just locked the door on her new minivan that she'd purchased with the drug money Johnny B had given her.

"You need to be convincing and really look like a single mom," Johnny B had told her when he handed her several thousand dollars in cash to pay for the vehicle.

Cynthia had just gotten Angel seated in her stroller and was about to free Anthony up from his seat when she noticed another car pulling up behind the van and blocking her from backing out of the parking space. She didn't think much of it at first because she thought it was just someone being dropped off. But a few moments later, she heard someone call her.

"Excuse me!" A woman stepped toward her. "Cynthia, I need to speak with you."

Cynthia was stunned that the woman called her by her name because she had cut herself off from everyone she knew because she didn't want them to be involved in any way with what she was doing.

"I don't speak to people who I don't know," Cynthia said as she held on to Anthony's hand. He jumped to the ground and landed in a small puddle of water, splashing up Cynthia's leg.

"Look at what you did!" she quickly scolded him.

"I'm sorry," Anthony answered innocently.

"You have beautiful children," the woman said as she continued to approach. Once she was close to Cynthia, she stopped and asked Cynthia a puzzling question. "Do you consider yourself to be a good mother?"

"What kind of question is that?" Cynthia snapped.

The woman identified herself as a police officer and showed her badge to Cynthia. Just as she identified herself another officer approached Cynthia from the opposite direction and blocked her in between her minivan and another parked car.

"It's the kind of question that the Department of Family Services will be asking you when they come to take your children away from you."

Cynthia felt her heart stop beating for a moment. *What in the hell is going on?* she thought, fearing that her life was about to change dramatically.

CHAPTER 18

"No one is going to take my children away from me," Cynthia declared. "Not you, or him or anyone. I will kill both of you before you lay a single hand on my children."

Cynthia quickly placed both Anthony and Angel back in the minivan and shut the door. Anthony began crying and slapping his hand on the window of the van.

"Out!" he cried. "Let me out!"

"Wait a minute," said the female officer. "I didn't think you'd want that to happen. I'm Officer Lisa Granger and I'm offering you a choice."

"I make my own choices," Cynthia answered defiantly.

"Good, because I hope that you make the correct one. You can be either an informant or a suspect into the investigation of police corruption and the sale and distribution of illegal narcotics."

"I wouldn't know a thing about that." Cynthia folded her arms just below her breasts, acting as if she were shocked. "I'm a single mother trying to raise my children the best way that I can."

"Cynthia, I don't have a lot of patience."

"How do you know my name? I never told you my damn name," Cynthia asked but then realized that someone probably ratted her out.

"Does the name Butch Clark sound familiar to you?" Cynthia was about to say no but her facial expressions told the truth.

"A few years ago, you came into the station to bail him out. Remember?" Cynthia began searching her memory and vaguely remembered the officer. "I was the one who arrested him."

"Yes, I remember that now," Cynthia answered.

"I should have arrested you, as well," Lisa said with an authoritative tone.

"What are you talking about? You're crazy."

"No, I don't think so. You see, Butch was picked up again for possession and when he was questioned about who his seller was, your name came up."

"You're kidding me." Cynthia couldn't believe Butch had dropped her name to the authorities.

Hell, I thought he was somewhere about to jackknife into his grave with a dialysis machine attached to his ass, not roaming around the streets looking for another hit to get high.

At that moment, Cynthia's emotions swung from all-out hatred for Butch and Hanna to feeling as if she'd been kicked in the stomach by a horse. She felt as if every breath of air had been squeezed out of her lungs. She had to place her hand against the side of the van in order to support herself.

"I can't do this anymore," she whispered, then began hyperventilating. When she caught her breath, she once again stood straight and looked at Officer Lisa Granger.

"This is the last time that I'm going to ask you. If you don't give me an answer, life could get very difficult for you. So what's it going to be? Door number one or door number two?"

Cynthia glared at Officer Granger for a long moment and then swallowed hard.

"I'm not really like this," Cynthia answered. "I'm a good person. I didn't have a choice. I felt trapped. If I didn't do it, I'd be out on the streets or sponging off my uncle Jo Jo for as long as he would allow me."

"Look, your history isn't important to me right now. What I care about is putting Johnny B behind bars. If you help us gather evidence on him, then you can walk away and start over. If not, chances are very high you'll be arrested along with him, charged, convicted and placed in prison. Your children will end up in foster care and at the mercy of strangers. Right now, we want Johnny B and the other officers who are running the drug house."

"I could be killed," Cynthia cried. "You don't know Johnny B like I do. He would kill me if he ever found out that I was doing this behind his back."

"The way I see it, if you don't help you'll end up behind prison bars, rotting for selling poison. If you do help, you'll at least have a chance at a new life."

Cynthia was silent again for a moment, but Anthony

once again began slapping the window and interrupted her concentration. “Let me out!” he demanded.

Cynthia looked at her son and felt her emotions welling up. *How did I get here?* At that moment, it was as if a switch had been thrown inside her mind. Something was happening to her, but she didn’t know exactly what.

“Okay,” she answered. “What do I need to do?”

“I need you to help gather information. Specifically, I want you to agree to wear a wire and tape your conversations with him. I need you to get him to talk about where he’s getting his supply from, and I also need to know who he’s working with and the layout of the apartment.”

“He doesn’t really like to talk about details like that. If I start asking questions, he’ll get suspicious.”

“Cynthia, whether you know it or not, he’s already suspicious of you. Johnny B has followed you from time to time.”

Cynthia didn’t know how to respond. She was shocked by how much Lisa Granger knew.

“I’ll be in contact with you,” Officer Granger said. Then she and her partner walked back to their unmarked vehicle and drove away.

When Cynthia returned home, she put away the food she’d gotten for the house but put more food for her and her children inside of a small refrigerator she had in her bedroom. Once all of that was done, she locked herself and her children in the bedroom. She knelt beside the bed. Anthony was on the floor beside her playing with one of his toy cars. Angel was asleep on her stomach atop the bed. Cynthia closed her eyes and began whispering.

"Dear God, I know that I haven't been living right. I know that what I've been doing is wrong and I know that a lot of souls only come to you when things have gotten out of control. I'm one of those souls. I need your help. I'm lost and I don't know what to do. I need you to show me a way out. I need you to guide me. Please. If you answer my prayer, I promise you that I will live right and do right by my children. I will be a good mother and love and raise them to be all that you intend for them to be. I need you to deliver me from the madness that I've been swallowed up in. Please, God, help me."

When Cynthia finished her prayer, she got atop the mattress and rested next to her Angel. She sat upright with her back resting against the bed's headboard. At that moment, she felt another light switch go off in her mind and suddenly she began looking at what she'd been doing and how she'd allowed herself to be manipulated and placed in this situation. Over the past years, she'd automatically done whatever Johnny B wanted. She didn't question him or challenge him or try to escape from what he was forcing on her. For some reason, she just went along with his program and somehow agreed to give up everything that was good and right in order to please him.

"Maybe I was looking to be saved," she whispered. "Maybe in some way I thought that Johnny B was my savior. Perhaps I thought that somehow he'd rescue me from all of my pain, heartache and disappointments like Elaine did."

Cynthia began to cry. "Mama, I miss you. How could I have done this? How could I have allowed all of this to take place in your home? I'm no better than Victor." Images of what she'd done flashed through her mind and it was like watching someone else.

She'd sold drugs for Johnny B and if that wasn't bad enough one night she'd gotten needy and longed for the company of a man. She decided that Johnny B, by some sort of right, should be the man to fill that void. She thought that a man with as much power and confidence as Johnny B would somehow make her feel good and take her to levels of pleasure that she'd never known. However, Johnny B was nothing like that. He was barbaric and cold.

"Come on, baby. I want you to turn me on. Kiss it for me," Cynthia purred, hoping for oral sex.

"I don't get down like that and you'd better never ask me again to put my face between your legs. That's nasty. You're one nasty-ass woman," Johnny B said.

"Excuse me?" She sat up in bed. "I can't believe you actually called me nasty. I'm very clean, I'll have you know."

"Naw, you're one of those nasty girls who needs to be turned out." Johnny B laughed at her. "Is that what you want? You want to be turned out, don't you?"

"You know what? Let's just forget this." Cynthia no longer wanted to be with him. She decided to get out of the bed, but he grabbed her arm and pulled her back down.

"I said no, Johnny!"

"No one says no to me." He pulled her down. "You know you want this. It's all in your eyes. You've been wanting me for a long time."

"Johnny, please stop."

"No. You know your pretty ass has been prancing around me long enough," he said. He forced her legs apart and then kissed her hard. At first, Cynthia resisted but some deep part of her consented and allowed Johnny B to have her however he saw fit. Afterwards, Johnny felt as if he owned her. He felt he could speak to her however he saw fit, and Cynthia allowed him to. She thought that it was his way of showing her how much he cared. She realized now that her thinking was twisted.

One day, she became curious about the drugs that she was selling and why people went to the lengths they did in order to get money to buy them. She asked Johnny B why he thought people were so hooked.

"They're weak," he explained. "They're weak mentally, physically and financially. They're like zombies. They don't know the sun from the moon. They only know that they need to do whatever it takes to get high."

"Have you ever tried it?" she asked.

"I don't mess with the shit. You know that. Why are you asking all of these questions?"

"I'm just curious, that's all."

"You want to try it, don't you? I can tell. It's written all over your face. You want to go down the crazy road."

Cynthia was silent for a moment as she thought about

what it would be like to have a drug alter her state of mind.

"If I did want to try, I would want it to be with you. I want to be around someone that I know. I want to be with someone who'll look out for me, to make sure that I don't do anything too crazy."

"Cynthia, you're entirely too beautiful. The hallucinogenic drugs will age you and have you looking old and worn out. Then I really wouldn't want you. I'd have to put you and those damn kids of yours out. I can't have an ugly woman with some ugly-ass kids riding around with me."

His comment hurt her feelings but she didn't say anything. She wanted to keep the peace.

"Do you think if I tried just once I'd get hooked?"

Cynthia wanted to prove to Johnny B that she could handle it all, that she could hang with the big boys. She thought that her enthusiasm would impress him. Instead, his reaction was the exact opposite.

Johnny approached her from behind and clutched the back of her neck, then spoke purposefully in her ear.

"I've already told you. I can't have some ugly crackhead and her neglected babies around me. Get one thing clear. The only reason I have you around is because you still have your looks intact and you know how to handle my business. Believe me when I say the moment you slip up in any way, I will put you and those snotty-nosed children of yours out on the street. Right now, you've got it good. You have the protection of the police department and you're making more money than most people make in a year. Plus, I still like getting between those thighs of yours."

Johnny B snickered.

"Something younger will come along, though, and you'd better pray that I don't like her better than I like you."

Once Johnny B had had his say, he left Cynthia standing where she was. She was crying at that point. She wanted to be tough, but she just couldn't.

As Cynthia continued to reflect on her complicated relationship with Johnny B, she came to realize that at some point she'd suffered some type of mental malfunction. Now that things were a little more clear, she didn't like what she'd become.

More than anything, she wanted out.

CHAPTER 19

After three long days of taking a critical look at her life and the choices she'd made, Cynthia made the commitment to herself and her children to make a change.

"One thing is for sure," she whispered to Angel who was resting comfortably in her arms and staring at her while Cynthia bottle-fed her. "I'd be stone-cold crazy to keep on doing what I'm doing and expecting to get a different result. I have to get tough, even though on the inside I'm scared as hell. I don't know what is going to become of us or how we're going to make it. But I promise you this—I'm going to do right by you and your brother. I'm going to get us out of here and start making my own decisions instead of letting other people make them for me."

To keep her children out of harm's way, Cynthia contacted the only man left that she trusted, Uncle Jo Jo. He'd agreed to meet with her at the food court of a local mall. When she arrived, he was already there waiting for her. She hadn't seen him in three years and he'd aged considerably. His hair was all gray and his eyes had the same worried look as Elaine's. In spite of that, she was very happy to see him.

"I was wondering when you'd come around to your senses," said Uncle Jo Jo in a raspy voice.

"I know that I haven't been living up to my potential, Uncle Jo Jo, but I want to change all of that."

He placed his hands on top of hers. "I know that you got lost after your mother passed away. I was so hurt after she died." Uncle Jo Jo paused in thought. "I wanted to do so much more for you, but I was unable to and that hurt my heart."

"Uncle Jo Jo, none of what has happened to me is your fault. You didn't do this to me. I did."

"I just feel so responsible. I've had a chance to think about things and, well, I'm just sad about the way things turned out."

"So am I," Cynthia admitted.

"Hanna." He spoke her name and Cynthia jaws got tight. "I know. I see how angry you are about what she's done. I'm angry about it to. I had to put my baby out of the house, you know." Cynthia saw the pain in his eyes and it saddened her. "She was stealing from me and I can't deal with that type of stuff. I know that in the past I've crossed the line in some areas, but I'm older now and understand things a little better. I blame myself for the way she turned out." Uncle Jo Jo paused in thought again. Cynthia didn't know what to say. "You know that she lost her baby?"

"No, I didn't realize that."

"Well, she did. It's probably for the better since she is in a bad way right now. Look, Cynthia, I know that there is a lot of bad blood between you and Hanna, but I want you to promise me that some day, you'll work toward healing that wound. I know it's an ugly one. But I want you to work toward it. Hanna is a good girl. She's just mixed up right now."

"Uncle Jo Jo, with all due respect, Hanna has crossed some lines and done things that just can't be undone."

"I know. Just consider it. If there ever comes a time when you start the healing process, promise me you'll do it."

"I don't think there will ever be a time like that, but if I see it I promise to do what I can to make things right between us."

"That's all that I'm asking."

Cynthia went on to explain about her current predicament and what she would be doing to get out of it. She asked that he watch Anthony and Angel for a few days so that she could work with Officer Lisa Granger to bring down Johnny B. She explained that she was making bold moves to get her life back on track and that she had no one else to turn to.

"I know that I've been estranged from the family for some time now," she told him. "But with God as my witness, I'm about to turn my life completely around and all I'm asking for is a little help."

Uncle Jo Jo agreed to watch her children for her and she offered him three hundred dollars for his trouble.

"I don't need that," he said to her in a soft voice. "Just

go do what you have to do and come back safely. If something happens, I'll make sure that your children are taken care of."

Cynthia hugged Uncle Jo Jo and thanked him for his understanding and support. Once her children were safe with him, Cynthia rushed off to meet up with Officer Lisa Granger so that she could be wired.

"I'm so nervous about doing this," Cynthia explained. "But I want Johnny B out of my life. He's toxic, corrupt and dangerous."

"Last time I checked the scorecard you weren't exactly a bed of roses yourself," said Officer Lisa. Cynthia stared at her, stone-faced.

"I don't know how I became that person. All I know is that I want out. I want a better life for me and my children and I'm going to do what I have to do in order to make that happen."

"Well, you have switched teams," said Lisa. "I hope that you mean what you're saying. For the sake of your children, I hope that you look at this as a second chance to get your life in order."

"I know that you're giving me a break because I'm not as big of a catch as Johnny B is. I don't know if it's right for me to sit here and thank you, but in case I don't get a chance to say it, thank you." Cynthia held Lisa's gaze. She wanted her to know that she was serious about turning her life around.

"Okay," Lisa said. "I believe you. I'm going to have the technician wire you up. Several agents will be able to hear your conversation with him. If you can get Johnny B to talk about how he runs the operation and get him to admit that he's the leader, that's all we'll need. Once that information is recorded, leave. Go to the front door and open it. Someone will get you out of harm's way while we go in and take him down."

"I'll do what I can," Cynthia said. "But what if he finds out that I'm wired? Then what?"

"Undercover agents posing as drug abusers will be stationed in the apartment across the hall from you and within the stairwell. If it appears that you're in danger, we'll move in."

Cynthia swallowed hard. She felt as if she wanted to vomit.

"Come on, now. I need you to hold it together," Lisa said. "You look like you're about to throw up."

"It's okay. I'll be all right. My nerves are just shot, that's all." Cynthia paused. "Once I do this for you, what happens then?"

"As I explained to you during our earlier conversation, the state prosecutor will review the evidence gathered and criminal charges will be filed against Johnny B and his crew. I'm certain the prosecutor's motion for denial of bail will be granted, so you will not have to worry about Johnny B coming after you."

"What about other officers who are loyal to Johnny B, what if they come after me? Johnny B has friends everywhere," Cynthia mentioned out of concern for the safety of her family.

"I'm confident that any person who will be a direct threat to you will be behind bars after today. If anyone has to worry about threats, it's me." Officer Granger paused for a moment. Cynthia could tell by the intense look in her eyes that her mind was processing something.

"You're worried, aren't you?" Cynthia thought she'd figured out what Officer Granger was thinking.

"No, I'm not. I'm going over all of the hard investigative work I've done to make certain I didn't miss anything." Officer Granger cleared her throat. "The prosecutor will call you as a witness during the trial. I'm not going to lie to you and say this experience is going to be a cakewalk. Johnny B's defense lawyers will attack your character in every possible way. It's going to get uglier before it gets better."

"God, I just want this to be done and over with. I want this nightmare to end," Cynthia said.

"We have to go through the judicial process before things will get better." Officer Granger placed her hand atop of Cynthia's and trapped her gaze. Once again she had an unyielding glare in her eyes. Cynthia admired her for her fearlessness. "I need you to be strong right now. Not just for me but for your children and yourself."

Cynthia exhaled and then closed her eyes searching for the strength to pull this off. After a moment, she went over to sit down in a chair next to the technician so that her wire could be installed.

When Cynthia entered the apartment, the foul stench of cigarette smoke was wafting in the air. She could hear the voices of Johnny B and the boys coming from the kitchen. She walked toward the sound of the men and greeted them.

"Hey," she said.

"Where has your ass been?" Johnny B was upset and irritated about something. "I've been paging you and you haven't returned my phone call."

"Johnny, I'm sorry. I had to take Anthony to the doctor," Cynthia lied.

"Doctor?" Johnny B was still suspicious.

"He has an ear infection," Cynthia continued. "He's been cranky for several days now, Johnny. You wouldn't let me out of the house over the weekend to go see about it, so I did it today."

"Where are they now?" asked Johnny B.`

"They're with my uncle. I thought you'd appreciate not having them around for a few hours. That way, I can focus on all of the business we need to handle."

"That's good thinking," Johnny B complimented her. "Come on up here with me into the front room. I have some dope that needs to be packaged." Cynthia followed Johnny B into the living room at the other end of the apartment. When Cynthia entered, she saw stacks of money and drugs piled on top of the coffee table. She'd seen Johnny with as much as thirty thousand dollars in cash, but there appeared to be much more than that before her.

"Where did you get all of this money?"

"You're asking too many questions," Johnny B said.

"Sorry, babe. It was only a question. I didn't mean

anything by it. I just get curious sometimes. Just like when I thought I wanted to try drugs. My mind just gets a little curious, that's all."

"Well, curiosity will get you killed," Johnny said as he picked up a stack of money and began separating the denominations. "For your information, this particular pile of money came from the evidence room at the station."

"Aren't the police going to miss all of this money?"

"Not if it was never logged in as evidence."

"Why wouldn't it be logged in?"

"Because the man who works in the evidence department is loyal to me, and the officer who made the arrest is sitting back there in kitchen."

"Well, who was holding the money in the first place?" Cynthia asked again.

"Girl, what's up with the one hundred and one questions? Shit, if I didn't know any better, I'd say you had on a wire."

Cynthia thought for sure she'd blown it and Johnny B was going to search her, but he didn't.

"You're such a smart leader," Cynthia said. "Those men are so loyal to you. They always listen to you," Cynthia said. "Have you always been their leader? Have they always worked for you?"

"Yes," Johnny B answered in an irritated tone. "They've always worked for me. Isn't this a bitch?" Johnny B seemed to be even more irritated.

"What?" Cynthia asked.

"I think some of this money is counterfeit. See. The color isn't right. Hang on. I'll be right back."

Johnny got up and headed toward another room calling out the name of one of his crew. Once she was sure that he was in the room, she moved toward the front door and opened it. She saw a small army of police officers. They waved for her to come out of the apartment; she was rushed down the stairs to safety. Once outside, she went into the communications van where Officer Lisa Granger was.

"You did good," Lisa said. "It's over now."

CHAPTER 20

Cynthia entered a large conference room at the downtown office of the state prosecutor. She moved toward the large conference room window and admired the birds-eye view of the Chicago River. A few moments later Officer Lisa Granger entered the conference room stating that the prosecutor had been delayed at the court building but was on his way.

"He should be here in about five minutes," she said. "I'm going to start and he can join in when he arrives."

"Okay," said Cynthia as she took a seat at the conference table.

"This is a big case that is going to expose some of the corruption in this city's government," Officer Granger said. "During my investigation I learned that Johnny B had elected officials on his payroll. This will be the type of case that has the potential to end the political careers of some influential people. Johnny B has a good defense team who will be merciless on you during cross-examination. You need to be strong on that witness stand. I want you to be ready to explain what happened. You need to give details about how Johnny B forced his way into your life. How he intimidated and threatened your life and the lives of your children. You need to tell them how you felt like a hostage and how he coerced you into a lawless lifestyle. We need the jury to understand you were under a great deal of stress at the time he entered into your life. You were a battered woman fleeing from an abusive marriage. You were expecting your second child, you were unemployed and to add to your complications, you had to deal with the loss of your mother."

"I'll do my best to explain it all, but I know I'm going to be nervous and when I get too nervous I don't explain myself very well."

"Just take your time and you'll be okay," Officer Granger reassured her. Cynthia exhaled as she tried to control her stomach, which was turning sour.

"I also want you to stay away from the media. Don't talk to them. When the trial begins the media will be swarming around the courthouse like bees at a honey pot. They may try to interview you or get you to say something about the case prior to the trial and I don't want a mistake like that to happen."

"I promise I will not say a word to anyone from the media," Cynthia reassured her.

When the trial finally began months after Johnny B's arrest, Cynthia was amazed by all of the media attention the case was receiving. Just as Officer Granger had feared, the media tried to contact Cynthia for an exclusive interview about her relationship with Johnny B. Cynthia held true to her word and didn't speak to them. She withheld all of her comments until she was sitting on the witness stand. The prosecution painted Cynthia as a good woman and mother who had little choice or defense against Johnny B. They explained how Johnny B had a pattern of taking advantage of individuals who were at the end of their rope and had little hope. However, the defense painted a completely different picture of Cynthia. They attacked Cynthia's character. They called her a seductress who used her beauty and charm to persuade men to take care of her. They called her a horrible mother for allowing her children to be raised in an environment surrounded by drugs and drug abusers. They argued that she could have left her situation at any time but decided to stay because she enjoyed the lifestyle she was living. Several times Cynthia got upset during cross-examination and disputed all claims about enjoying being trapped in the environment she was in. The trial went on for days and exposed a complicated network of drugs, money, power and politics. At the trial's conclusion, the jury reached a verdict of guilty against Johnny B.

Cynthia watched as Johnny B was escorted out of the courtroom. He glared at her for a long time and wouldn't unlock his gaze from her. If he could have stabbed her with his eyes, she'd be dead by now. Once Johnny B was out of her sight, she decided to exit the courtroom but stopped when she noticed a horde of reporters waiting for her. There were cameras on her and photographers taking her photo.

"Damn," she hissed.

"You don't have to go out through that door," Officer Granger approached her. "Come on, follow me. We'll go out another way." Cynthia followed Officer Granger through a series of doors and down a rear stairwell. They exited the court building and Officer Granger escorted Cynthia to her car.

"You did well," said Officer Granger. "I'm proud of you." Cynthia was feeling very emotional and embraced her.

Cynthia had a renewed sense of hope about the second chance that she'd been given. She now believed without a doubt that there was a God who listened and answered prayers. She was convinced of it. Cynthia purposefully didn't follow the local news coverage about Johnny B and the corrupt officers who worked for him. She didn't care to. None of that mattered to her. She learned something about herself when she made the decision to turn her life around. She learned that when she said that it didn't matter or that she was leaving the past where it was, she meant it. Now that the illegal lifestyle she'd led was buried, she saw no need to dig up its bones for further analysis.

The first thing that Cynthia needed to do was locate a new apartment. This was going to be difficult since she didn't have a legal source of income. She did, however, have close to nineteen thousand dollars that she'd secretly saved up.

Although the money was from the sale of Johnny B's drugs, she justified using it to start her life over. "The money is just payment for the years of verbal abuse that I endured with him," she told herself.

Uncle Jo Jo offered her a place to stay until she got back on her feet, but she knew that with two small children and herself, they'd be cramped. Besides, the last thing she wanted was to fall into another situation where she was dependent on someone.

"Uncle Jo Jo, all I need is about two weeks to locate an apartment. Maybe less, if I'm lucky. I know the neighborhood that I want to move to and I've already picked up an apartment guide. First thing in the morning, I'm going to start calling some of the leasing offices. I have to pay the cost to be the boss. I need to make it on my own. I've never done that and I'm scared as hell, but that doesn't matter to me. I have to stop waiting to be rescued by someone and start rescuing my damn self."

Cynthia snickered and then smiled. "I feel stronger, Uncle Jo Jo. I feel like singing that 'I Will Survive' song by Gloria Gaynor. You know, the one where she's singing about how she's going to make it after her lover has wronged her."

"Yes, I know the song," he said, smiling.

"I think that song was written especially for me. I feel like a survivor."

Uncle Jo Jo began to cough uncontrollably. When he finally got himself together, he said, "I wish Hanna would find her way just like you have."

Cynthia could see the pain in Uncle Jo Jo's eyes. They had turned red and were glassy. She knew that what his daughter was doing out there in the street was eating him up on the inside.

"My baby is out there, strung out." He paused. "I've been praying for her to find her way out of darkness and when she does, I want you two ladies to make amends. I want you to forgive each other and love each other. Y'all grew up together. You're as close as sisters."

"Uncle Jo Jo," Cynthia interrupted him. "I don't mean to be hurtful or disrespectful, but right now I don't know if it's possible for me to forgive Hanna."

"Cynthia, when you've been around for as long as I have, you learn that you should never say never. You may feel that way now, but some day when you're tired of carrying around the anger you may find that your heart is ready to forgive her."

Cynthia hugged Uncle Jo Jo and then kissed his cheek.

"I love you, Uncle Jo Jo," she whispered.

"And I love you, too."

Cynthia's plan was to rent a two-bedroom apartment and pay one year's rent in advance. She rationalized that through diligence and unwavering effort, she'd be able to find some source of employment within twelve months. Once she got an apartment, she hoped that she could locate a clerical job at a day care facility so that she wouldn't have to worry about Anthony and Angel. However, after eight days of being rejected by leasing offices, her hopes of getting out of Uncle Jo Jo's tight apartment were fading. Today she'd looked at five different apartments and tried to sign up for three of them but she had been quickly turned down when she couldn't provide a source of income. Even with her offering to pay a year's rent in advance, no one was willing to give her a break.

She had one more building to check out over in the Ravenswood neighborhood, which was on the north side of Chicago. It was a large, three-story building with six apartments, two on each floor. When she arrived, she saw that the outside of the building looked decent and well maintained. The neighborhood seemed to be very quiet, and no one was loitering. She pressed the doorbell that had the word Office typed on a sticky label.

Cynthia was buzzed into the building and noticed the intense smell of Pine-Sol right away, someone had just mopped the floor.

Cynthia walked over to the door that said Office and opened it. A doorbell chimed. Once inside, she saw a woman in her midsixties sitting at a desk. The woman looked up at Cynthia.

"What can I do for you?" the woman asked.

"I'm the one who called about the two-bedroom apartment," Cynthia said. "Is it still available?"

"It sure is," the woman said as she stood up and walked toward Cynthia. "My name is Helen Hope, but my friends all call me Hope."

"Hope. That's a pretty name. I'm sure full of hope

right about now," Cynthia whispered. Hope smiled at her as she shook her hand.

"Let me get the key to the apartment. It's on the second floor," Hope said as she went to retrieve the key. "The apartment has been vacant for about four months now. It's been repainted and I've had some new kitchen cabinets put in," said Hope as she led Cynthia back out into the hallway and over to a side door.

"The building is real secure. The outside is lit up pretty good at night and this here vestibule, as well. Not much happens around here. The neighborhood is very quiet and they are a lot of nice people staying here."

The two women entered the stairwell and walked up to the second floor. Hope opened the door and let Cynthia in.

"I love the hardwood floors," Cynthia said upon entering. It was the first thing she noticed.

"Well, some folks like wood floors and some like carpet. I like wood floors, myself. I had them redone about a year ago. Feel free to take a look around the place."

"Okay," Cynthia said and walked through the apartment. The space was nice and it certainly was more than enough room for her and the kids. Cynthia made her way back toward the front door where Hope was standing and waiting.

"This one rents for eight hundred dollars a month, right?"

"Yeah, that's what I'm letting it go for," Hope said.

"You own the building?" Cynthia asked, surprised.

"Yup. I bought it when I retired from the public school system. I was a teacher for thirty-seven years. You have any children?"

"Yes. Two. A boy and a girl. Why do you ask? Children aren't going to be problem, right?"

"Oh, no. Children are fine. I'm asking because I turned one of the apartments downstairs into a day care facility. It's nice for the tenants who have children because they just drop them off to me before they head out to work. The facility is licensed by the state and the children are well taken care of."

"You wouldn't happen to be hiring, would you?" Cynthia tried to smile but it was difficult because she knew that her question would cause Hope to pause.

"No. My granddaughters and I run the place. Most of the kids who come there go to the school up the street. We have a van out back. We take kids to school and pick them back up. We feed them and even help most of them with their homework. We have a couple of computers to help them learn. So, do you like the place?"

"I love it. It feels like my home. It feels like I'm supposed to be here."

"Well, the place is available. All I need is first and last months' rent, your last paycheck stub and a quick credit check. We can go back to the office and fill out the paperwork."

"Look. I'm going to be honest with you. I'm not working right now but I plan to get job."

"Well planning to get a job and having one are two different things, sugar."

"I know, but I can pay you one year's rent in advance and in cash." Cynthia noticed Hope's eyebrows go up.

"So, who are you running from? The police?"

"No," Cynthia answered

"A boyfriend? Ex-husband, ex-convict, what?"

"I've just gotten out of a very bad relationship and I'm trying to start over. I've saved up enough money to keep myself going for a year."

"So what type of work did you do before you became unemployed?"

"Well..." Cynthia paused. Hope's eyes reminded her of her mother's. She realized that Hope was no fool and would be able to spot a lie a mile away.

"I was married for a while and working as a clerk. But then I got pregnant with my first child and became a stay-at-home mom. My husband and I drifted apart. He beat me, so I left and divorced him. After that my mother passed away, I got depressed and ended up in a relationship with the wrong type of man."

"Did he beat you, too?"

Cynthia was encouraged by Hope's interest in what she was explaining to her. "Yeah, he did hit me once or twice."

"Bastard!" Hope said.

"Anyway, some things happened and he ended up in jail."

"What did he do for a living?" Hope asked.

"He was a police officer."

"Is that a fact? You know, just a few days ago, they

had this big thing in the news about corrupt police officers. It was a big mess. The mayor and everybody were talking about it."

"Yeah, I know. That's the situation I just left," Cynthia said, ashamed, and then hung her head. "Look, I don't want to waste your time. Thank you for showing me the place."

Cynthia walked down the stairs and out the bottom door. Once inside the vestibule, she made her way to the front door.

"Cynthia!" Hope called.

"Yes?" Cynthia turned to face her.

"Come here, child."

Cynthia walked back over and stood in front of Hope. Hope placed her hands on Cynthia's shoulders and looked her directly in the eye.

"Are you truly done with those men?"

"Yes," Cynthia answered. "My ex-husband has dropped off into the deep end, if you know what mean."

"And the other fella is behind bars."

"Yes. I've turned my life around. I'm just trying to start over. I just want to do it right this time, and all I need is a chance."

"Do you have a church home?"

"No, but I certainly need one."

"Come on back here into my office and let's see what we can work out."

Cynthia closed her eyes for a moment and then exhaled. "Thank you," she said to Hope. "You won't regret this."

"I know. I've had my run-ins with domestic violence myself. I understand what you're going through. When push comes to shove, you have to do what you've got to do."

CHAPTER 21

Cynthia couldn't believe how quickly five years had passed. She was now twenty-eight years old but felt older than her years. She blamed both Butch and Johnny B for stressing her out during the course of their relationships. However, neither one of them mattered to her anymore. Both Butch and Hanna were still drug addicts and, according to her uncle Jo Jo, neither one of them could be trusted. In Cynthia's mind, they deserved one another. Butch hadn't been around to see his children or offer any support. His absence didn't matter to Cynthia because she really didn't want Butch coming around her children. She didn't want to have to explain to them how their father had become a drug addict. Hope, who Cynthia considered to be a godsend, had on occasion asked her if Butch had made any efforts to see the children.

"I wouldn't want him to, Hope," Cynthia said. "The very sight of him would probably scar them for life."

"Well, just keep him in your prayers. He may find his way out of the hell that's he's living in," Hope said.

Cynthia had adopted Hope as her surrogate mother

and had developed the utmost respect and love for her. The kids loved her, as well, and considered Hope to be their grandmother. They genuinely enjoyed being around her, primarily because Hope let them have their way as long as they behaved in an acceptable manner. Hope had an infectious personality and it was hard to hold a grudge against her, even when they had differences of opinion.

Hope had helped Cynthia tremendously when she first arrived five years ago. She babysat her children free of charge while Cynthia searched for a job, and even helped her with her résumé. Cynthia was willing to do whatever it took to remain independent. Falling into her cycle of dependency was not an option for her. After nine months of searching, hoping and praying, a position as an office secretary became available at the neighborhood grammar school. Since Hope knew the principal, she put in a good word for her and Cynthia was offered the job. The pay wasn't much, but with it she was able to manage her bills, keep food on the table and clothes on the backs of her children, and that's what mattered most to Cynthia.

Her son, Anthony, was now nine and Angel was seven. Cynthia was amazed at how different they were from each other.

Anthony was the most organized little boy she'd ever known. It amazed her that he couldn't stand clutter or things in disarray. Anthony was also very smart, and math was his favorite subject. He could calculate numbers and provide you with an answer while playing with his toys, all without missing a beat.

"I believe he's gifted," Hope explained one afternoon when Cynthia had come home from work. Hope sometimes pitched in and helped the kids with their homework when Cynthia had to work late. "You need to look into placing him in a school that has a strong math and science curriculum. He needs to be challenged so that he doesn't get bored."

"Hope, he's only in fifth grade. I don't want to put that type of pressure on him."

"Cynthia, I'm telling you from experience. Anthony can and will run circles around other students. He's already understanding algebra and some trigonometry. All I'm saying is, he should be tested to see just how beautiful his mind is."

Cynthia finally agreed and had Anthony tested. Although he scored well, it wasn't enough to convince educators that he should be placed in an advanced program.

Angel, on the other hand, hated math and science. What she liked to do was make up stories and tell lies on her brother, which drove Cynthia crazy.

"She's going to be a writer," Hope said, laughing at Cynthia one morning when she had to discipline Angel for lying.

"I don't know what I'm going to do with her little behind," Cynthia said. "I don't know how she can look me in my face and lie to me like I'm some kind of fool."

Hope chuckled again. "Boy wait until she becomes a teenager. You're going to have your hands full."

"She might not make it at the rate she's going," Cynthia countered.

"She just has an active imagination, that's all. I'm telling you, it's a sign that she may have talent for becoming a writer."

"Or a politician."

Both Cynthia and Hope laughed.

It was Saturday morning and Cynthia was intending to fully enjoy sleeping in late. She was resting comfortably in her bed when a loud crashing noise startled her.

"Oooo." She heard Anthony's voice.

Oh God, Cynthia thought. *Now what in the world have they done?*

"Mama!" Anthony called. She heard the sound of feet rushing toward her bedroom door. Cynthia pulled her blanket over her head.

"Mama!" Anthony shook her shoulder. "I was in the kitchen making me some cereal and milk and Angel come in there and made me drop my bowl on the floor."

Cynthia removed the blanket and looked at both her son and daughter, who were standing next to her bed.

"No, I didn't. Mama he's telling a big old story," Angel complained. "He was in the kitchen and—and—he was spinning the bowl around on the table like a spinning top and it spun off the table and onto the floor. And that's what happened. I didn't make him do anything."

"Mama, she's lying again." Anthony glared at his little sister. "You're always making up stories. One of these days, they're going to put you in jail for making up stories about people."

"Anthony, stop it," Cynthia said as she sat up. "All I want to know is did anyone clean up the mess?"

"I didn't do it so I shouldn't have to clean it up," Angel said.

"You did do it!" Anthony said.

"Both of you, be quiet." Cynthia glanced over at the clock on the nightstand. It was six forty-five in the morning. "Why is it that during the week I have to fight with you guys to get out of bed early so that you can get ready for school, but on Saturday you're able to get up early in the morning just to fight?"

"I couldn't sleep," Anthony said. Cynthia was about to ask another question, but she was interrupted by a knock at the front door.

"I'll get it," Angel said and rushed toward the front door.

"Don't open that door, Angel!" Cynthia hollered after her as she got out of bed and moved toward the front door.

"Who is it?" she asked.

"It's me, Hope. Is everything okay? I heard a loud noise."

Cynthia opened the door.

"Yeah. Angel and Anthony were in here fighting first thing this morning. Come on in and have a seat. I'll be right back," Cynthia said and headed toward the bathroom to freshen up.

Cynthia and Hope's relationship was a strong, loving and supportive one. Cynthia had gotten completely comfortable with Hope coming over at the drop of a dime. Although Hope could never be a replacement for her mother, there were many things about Hope that reminded Cynthia of Elaine and that was a welcome feeling.

Once Cynthia had freshened up, she went back into the front room where Hope and the children were sitting together watching cartoons. Angel was snuggled underneath Hope's left arm and Anthony was on the floor resting flat on his belly.

"Watch yourself, Angel," Hope said as she got up from Cynthia's cozy sofa. "I made them clean up the mess they made in the kitchen."

"Thank you. Come on into the kitchen with me," Cynthia said. "I'll make breakfast and coffee for us."

"I've already eaten," Hope said. "You know that I get up at the crack of dawn. But I will have a cup of coffee with you."

Hope trailed Cynthia into the kitchen and took a seat at Cynthia's kitchen table. Hope slid the salt and pepper shakers over to the side, then focused her attention on Cynthia, who was pulling down coffee filters from the top cabinet.

"I told those children that after they finished watching cartoons, we should all go to the library and pick us out a book to read."

"Well, I know that Angel was all for it," Cynthia commented.

"Yeah, she was. I'm telling you, that girl is going to be writer. She just loves reading and she's a strong reader, as well. I love it when children are interested in learning. Because let me tell you, over the years I've had to teach some of the dumbest children God ever placed on the earth."

"Hope, stop that," Cynthia said, laughing. "You shouldn't talk about kids like that."

"Well, it's true."

"We'll all have to go to the library later. I'm glad you mentioned that because Anthony needs to work on his science project. He wants to do it on the life cycle of the monarch butterfly, so we have to go find some books on butterflies as well as stop and pick up some poster board. We can do it after choir rehearsal."

"That sounds fine. Say, speaking of choir rehearsal, you know that Bryan, the choir director, asked about you again."

"I'm not interested in men," Cynthia quickly answered.

"I don't see why not. He's a very handsome man and a good catch," Hope said.

"I think he has some interest in you but doesn't want to offend you," Hope continued.

"Hope," Cynthia said, turning to face her, "I know that you're not trying to play matchmaker again."

"Baby, you're so young. I worry about you sometimes. You shouldn't write men off totally because you picked two bad apples from the barrel. There are still plenty of good men out there. You just have to learn how to spot the good apples from the ones that are rotten to the core, that's all."

"Hope, this is where you and I have our conflicts. I'm perfectly fine just being with my children."

"But what happens once they've left the house to start their own lives? You don't want to be the type of mother who can't let go. Your children will resent you for that."

"I'm not going to be like that at all. Once they're ready to leave, they can," Cynthia said, even though she knew she'd feel pretty lonely once they left home.

"It's been five years. That's a long time. Hell, I'm seventy and I still long for the touch of a man from time to time. You can't just stop living. I know that I didn't."

"I don't want to be bothered with men. They're too much damn trouble, and my heart just isn't into the whole falling-in-love madness. Besides, when I have urges for a little action, I have Killer, my vibrator. He does the trick and he doesn't give me bullshit. That suits me just fine."

"You're going to mess up your stuff messing around with that mechanical contraption. Either that, or you're going to reach a point where you're going to forget what it feels like to be with a person."

"Why are we having this conversation?"

"Because I want you to be happy. You've come such a long way and you deserve some happiness."

"I am happy," Cynthia insisted.

"Okay, call me old-fashioned but I want you to experience at least once in your life what it feels like to have a man love you back just as much as you love him. I had that with my second husband, and I feel that every woman and man should experience the glow of love at least once in their lives."

"All I need is the love of my God and the love of my children. I don't need anything else," Cynthia said, quickly switching the topic of the discussion to her plans to shop for some new spring clothing for the children.

"I told Bryan Jones that he should ask you out on a date," Hope quickly added, interrupting Cynthia's rambling.

"You did what?"

"It's just a little dinner for singles at the church. He didn't want to go alone and he didn't want to go through your children to ask you, although Angel was going to tell him that he should just come up to you and ask you for a date outright. That child is too grown for her own good sometimes."

"I'm not going to some church dinner for singles with him and that's final." Cynthia was now mad and ready for Hope to leave.

Hope sensed Cynthia's irritation and thought that it was best for her to pass on the coffee for now. She made her way back toward the front door, Cynthia trailing behind her.

"What time do you want to head over to the library?" Hope asked before she left.

"We can leave right after rehearsal. I'll come back and pick you up."

"All right. I'll make sure that I'm ready," Hope said and then left.

Cynthia shut the door and then locked it. She rested her back against the door, closed her eyes and exhaled.

I'm afraid of men. I refuse to allow any man to get close to me. It hurts entirely too much to nurture a relationship only to have it fail.

CHAPTER 22

Cynthia had arrived at the church late for Anthony and Angel's choir rehearsal session. When she entered the sanctuary, the youth choir was in the middle of practicing the song "Shombock." Bryan Jones was playing the gospel melody on the piano but suddenly stopped when he wasn't getting the emotion he needed from the youth choir.

"Hold on, hold on," Bryan said. "Okay, listen. I need you all to be quiet for a moment and listen."

"Go on up there." Cynthia rushed Anthony and Angel off so that they could join the rest of the choir in the stands. When Bryan saw them take their place, his train of thought was interrupted. He looked at them briefly and then turned to find Cynthia. She acknowledged him by waving hello to him. Bryan smiled and then turned his attention back to the choir.

As soon as Cynthia sat down she felt the begrudging eyes of a few women in church all over her. She felt as if she had a target hovering above her head. Why the hell are they staring at me like that? Cynthia wondered.

"I need you all to wake up this morning," Bryan said.

"I'm hearing a lot of lazy voices." Bryan pointed to his right. "Altos, you sound very flat this morning and I need you to pull it together. Okay. I know what we're going to do. Let's do some exercises. Everyone stretch your arms way up high. Now, to the left. Hold it. Now lean to the right. Your body is your instrument, and we need to make sure that it's ready to be heard."

Cynthia had to admit that Bryan was very good with the Little Worriers Youth Choir, which consisted of children between the ages of six and thirteen.

"Okay, come on we have about five songs to learn today so we don't have time to mess around," Bryan said as he sat down behind the piano, which faced the choir stands. He struck the piano keys a few times and asked them to sing "Fa La So Do Me."

Bryan was pleased with their response. "Good," he said excitedly. "A little louder this time. Good. If you give me one hundred percent today, we'll be out of here in no time."

Cynthia watched, listened and allowed the beautiful young voices to fill her heart and soul. She also had to admit that Bryan was extremely talented and was blessed with a magnificent singing voice. He was also very expressive with his hands in order to make sure that the choir understood how much emphasis he wanted on a particular note.

One of the things that she loved about coming to church was that no matter how bad things seemed, whenever she came to church and listened to the sermons and the music, she always left with a sense of renewed hope that everything in her life was going to be all right.

After rehearsal was over, Bryan asked all the parents and children to come together and form a large circle so that they could all pray together.

"Okay, which member of the Little Worriers would like to lead the prayer?"

"I'll do it," Anthony quickly answered. Cynthia smiled at him and felt a sense of pride that he was confident enough in himself to lead the prayer.

"Thank you, Father, for waking us up this morning and blessing us with family and friends who love us. And thank you for all of the good things that you've done for us and thank you for making all of the beautiful voices so that we can sing and praise you. Please watch over us and make sure that we all arrive home safely. Amen."

Everyone said amen afterward and then began gathering their belongings. Cynthia was about to go back to where she was sitting to gather her things, but Bryan stopped her.

"Ms. Clark," he said. "How are you doing today?"

"Fine." Cynthia looked at him suspiciously. She still felt all of the evil eyes studying her every move.

"I was wondering if Ms. Hope spoke to you about the dinner that the singles ministry has organized." Cynthia exhaled, then looked at the floor for a moment. She didn't want to hurt Bryan but she needed to make it clear to him that she just wasn't interested in anything remotely close to dating. She also didn't want to deal with the gossip and rumors that would buzz around the church.

"Bryan," she said gently, "Ms. Hope has a good heart and good intentions, but if she's given you the impression that I'm interested in the singles ministry, she has misled you."

"Oh. I see." Bryan paused in thought for a moment, she feared she'd just destroyed every ounce of courage that he had.

"I didn't mean to come on to you like that," he said. "I just thought you might enjoy it. It's just a group of adults gathering at Jazz and Java, which is a new black-owned coffee shop not too far from here. On Saturday evenings, they have a live jazz concert by a local band. They also have an open mike session where poets get the opportunity to read their work. It's a completely comfortable setting and you can leave anytime. Ms. Hope said that you don't go out much and thought that it would be okay for me to ask if you were interested."

Cynthia was about to tell him that her answer was still no, but she paused because she was somewhat interested in listening to poets. She'd always loved poetry and admired those who could write it. She'd tried it a few times, but was unsuccessful because she couldn't get her words to flow right.

"It sounds like a really nice time, but I'm just not interested," Cynthia answered conclusively.

"I tell you what," Bryan said. "If you change your mind, here's the address." Bryan pulled out his wallet and gave her a card. At that moment, both Angel and Anthony came over to Cynthia.

"Can we go to the library now?" Anthony asked.

"In a minute, honey," Cynthia said.

"Well, did you ask her yet?" Angel came right out and asked.

"Angel!" Cynthia glared at her daughter. "Go sit your tail down over there."

"It's okay." Bryan smiled. "You have beautiful children."

"Thank you," Cynthia said.

"They're well-mannered and behaved. They also look just like you. Especially Angel."

"Actually, she really resembles her father more," Cynthia admitted.

"Well, he has to be one proud father to have such a beautiful young daughter." At that moment, Cynthia felt something inside her break. It was fragile baggage of Butch's that she was still carrying around.

"I have to go now," Cynthia said abruptly and then walked away from him.

"Tell me more about yourself. Where are you and your family from?" Bryan attempted to continue their conversation, but Cynthia wasn't about to disclose anything from her past.

Later that evening, Cynthia was at home spending time with her children. The three of them were sitting at the kitchen table working. Cynthia was helping Anthony look through some nature magazines so that he could cut out pictures of butterflies for his science project. Angel was sitting at the other end of the table practicing writing. Cynthia got up for a moment and turned on the stereo, which was in the other room. She turned the music up a little so that she could hear it in the kitchen. Toni Braxton was crooning about how love should've brought her man home last night. To Cynthia's surprise, when she returned to the kitchen Angel was singing the words to the song as if she'd experienced everything that Toni was crooning about.

"You need to be quiet because you're not doing nothing but messing up that song," Anthony said to his sister.

"Don't be mad because I sound better than you do," Angel fired back. Angel and Anthony seemed to enjoy competing with each other, but at times Cynthia wondered if it was healthy.

"Stop it, both of you," she said as she sat back down with them.

A short time later there was a knock at the front door.

"Anthony, go answer the door. I know it isn't anyone but Hope, but make sure you ask who it is before you open the door," Cynthia said.

"I'll do it," Angel said, trying to beat Anthony to the front door.

"Angel, I told him to do it," Cynthia shouted and stopped her daughter in her tracks. "Come sit back down and finish practicing." Angel came back to her seat.

"What are you in here doing?" Hope asked as she entered the kitchen.

"Homework," Cynthia answered as she found a photo of several butterflies that Anthony could cut out. At that moment, a radio advertisement for Jazz and Java played and Cynthia paused to listen.

"Isn't that the place Bryan was talking about?" asked Hope.

"Yeah, I think it was."

"It sounds like a nice place," Hope said and then paused for a long moment.

"What?" asked Cynthia.

"Bryan called me to ask if you were okay."

"Why would he do that?"

"Because he says that he thinks he's offended you. He says that you just turned and walked away from him in the middle of your conversation today."

Cynthia thought about how quickly she'd left when Bryan had made her remember that Butch was the father of her children.

"I didn't have anything more to say," Cynthia said.

"Well, you didn't have to be rude to the man. He's a good man. He has Christ in his heart. In fact, that's probably the first thing you need to find out about a man before you get serious with him. You need to find out if he lives by and believes in the word of God. If there ever was a right man to be interested in, it's him."

"I wasn't trying to be rude to him. I just had something on my mind at that particular moment. I..." Cynthia lost her train of thought.

"What were you thinking about, Mama?" Angel asked as she concentrated on her writing.

"Nothing that concerns you," Cynthia answered her

daughter. She began to reconsider and turned back to Hope. "Have you ever been down to that Jazz and Java place?"

"No, but I've heard that it's a very nice place. I'm sure you'd like it. You should treat yourself," Hope said. "You should just go and enjoy yourself. Do you realize that I've known you for five years and you've never gone out on a date? You don't even treat yourself. You don't take vacations or anything. You just go to work and come home."

"Well, when my daddy gets better he's going to fly my mama off to Paris," Angel said. On several occasions, Cynthia had explained to her children that their father was very ill and was unable to see them. She said that when he got better, he'd come around to see them. Angel, who'd never met him, still fantasized about the day she'd meet him.

"That'll be the day," Anthony responded to his sister's comment.

"Anthony! Don't be like that, you hear?"

"Yeah, I hear you."

"Hope, my money is always tight and I just don't have extra cash to spend on entertainment."

"Well, from what I heard, the Jazz and Java place is free to get into. And a cup of coffee isn't going to cost you more that two or three dollars, and it certainly won't cost you anything to sit and listen to music."

"So what are you trying to say, Hope?"

"It's Saturday night. I'll watch the kids for a few hours while you go down there and enjoy a night to yourself."

"I don't know." Cynthia was still hesitant.

"Goodness, child. What do I have to do in order to get you to live a little bit for yourself?"

Cynthia paused and thought once again. "I would like to hear some poetry." She smiled.

"Then go and listen," Hope said. "Come on. Go into your room, find you some comfortable clothes and take your behind on out of here."

Hope pulled Cynthia to her feet and forced her to go and change her clothes.

When Cynthia arrived at Jazz and Java, it was like stepping into a different world for her. There were no children to take care of or keep up with. In some ways, she felt a little out of place. She felt awkward, thinking she should have come with a date. As she looked around the café and noticed the couples, she suddenly got cold feet. She was about to turn and leave when, out of nowhere, Bryan appeared.

"You're not going to leave so soon are you?"

Cynthia felt completely out of place and nervous. "This really isn't for me. I don't even know why I came down here."

"Give it chance," Bryan encouraged her.

"No. You don't understand. I've never done anything like this."

"What, you've never gone out to a coffee shop before?" Bryan looked at her, confused.

"No, I mean—" Cynthia was suddenly at a loss for words.

"Come on. Have a seat and enjoy the show."

Cynthia reluctantly followed Bryan to the table where he was sitting, which was situated near the stage.

"This is a good seat. You'll be able to see and hear well from right here. Would you like something to drink?"

"I don't know what to order."

"Let me order something for you, then. I'll be right back." Bryan returned a short while later with an espresso.

The two them sat and listened to the music and Cynthia, for the first time in a long while, felt alive. She felt like a hermit who'd come of a cave after a long slumber. The soft music was wonderful and the atmosphere was more relaxing than she'd thought it would be. There was no pressure and no toxic souls walking around trying to control her. In fact, as she looked around the room, she saw nothing but beautiful people of color.

"Do you come here a lot?" Cynthia leaned in toward Bryan.

"I have to let you in on a secret. My cousin owns the place."

"Wow." Cynthia was impressed. "It's a very nice place he has."

"He and his wife were in the restaurant business for a while, but then decided that it was time to strike out on their own."

"Well, I've always admired people who could make their dreams come true," Cynthia said as the band ended their session.

"Now comes the poetry part. Do you like poetry?" asked Bryan.

"Yes, I love it. Although I must admit that I haven't read any in a very long time."

Bryan smiled at her, and the beauty of his smile warmed her heart.

"I'm so glad that you came."

"Well, I'm glad that I came, too."

Cynthia sat and listened as various poets stood in front of the microphone and recited their work. She allowed their words to dance freely around her and bring forth feelings of warmth and joy. She was so into the poets that she hadn't noticed that Bryan had left the table and was now on stage. He approached the microphone and cleared his throat.

"This one is for a very special woman." He deepened his voice and Cynthia liked the sound of it. His voice made the air around her ripple and tickle her skin. "This piece is called, 'Let Me Dry Your Tears.'" Bryan closed his eyes and began reciting.

> Baby, let me dry your tears, and defeat your fears so that we can be with each other year after year.
> Baby let me dry your tears so that I can hold you near and make you understand my dear that I will always be here even if God makes me disappear.
> Let me dry your tears and kiss your ears with sweet music that I know you yearn to hear.
> Baby let my dry your tears and fulfill your years with happiness love and loud loving cheers.

Baby let me dry your tears so that everything becomes clear that I am the man you've been longing to endear.
Baby let me dry your tears to that you don't mishear that I want to be your man by the middle of this year."

After Bryan said that, he opened his eyes and focused on Cynthia. There was no mistaking the warm look in his eyes. She knew that he had more than a passing interest in her. The audience clapped and cheered Bryan for his wonderful work, but he didn't acknowledge them right away.

Cynthia was awestruck. No one had ever read poetry to her. No one's words had ever made her feel the way that Bryan's words did. No man had ever been that nice to her, and she didn't know what to do with these new feelings Bryan was bringing out in her.

The only thing that she knew at that moment was that she felt very special. She sensed that there was much more that he could've said but that he'd held back. Cynthia didn't want him to, she wanted him to keep on going because she thought that she'd never tire of listening to him.

Cynthia smiled at Bryan and then began clapping and cheering for him along with the rest of coffee shop patrons.

Something new and wonderful had happened to Cynthia. A man whom she barely knew had broken through her defenses and hugged a part of her that had been locked away for years. At that moment, she realized that Bryan was a very special man and that she might be missing out on something wonderful.

CHAPTER 23

A few weeks later, Cynthia was standing in front of her bathroom mirror putting the finishing touches on her makeup. She'd finally agreed to go on a real date with Bryan, something that was still foreign to her in many ways.

As she thought about dating, she realized that it was something she'd never done. At least not in the traditional sense, because Butch had never taken her out anywhere because he'd always hosted house parties. Johnny B was no better and could have cared less about spending any real time with her in order to get to know her.

So, in many ways, at the age of twenty-eight, Cynthia felt as if she was going out on her first date.

Angel, who was excited about seeing her mother dressing up, entered the bathroom and began toying with a tube of lipstick that was on the countertop.

"Angel, put that down," Cynthia said to her as she put on her eyeliner.

"I want to try it," she whined.

"You're too young for lipstick," Cynthia told her. But

before she could stop her, Angel had placed a healthy amount on her lips.

"Do I look as pretty as you?" Angel asked.

Cynthia glanced down at her daughter and smiled. "You look even prettier," she said then kissed Angel's forehead.

Cynthia was finally satisfied with the way she looked, so she returned all of her makeup items and went into the front room where she found Hope and Anthony glancing out the front window waiting for Bryan to pull up.

"He's here!" Anthony announced.

"Why are you screaming like that, boy?" Cynthia asked. "You act as if you've never seen him before."

"Mr. Jones is just cool, that's all," Anthony said. "Besides, I'm glad that he's taking you someplace nice."

"Oh, Lord," Cynthia said as she walked over to the closet to get a coat.

"What's taking him so long?" Cynthia heard Anthony ask.

"He just finished parking his car," Hope answered. By the time Cynthia had retrieved her coat, Anthony was letting Bryan into their apartment.

"Hello, everyone," Bryan greeted them all.

"Now, you know if you mess up, I'm going to have to cut you, right?"

Cynthia couldn't believe that Anthony had just said that. "Anthony!" She gave him a look that said he was going to get it when she returned home.

"Uncle Jo Jo told me to tell him that," Anthony quickly explained.

"Oh, Lord, Uncle Jo Jo knows about this, too?"

"Yeah, I told him," Anthony admitted.

"Bryan, don't pay him any attention. My uncle Jo Jo is just plain old crazy."

"It's okay," Bryan said, laughing. "It's just a sign of a good family who cares for each other."

"Okay. I'm ready," Cynthia said.

"Well, go on, get on out of here," Hope said. "I've got everything here covered. You two go and have a good time."

"And you'd better bring her back the same way she left here," Anthony said to Bryan just before he walked out.

"Anthony, you're pushing it!" Cynthia yelled back from the stairwell.

Bryan was taking Cynthia to a new comedy club that had just opened called All Jokes Aside. He'd learned through a friend of his that it was a great first date location.

Cynthia had a wonderful time. She laughed so hard at the jokes that her stomach ached. It was strange to her to have a man who treated her as kindly as Bryan did.

She'd never truly known that a man could be so considerate and caring. She was used to arguments and power struggles in a relationship.

One of the things that she was attracted to was Bryan's attitude and outlook on life. He was easygoing and easy to talk with, and her kids were crazy about him.

After they left the comedy club they went out to dinner at Carmen's, a great Italian restaurant on Rush Street. She learned a lot more about Bryan during dinner.

"I have a soft spot for single moms," he admitted. "My dad left my mom before I was born."

"Why did he leave?" Cynthia asked.

"From what I understand, he'd lied to my mother and told her that he was single when he was actually married with three children."

"Oh, I'm so sorry to hear that."

"Don't be. It is what it is. Anyway, my mom and uncles raised me and even put me through college."

"What school did you go to?" Cynthia asked.

"Chicago State University. I went there for music," he said. "My grandmother was a church-going, God-fearing woman who made sure that my behind was in church with her every Sunday all day long." Bryan laughed at the memory.

"I'm telling you, I'd want to be outside running around with my friends but I couldn't. Eventually, I took an interest in the piano and learned how to play by ear. That made my grandmother very proud."

"So do you still play by ear?"

"No. I learned how to read music and after I graduated I gave lessons."

"So what do you do for a living? I know that you're a deacon and you work well with children."

"I work for the IEMA. You ever heard of it?"

"No."

"It's the Illinois Emergency Management Agency. You ever watch the news after a bad storm and learn the governor has to declare a certain area a disaster?"

"Yes, I hear that from time to time."

"Well, when that happens, the IEMA enables the state to assist affected communities with debris removal and other storm-related issues. Many times I have to drive to smaller counties in southern Illinois and set up an office. I then go out to survey affected areas and give direction to local civic and community leaders."

"Southern Illinois has a lot of flooding problems, right?" Cynthia was fascinated by what Bryan did for a living.

"Flooding has been a problem, but southern Illinois gets hit by tornados a lot, as well, and that can be devastating to communities."

"So how did you go from majoring in music to doing a job like that?"

Bryan laughed. "I believe in doing good service for the community. When my musical aspirations didn't turn out as I'd hoped, I got involved with an organization that helped to build affordable housing in under-served communities. I became the fiscal manager and made sure the funds got to the right people. The projects turned out to be very successful, and we placed a lot of families in good homes. Then a college buddy of mine who was working for the state asked if I'd be interested in coming to work for the Illinois Emergency Management Agency. It was a good career move."

Bryan paused. "But I still had my love for music and for working with children so I love to volunteer my time to the church, my God and my faith. What about you, Ms. Clark? What's your story?"

Cynthia thought that her life was so different from his and for a moment felt that she might be wrong for him.

"Did I say something wrong?" Bryan asked.

"No." Cynthia put on a fake smile. "My life was rather complicated."

Cynthia said, "My mother didn't have any advantages in life and she never finished high school. She only got as far as her sophomore year before she had to take a job to help put food on the table. She worked for a nursing home, bathing elderly people. I thought I had it all figured out when I was young. I knew that I didn't want to stay in the house with my mother and struggle and I thought that my ticket away from that life was to get married. I chased after this neighborhood guy for about two years and finally got him to marry me. I was happy at the time because I thought I'd made it. I thought I'd been rescued and would live happily ever after."

At that moment, a waiter interrupted them. Cynthia and Bryan gave the waiter their orders. Once he'd taken everything down, he said he'd return with their drinks.

"Go on," Bryan said.

"There is really not much to tell, Bryan. My life is nothing compared to the good things you do. I mean, you help people survive the most horrible situations imaginable."

"This isn't about me. I already know all about me. I want to know everything about you."

Cynthia knew that there was no way she was going to tell him everything about herself. There was no way she was going to mention the three years of her life that she'd spent as a drug dealer. She knew that would turn his stomach and he'd take her home.

"My ex-husband became abusive. He'd beat up on me and make me feel really low. I felt like I was nothing to him." Cynthia lowered her head for a moment as she gathered her thoughts.

"Here are your drinks, folks," the waiter said as he placed their drinks before them and then went to another table.

"So you divorced him, right?"

"To make a long story short, yes. I divorced him and the rest, as they say, is history."

"It just sickens me to learn that some man was beating up on you. You're so beautiful and warm."

Bryan's kind words made Cynthia feel both good and uncomfortable. "Wife beaters are scum of the earth. They're just as low as drug dealers. I wish that there were a way I could rid the planet of people like that. Wife beaters, drug dealers and criminals, every last one of them needs to be placed in front of a firing squad."

"Wow. That's a pretty decisive position," Cynthia said paying close attention to this new side of his personality.

"I don't have any tolerance for certain types of individuals."

"Maybe a person didn't have a choice or perhaps they were forced into something," Cynthia said.

"In my opinion, life is about choices. In my heart I feel most people understand the difference between right and wrong, as well as good and evil. I think a person at some point makes a conscious choice to do what's right or wrong."

"Okay," Cynthia answered not wanting to continue that conversation. It was clear to her that Bryan's position on certain things was fixed. She quickly changed the subject. "Let's not talk about that anymore. I want to know more about you. Have you ever been married? Do you have any children?"

"I was almost married once but my would-be bride got involved with another man. So my wedding plans were tossed out of the window. It took a while for my heart to recover from that one because I really thought she was the woman for me."

"So you've been hurt?"

"Yeah," Bryan admitted.

"It looks like we've both been wronged to some degree," Cynthia added. "What about children?"

"I don't have any. One day I hope to be blessed with a child."

At that moment, Cynthia wanted to know why he was interested in her and not a woman without children.

"So why aren't you out there searching for a woman who doesn't have kids? I mean, I have two and I'm not saying that I couldn't have more, but..."

"I told you. I have a soft spot for single moms. Besides, I like your kids and I can tell that you're a good mother just by the way they carry themselves. So, honestly, I could meet a woman without kids, but she may not have the nurturing skills that you have. I've seen far too many mothers who will drop their newborn children off with someone in order to go out and run the streets to chase something that isn't worth the time they're wasting."

"So you're saying that you think I'm a good mother?"

Cynthia wanted to tell him that she hadn't started out that way. She wanted to tell him that she could have lost her children had she not turned her life around, but she just couldn't bring herself to do it.

"I think you're doing a fine job," Bryan said, and that made Cynthia feel good about herself.

During the next several months, Cynthia and Bryan spent a lot of time with each other and the kids. Cynthia enjoyed being around him. She loved the way that he made her feel about herself. She eventually began assisting him with the Little Worriers Youth Choir and got more involved in community activities with him.

They became a couple and everyone within their closely knit church family knew the two of them were made for each other. However, not everyone in the church was happy about the relationship. Other single female church members who wanted to lasso Bryan for themselves became envious and suspicious of Cynthia. It wasn't long before inquiries about her past and where she'd come from surfaced. For the most part, Cynthia did what needed to be done to keep the nosey members from finding out about her life. Then one day, directly after choir rehearsal she overheard big mouth Hester Brown and pigeon-toed Patty Picket talking about her.

"There is something about Cynthia that doesn't sit well with me," Patty said.

"It's because no one knows a damn thing about her except for Ms. Hope and she won't give up any type of information on her," replied Hester.

"She's hiding something," Patty concluded.

"Or lying about something. I've seen Cynthia someplace before, but I can't remember where," Hester said.

"She never talks about the father of her children, and whenever I've tried to be cordial and talk about any brothers or sisters she may have, she gets an attitude. I think she feels as if she's a queen or something. I mean, just because she's pretty and has all the men in church, married and single, drooling over her doesn't give her the right to treat people like they're beneath her," Patty said.

"Well, one thing is for sure. Someone is going to have to speak with Bryan about her. Somebody is going to have to warn him to be careful and keep a close eye on her. I just wish I could recall where I've seen her," said Hester.

"Bryan is such a good man," Patty said. "I certainly hate that he's blinded by her pretty looks and shapely figure."

"Just because the package is pretty on the outside, doesn't mean it's pretty on the inside," said Hester.

"I know that's right," Patty supported Hester's viewpoint. "I think we should warn Bryan. We should let him know something is very strange about Cynthia."

"Hello, ladies," Cynthia interrupted them. Hester and

Patty quickly spun around and placed plastic smiles on their faces. Neither one of them had heard Cynthia approach them from behind.

"Hello, Cynthia," they both chimed.

"You two look as if you've just been shot with horse crap and left hanging to stink." Cynthia felt catty and wanted Hester and Patty to know it. Cynthia felt bad about using inappropriate language inside the church but a very wicked part of herself surfaced without warning.

"Excuse me," said Hester who had a confrontational glare in her eyes.

"It's a shame there are toxic souls buzzing around the house of the Lord like flies at a picnic," Cynthia said. Hester and Patty were about to respond but Angel came up beside Cynthia.

"Mom, Bryan wants to know if it's okay with you if I sit in on one of his piano lessons. Can I stay and watch for a little while?" Cynthia didn't acknowledge Angel right away because her glare was locked on Hester and Patty.

"Come on, Hester, we've got better things to do other than worry about filth floating around this church."

"What's wrong with them, Mama?" Angel asked.

"They just got scratched up in a catfight, that's all."

"Catfight? What's that?"

"Nothing that you need to worry about," Cynthia said.

During their courtship, the issue of lovemaking arose but Cynthia just wasn't ready for that yet. She thought it would be the end of her relationship with Bryan.

"Bryan, I love all of the kissing and touching and believe me, baby, I want to but I'm just not ready to go there yet. I'm nervous, Bryan. I want to make sure that I get it right this time. I don't want to go down this road again until I'm married."

"I understand," Bryan said, "and I respect your decision."

"Does this mean you're going leave me now? Because I know that you have your needs, and if I'm not providing you with them, I—"

"Cynthia, why are you trying to get rid of me? I'm not going anywhere. Don't you know that I like you? Don't you know how my heart feels when you're around me? I will wait for you. You're worth waiting for and I'd be a fool if I were to turn my back on my best friend."

Bryan's words went straight to Cynthia's heart and she embraced him tightly. But she still hesitated to give herself fully to him because she still harbored baggage from her previous relationships.

One year after they'd officially begun dating Bryan took Cynthia and the kids to a Chicago Bulls basketball game to celebrate the day. Once they were all settled in their seats Cynthia asked how Bryan had gotten such good seats.

"I won the tickets at an office raffle," Bryan said. "Besides, I know how much Anthony has grown to like basketball and I thought that this would be something that he'd enjoy, as well as the rest of us."

"Mama, he brought us here for something else, too, but I can't tell you what it is," Angel said.

"Angel, if you don't be quiet, girl, I'm going to flip your eyelids inside out and watch you go blind," Anthony blasted his sister.

"I know one thing. You two had better not get out of hand or you're going to have to deal with me," Cynthia quickly admonished to nip their little argument in the bud.

The four of them sat and enjoyed the game. Cynthia enjoyed it more than she'd thought she would. In fact, she enjoyed it just as much as Anthony and Bryan. Cynthia was glad that Bryan was around because she realized that Anthony needed a good man in his life to help him deal with the pressures the world would place on his shoulders.

At halftime, Angel got excited and suddenly blurted, "Ooo, look, Mom! At the marquee sign. Read what it says."

Cynthia focused her attention on the sign and damn near had a heart attack when she read what was written in bright letters.

"Cynthia Clark. Bryan Jones would like to know if you'd marry him." The next thing Cynthia knew was that a camera was being aimed at her because she saw her face on the giant marquee screen. She was stunned and tried to avert her eyes from the screen. But when she did, she noticed that Bryan was down on one knee holding a ring. The capacity crowd began chanting "Say yes!" Cynthia started crying and just couldn't get the word *yes* to come out of her mouth, so she shook her head and acknowledged that she'd accepted his proposal. Everyone in the stadium began clapping and strangers sitting around them began congratulating her and Bryan. Cynthia had never felt so loved and special in her life.

Later that evening, at his home, Bryan explained to Cynthia his plans for them. He was going to sell his small two-bedroom home and have a four-bedroom house built for them.

"One of the developers that I worked with years ago when I was the fiscal manager for the city is building a new home community in the south suburbs. They've just put the finishing touches on the model and I want all of us to drive out there to see what they look like."

"How long have you been planning this?" Cynthia asked, feeling as if she were on top of the world.

"Well, okay. I'm going to come clean. Hope, Angel, Anthony and I have been planning this for a few weeks. It was hard to get Angel to keep quiet about it because you know she can't hold water."

Cynthia laughed. "I'm so surprised that she was able to keep this away from me."

"Are you happy, though? I want to make you happy, Cynthia, and if you're not happy just let me know."

"Baby, I've never been happier in my life."

"Good. Because when you see the new development I know you're going to love it. The school district is great and the homes are even greater. If you like the new home community, which I know you will, we'll have our home built from the ground up. We'll get to choose the types of cabinets and flooring and—"

"My God, Bryan, I love you," Cynthia interrupted him. "I love you so much."

"I love you, too," Bryan reaffirmed. "I want to build a life with you. I'm so ready to take our relationship to the next level. I love your kids, and I love you, and perhaps one day we'll be blessed with one more child."

"You know, sometimes I pinch myself because I can't believe the impact you've had on my life," Cynthia said. "Sometimes I wonder if you're real. Sometimes I think this is all some grand fantasy of mine and I'll eventually wake up."

"Why do you think that?"

"Because before I met you, my life was complicated, and—" Cynthia caught herself. She didn't want to inadvertently reveal the truth about her life with Johnny B.

"And?"

"Nothing, baby. Go on. Tell me more about how you want to build a life with me. I love it when you talk to me like that."

The following Sunday the pastor announced that Bryan and Cynthia were engaged. When the church applauded the news Cynthia felt herself glowing on the inside. The pastor allowed Bryan to say a few words to the congregation that knew him so well.

"A man is supposed to find a wife. For me, this search has taken many years, but in my heart I believe I've found my soul mate. The warmth, love and respect I feel for Cynthia is beyond words. She is the air I breathe and my light in the darkness. God truly blessed me when He brought Cynthia into my life." Bryan then stepped down and Cynthia felt her heart soaring with love. After the service Cynthia excused herself from Bryan and the children to head to the ladies' room. She was buzzing with much joy as members congratulated her. As she returned from the ladies' room she noticed big mouth Hester Brown and pigeon-toed Patty Pickett talking to Bryan. Angel and Anthony were nearby talking with some other children.

"Cynthia, go get your man from them," said Hope who seemed to appear from thin air.

"When did you get here?" Cynthia asked. "I didn't see you."

"I overslept this morning and was running late. I had to sit in the back next to Hester and Patty. But that's not important right now. You need to go pull him away from those two. I overheard them asking him how much he knew about your past." Cynthia's heart began racing.

"Have you told Bryan about Johnny B yet?" asked Hope.

"No. I'm going to but I just haven't found the right moment to tell him. Then again, I'm not even sure if I want to tell him. That life means nothing to me. That happened years ago and that's where all of that drama needs to stay."

"Well, Hester and Patty are working as a tag team trying to dig up bones in your backyard. You need to get them out of your business once and for all."

"Why are they snooping around so hard?" asked Cynthia.

"Because they don't have anything else to do. Besides, Hester was working on trying to get Bryan for herself, until you came along." Hope paused for a moment. "Hester's head damn near twisted off her head when the pastor made the announcement of your engagement. I heard her whisper to Patty that she was going to ask Bryan if he was sure you were the right one. She wants Bryan to notice her instead of you."

"I need to kick Hester Brown's ass," Cynthia said through gritted teeth.

"Shh, watch your language. You're still in church," Hope scolded her. "Now go get your man before they fill his head with all types of nonsense."

As Cynthia approached she could hear Hester asking him questions about her.

"Here she is," Bryan said as he embraced her. "You have to save me," he whispered in her ear.

Cynthia rubbed the palm of her hand up and down his spine to acknowledge she'd received his request for help.

"Hello, Hester and Patty," Cynthia greeted them. "Aren't you going to congratulate us, Hester?" Cynthia captured her gaze.

"You're not married to him yet," said Hester, and then turned her back and walked away. Patty trailed behind her.

"Why are they all up in the church acting like that?" Bryan asked.

"Baby, it's not even worth discussing," said Cynthia.

Bryan chuckled a little. "Those two ladies are what my

grandmother would call busybodies. Hester tried to convince me that you were an ex-convict and had been imprisoned. Can you believe that, they think you're some type of smooth criminal." Bryan continued to laugh.

Cynthia's mind began to race. Her first thought was to call up Uncle Jo Jo and her other uncles and have them deliver a message to Hester Brown, but she dismissed the thought because she felt that it would backfire. I'll have to deal with Hester and Patty in my own way, Cynthia thought to herself.

Cynthia had no idea of how the process of purchasing a home worked because she'd never in her wildest dreams thought that she'd actually be a home owner. She was explaining this to Bryan late one evening when she and the kids were visiting him at his home. They had all piled into Bryan's king-size bed to watch a movie. The movie had ended and the kids had fallen asleep at the foot of Bryan's bed.

"I've always been told that buying a home isn't easy and you have to have a lot of money to put down," Cynthia said.

"There are some programs out there that allow first-time home owners to put very little or no money down at all. It just depends on what a person qualifies for."

"Tell me again what you're going to do and how everything works. I like hearing about how you're going to make things happen."

"Well, I'm going to sell this house. We'll have to put a fresh coat of paint on everything and I'll update the fixtures and give the kitchen cabinets a facelift. The carpet is pretty new, so a good shampoo job is all it needs. I'll have a landscaper come out and give the house some curb appeal so that buyers will becoming interested enough to stop in."

"Now, how does the real estate agent work?"

"You just sign an agreement with them, baby. They'll get a commission from the sale of the house. They'll come by and look at the house and make a recommendation as to the listing price. Then they'll bring in potential buyers and hopefully someone will like the place enough to make an offer on it."

"Now does the buyer pay the price that you ask for?" Cynthia asked. Bryan shifted his neck and looked at her strangely.

"I'm serious. I have no idea but I'm trying to learn," Cynthia said defensively.

"I'm not looking at you because of your question. I'm looking at you because I adore you," Bryan said and kissed her forehead. "Now, getting back to your question. No, a smart buyer is never going to pay the asking price. Me and the buyer will negotiate the price."

"So once you sell the house, then you'll move out and stay with me if the new house isn't completed yet, right."

"That's the plan."

"Now when we get the new house, tell me the steps we'll go through."

"Well, we'll go to a lender and they'll do a credit check. This will not be a big issue because I have strong credit."

"But I don't have any. I've never had a credit card or anything. I don't even have a credit history."

"That's okay. Once you sign up for a home, creditors will be busting down the door trying to give you credit."

"You don't think they'll turn us down because I don't have any credit, do you?"

"No, it should be fine. The only thing that might raise a red flag with lenders are previous lawsuits, judgments or liens against you. And since you don't have any of those things, we'll be fine. So once the bank approves us, we wait for the builder to finish the house. Then a home inspector comes out to make sure that everything is in proper working order. After that, an appraiser comes out to make sure the property is worth the money we'll be spending on it. After that, we set a closing date and the rest, as they say, is history."

"Wow. It's hard for me to believe that I'll actually be moving into a home."

"Well, believe it, because that's what we're going to do."

Bryan had been right when he told Cynthia she'd love the model home in the new community that he wanted to move to.

Cynthia was impressed with the suburban community. She loved how the developer planned the new home development. There was going to be a community park where the kids could play and a walking trail for the adults.

The homes were even more dazzling to Cynthia. All four models they saw were spacious and well thought out.

After some discussion and a few more visits to the model homes, Cynthia and Bryan decided to go with the thirty-two-hundred-square-foot, four-bedroom home. It would have a family room, living room and dining room, two full bathrooms and a small den where Bryan would be able to do some work from home. They agreed that one of the upgrades should be the whirlpool in the master bedroom, as well as granite countertops in the kitchen.

The process of selling Bryan's house went smoothly. He did the updates like he said he would, and he and his agent set the asking price. Once that was done, he and Cynthia went to a lender to get prequalified for their new home loan. However, Cynthia got a big surprise when her credit report came back.

"Now, run this by me again," Bryan said once they returned home from the lender. "Who is Jacobson Realty? And why do they have a lien against you for two thousand dollars?"

"They're the real estate company that owned the apartment building my ex-husband and I lived in." Cynthia was humiliated and embarrassed when the lender came back and told her about this problem.

"When I left my husband, I just left. I didn't worry about paying the rent and I guess he didn't, either. I just wanted to get away from him. Damn," Cynthia said, feeling as if Butch had once again screwed up her life. "I'm sorry, baby, but I honestly didn't know about this. I know that I should've been checking into stuff like this, but my mind just wasn't programmed to think like that after I left him."

"You never received any letters or phone calls from them about this?" Bryan asked.

"No," Cynthia answered. At that moment, she wanted to give him the most likely reason she hadn't received notification but still feared that if he knew the entire truth, he'd leave her and she just couldn't bare the thought of losing him.

"Okay. This isn't going to stop us from moving forward. We're going to straighten this out. We'll call the real estate company and explain what happened. Then we'll see about negotiating a settlement with them."

"Do you think they'll do that?"

"Hey, it doesn't hurt to ask."

"I can come up with half of the money," Cynthia said. "I could take a second job and make more money to make up the difference."

"No, you keep your money. If the full price has to be paid, I'll take care of it. Keep your extra money to do something for the kids, okay?"

"Bryan, I can't let you do that. I can't let you pay a debt that large."

"Baby, I got it. I can handle it. We'll get through this."

"I just wish there was another way," Cynthia said. "God, I just want to scream. I want to find Butch and just beat his ass."

"Stuff happens, but you can't let it get to you. Let me tell you something my mother always said to me when things didn't go her way. She said, 'Baby, it's not the load that breaks you down, it's the way you carry it.'"

"I wish that I could have met her."

"So do I. She was good woman," Bryan said. "Don't worry, this is just a small wrinkle that can be ironed out."

In Cynthia's mind, Bryan was brilliant. They contacted the real estate company and, just like Bryan thought, they negotiated a settlement. Bryan paid off Cynthia's debt and then they returned to the bank, presented a paid-in-full letter to the lender and were pre-qualified for their home loan. Afterwards, Cynthia decided that Bryan was a more than honorable man and deserved to have a fiancée who wasn't afraid to make love to him. Cynthia lifted her vow of celibacy and made love to Bryan.

Bryan was able to sell his house for twenty thousand dollars above the asking price and was overjoyed when he got the news.

"Baby, we're going to be just fine," Bryan said. "Now all we have to do is plan our wedding."

Eleven months later, Cynthia and Bryan were married. Their wedding ceremony was one of the best the church had ever hosted. All of Bryan's and Cynthia's family and friends attended the wedding. At the reception, Cynthia and Bryan danced to their wedding song. Afterwards, Uncle Jo Jo and her other uncles came up to Bryan and pulled him away from her

"Uncle Jo Jo, that's not necessary," Cynthia complained.

"This is a man thing," Uncle Jo Jo explained. "He needs to know that I'll cut him if he screws up."

"Uncle Jo Jo!" Cynthia wanted to be mad with him but she couldn't. She knew that he was only doing it out of love for her.

"Don't worry, baby," Bryan said, laughing. "I'll be okay."

"Uncle Jo Jo, don't y'all hurt him. I need him to be in tip-top condition for our honeymoon," Cynthia shouted out to her uncle. Uncle Jo Jo turned to her and smiled.

"Don't worry. I won't hurt him," he said and smiled at her.

"Come on, Mama. I'll dance with you." Anthony came up and Cynthia felt her heart soar.

"Don't worry about them. They'll be back before you know it," Anthony said as he locked his fingers with hers and danced with her. "Are you happy, Mom?"

"Of course I am, honey. Why do you ask?"

"Because I can tell. I know that I was real little when you were with that other guy, but I remember him yelling all the time."

"You remember that?" Cynthia asked, surprised.

"Yeah. A little bit. I remember how afraid I was of him and how I had to stay out of his way."

"I'm sorry that you even remember any of that. The important thing is that is behind us now."

"I know. It just feels good to be a family."

"I believe I know what you mean."

"So, about your honeymoon. I want you to have a good time in St. Thomas. I don't want you to worry about me and Angel. Hope will take good care of us. Plus, I'll look out for Angel to make sure she doesn't get into mischief."

"You're such a smart young man," Cynthia said as she studied her son. "I'm so blessed to have such a wonderful son and daughter."

Angel came over. "I want to dance with Mom now."

"Come on, honey. We can all dance together," Cynthia said and made space for Angel to join them.

CHAPTER 24

Cynthia could hardly wait for the plane to land in St. Thomas late Monday evening. She'd never been so excited in all of her life and she had Bryan to thank for it all. He'd taught her how to love and trust again. He made her feel good about herself and she loved him for it. When they arrived in St. Thomas, Cynthia wanted to explore every part of the island and she wanted to do it immediately.

"Slow down, Cynthia," Bryan said to her as she rushed through the airport toward the baggage claim area.

"I can't. I'm too excited," Cynthia said. "Being here is so wonderful and I just feel like screaming out with joy."

When they arrived at their hotel, they checked into their honeymoon suite, which was everything Cynthia had imagined. It was a one-of-a-kind, four-level suite that provided a unique setting for an unforgettable romantic honeymoon. The room was decorated in shades of burgundy and sandstone, with an Egyptian theme. Cynthia was blown away by the seven-foot-tall champagne-glass whirlpool bath for two. There was a cozy log-burning fireplace, along with a private, enclosed, heated heart-shaped swimming pool. The room also had a massage table with a heat lamp.

"Oh, my God! This room is beautiful, Bryan." As she walked around, she came across Bryan who was laying down on the king-size round bed.

"Look at that, baby," Bryan said pointing to the ceiling.

"Wow," Cynthia exclaimed as she looked at the ceiling, which gave the illusion of sleeping under a star-filled sky.

"We're never going to leave this room," Cynthia said. "I want to see the island, true enough, but first I'm going to have to enjoy this room and you." Cynthia gave Bryan a seductive look.

"You're glowing," Bryan said. "I've never seen you like this, I mean this happy." Bryan stood up.

"That's because with you all of my dreams have come true," Cynthia said as she stepped into his embrace. She cupped the back of his neck and kissed him. When their lips met, she quivered. There was no doubt about it in her mind. Cynthia knew that she'd matured. With previous lovers, she couldn't express herself and be who she wanted to be sexually. But Bryan changed all of that. She was now able to explore and share a side of herself that was special and unique.

"Oooo," she cooed as she exhaled. "You taste good."

"I like the sound of our kisses," Bryan said. "It's a special kind of sound."

"I can't wait to climb up on you. I can't wait to feel you inside of me." Cynthia was hot and she couldn't help the way she felt.

"Why don't we go and put that champagne-glass whirlpool to good use," Bryan suggested.

"Baby, that sounds like a plan to me."

Cynthia and Bryan prepared the room for an evening of lovemaking. Bryan placed the Do Not Disturb sign on the door and Cynthia filled the whirlpool and put in a healthy amount of her lavender-scented bath gel. Bryan placed candles around the room to give a special glow and put a lovers' disc in the CD player. The smooth, sensual voice of Luther Vandross singing "Superstar" filled the room.

"Damn," Bryan said as he popped his fingers and grooved to the music.

"Woo, that's my man there," Cynthia shouted out. "Woo, Bryan, you shouldn't have put that song on."

"Come here and dance with me for a moment," Bryan said. Cynthia stepped into his embrace and they swayed to the music. Cynthia cradled the back of Bryan's neck and spoke in his ear.

"Oh, baby, do you know what you've done to me? Do you realize how much my life had changed since you've entered into it. Baby, I love you. I love you with all my heart."

"And I love you, too. You are all that I've ever searched for in a woman and much more. You're wonderful, smart and you complete me."

"Do you really mean that?"

"Yes I do," Bryan answered as he nibbled her earlobe. Cynthia melted. She felt a tingling sensation consume her body. She was caught up in the rapture of the moment and didn't want it to end. "Oh, yes, kiss my neck," she said and tilted her head for him. Bryan placed his soft chocolate lips on her neck. The wetness of his touch and the sound that his lips made when he kissed her skin caused goose bumps to form all over her body.

"Come on. Get out of your clothes and come get in the whirlpool with me."

Bryan did as she requested and joined her inside the bubble bath.

"Oh these water jets feel so good," Bryan said, allowing himself to relax completely. Cynthia studied him. She studied his wet chocolate skin, his handsome face and strong shoulders. She got caught up in the music, the scent of the room and the fact that she was in paradise with the man she'd fallen in love with. A good man, who loved, respected and admired her. Cynthia exhaled and closed her eyes for a moment, just to enjoy the feeling of being loved.

She noticed that his manhood was solid and breaking through the surface of the water. The sight of his erection made her ache. She maneuvered herself through the thick white foam over to where he was relaxing. She mounted him.

"Oooo," Bryan cooed as he entered her. Once he was inside her, Cynthia began moving her hips in a slow circular motion. She felt Bryan place the palms of his hands on her ass.

"Oh, yes," she sighed

"Damn, baby, you've got me worked up," he murmured, squeezing her behind just the way she liked it. Cynthia stopped her movements for a moment and looked down at him. She caught his gaze and held it for a long moment.

"Hey, you," she said, enjoying the sensual glow of his eyes. She could see directly into his soul, and she loved what she saw. She craned her neck down and kissed him fervently. Their tongues did a slow passionate dance, and the sweet taste of his lips made her come.

"Oh, I feel you squeezing me," he said and Cynthia felt him flex against her contraction.

"Oooo, oh God, what are you doing to me? How can you make me feel this way? How can you feel so good?"

"Because we're meant to be with each other. That's why it feels so good."

The words sent Cynthia over the edge. It was the way that he was into her that turned her on. Her orgasm was strong, and it consumed her. Once her orgasmic contraction subsided, she exhaled loudly and then tossed her head back. Shortly after she enjoyed the sensation of several more short quick orgasmic contractions. He was draining her, and it fell heavenly. When the orgasm subsided, Cynthia once again held his gaze and studied him.

"How did I get so lucky?" Bryan asked.

"It wasn't luck, baby," Cynthia answered. "It was fate. I've been searching for a man like you all of my life and now that I've found you, I'm not ever letting you go."

"Good," Bryan said, "because I don't want you to let me go."

"Never, baby," Cynthia said to him and held him tightly.

"I want you to get yours, baby," she said. "What do you want me to do?"

"Ride me," Bryan answered. "Ride me hard."

Cynthia smiled at her husband and then complied with his request.

Early the following morning, Cynthia was the first one out of bed. She went over to the patio window, drew back the curtains and witnessed the most spectacular sunrise she'd ever seen.

"This is heaven," she whispered to herself.

The honeymoon suite they'd rented had an oceanside view and came complete with its own private deck. The deck overlooked a white sand beach, and the sound of the water rushing ashore was just too romantic and relaxing for words.

"Oh, I could live here with you forever," Cynthia whispered to herself.

"So could I," Bryan said as he joined her.

"I didn't even hear you get up," Cynthia said as Bryan eased up behind her and embraced her.

"I am so happy to be with you, Cynthia. I cannot tell you that enough."

"And I can't hear it enough," Cynthia said.

"Are you hungry?" Bryan asked.

"Yeah, I'm starving," Cynthia admitted. "We should go down and see what they have for breakfast."

"You don't want to order room service?" Bryan asked.

"We'll order room service later. I promise," Cynthia said as she rested the back of her head on his shoulder and enjoyed being held by him.

After breakfast, Cynthia and Bryan spent the day enjoying each other's company. They went shopping and found gifts for the kids, Hope and Uncle Jo Jo. After that, they went out on a catamaran boat tour with other guests who were vacationing at the resort. When they returned from boating early in the evening, Cynthia suggested that they take walk.

"I'm not ready to call it a day just yet," Cynthia said. "I'm having way too much fun."

"I'm game for whatever you want to do. However, I would like to stop by the room just so that I can freshen up," Bryan said as he slipped his arm around her.

"That doesn't sound like a bad idea," Cynthia agreed. They went back to the room, freshened up and then headed back out.

As they walked around the lovers' resort property, they found a nature trail that they decided to explore. Once they were deep into a wooded area, they came across a wooden bridge that had a relaxing stream of water flowing beneath it.

"Let's stop right here for a minute," Cynthia suggested. "I want to look at the water and just listen to it for a moment." Cynthia placed her hands on the bridge railing and glanced down at the running water beneath her.

"You know what? Being alone out here like this with you just has me feeling like I want to do something freaky," Cynthia admitted.

"Something freaky?" Bryan chuckled. "Something freaky like what?"

"Just wild stuff. I don't know how to explain it." Cynthia paused. "It's like you've opened up an entirely new world to me and it's like I want to see and experience everything with you. I feel comfortable with you because you allow me to be who I am and I love that about you."

"I like knowing that you feel comfortable around me. That's the kind of thing that makes for a healthy and strong marriage."

"So can I express all of my sensual sides with you?" Cynthia asked, even though she knew the answer.

"You'd better," Bryan answered with a smile.

"Good," Cynthia said. "Lift me up so that I can sit on the rail."

Bryan helped to lift Cynthia up so that her behind was resting on the rail of the bridge.

"Now I want you to put your face between my thighs and get you some."

"What?" Bryan said, laughing. "Are you serious?"

"Yes. I have on a sundress and I'm not wearing any panties."

"It's still daylight and someone could walk by," Bryan said nervously.

"Come on. Let's be daring," Cynthia said, encouraging him. "Let's be bold and toss our caution to the wind."

"You are so damn crazy," Bryan said as he kneeled down on one knee. Cynthia lifted her dress up so that he could place his head up under it. She braced herself on the rail, opened her thighs and draped her legs over his shoulders. The moment she felt his warm tongue sweep across her, she exploded. Cynthia loved the way that he ate her pussy. The way he kissed it, sucked it and rotated his tongue around in slow deliberate circles. She never knew that lovemaking could make her feel this way. Cynthia clapped her thighs closed around his cheeks as another orgasm hit her and made her shout out.

"Ooo, shit," she said, louder than she intended to.

"Ummmm," Bryan cooed as he continued to flick the tip of tongue up and down her clit. He maneuvered his middle finger inside of her. He pressed the tip of his finger against the inside back wall of her clitoris, and the sensation that she felt was like being struck by lighting. Cynthia's body shivered with ecstasy.

"Oh, baby." Cynthia couldn't help the way she was feeling. "Okay, stop," she begged him. "Please, baby, stop. You're driving me crazy," Cynthia said as she forced him to come from underneath her sundress.

"Damn, you taste good," Bryan said, licking his lips. "I love the scent of you. It drives me wild."

Cynthia studied the beauty in his eyes. She loved how compatible they were and how free she was to express herself with him.

"How freaky do you want to get?" Bryan asked.

"We can't get any freakier," Cynthia said with a laugh as she jumped down from the railing. "People are coming our way." She laughed.

"Oh, no. You're not going to get off that easily. You started this and we're going to finish it."

"Okay, baby. Let's go back to the room. That way, you can have me any way you want me."

Bryan smiled and then laughed. "I want you out here. I'm going with the flow. Come on, follow me."

"Where are we going?" Cynthia asked. She was both nervous and excited.

"I don't know, but I'm sure I'll find a spot," Bryan said. Cynthia followed her love off the trail and deeper into the woods. Once they were a good distance from the trail, Bryan unzipped his shorts.

"Well, check you out," Cynthia said, surprised to see that he wasn't wearing any briefs.

"You're not the only one who has a daring side," Bryan said. "I want it from the back."

The way Bryan said how he wanted her made her even hotter. Cynthia turned and leaned over. She bent down to waist level and placed the palms of her hands against a tree for balance. She felt Bryan lift her sundress up so that it came above her hips and rested on her back. He brushed the tip of his manhood up and down the entrance of her love cave, making sure that she was moist and ready for him. Once he was confident she was ready to receive him, he penetrated her.

"Oh, damn!" Bryan cried out as he pumped her from behind.

"Slap my ass," Cynthia said and Bryan complied.

"Look at you. I've got all of your caramel ass up in the air. I've got you wide-open," he said as he found the perfect rhythm which they both enjoyed. The sound of their skin slapping and popping drove Cynthia wild.

"I can't believe you have me out here in the woods getting down like this," Cynthia said as an orgasm exploded from within and made her legs tremble. Bryan's hands were all over her ass, and she loved the way he was controlling her.

"Come on, don't cheat me," Bryan said. "Give it all to me."

"I am, baby. You're getting all of me," Cynthia said as the force of his thrusts became more aggressive. She felt him swell inside her and knew that he was about to release. She flexed her vagina muscle purposefully and held on to his manhood.

"Oh, damn!" Bryan cried just as he exploded inside her. Cynthia wiggled her behind around so that Bryan would enjoy his orgasm a little longer. She listened to his labored breathing and wondered if he was okay.

"Are you all right back there?" she asked, suddenly feeling energized.

"That was a big one," Bryan admitted. "You've drained me."

"I hope not. I'm all wound up now. I want some more of you later," Cynthia said as they recomposed themselves. "You have me out here in the middle of the damn woods acting like some overzealous teenager."

"Yeah, we are acting wild," Bryan admitted as he fastened his shorts. "I'm going to just chalk this up as jungle fever."

Both Bryan and Cynthia got a kick out of the phrase and laughed as they made their way back to the main path.

Cynthia and Bryan enjoyed the rest of their time on the island of St. Thomas. They had romantic dinners and went dancing. They spent time at the spa getting pampered and enjoyed lazy afternoons on the beach. In Cynthia's mind, her life was finally on track, with Bryan by her side, she knew that anything was possible.

CHAPTER 25

Cynthia loved her new life with her husband and children. She also loved her new home, often she just stood in the center of a room and did her happy dance to celebrate the fact that she was actually living in a home.

Bryan's income covered the mortgage and utility bills, so she used her income to cover everything else, such as new furniture, food and clothing for them and the children. She was also now able to save more of her income for the kids' college education as well as for a rainy day. The kids also loved the new home and were overjoyed at having their own space. Cynthia looked forward to decorating all of the rooms and having the freedom to do whatever she pleased.

The very first night that she was in her new home, she made the entire family stand in the middle of the family room and give praise to God for all of the blessings he'd given them.

In Cynthia's mind, she and Bryan had achieved the American dream. She was now a home owner with two beautiful children and a loving husband. It was a far cry from where she'd come from. It was a far cry from Larry the cockeyed landlord, wife beater Butch and Johnny B.

Cynthia and Hope still remained close friends and Cynthia told Hope that if she ever needed a place to stay, the spare bedroom in her home was hers.

"Child, I'll be okay. I've got this building and it's more than enough home for me. But I may want to come out here and spend the weekend with you every now and again," Hope said one afternoon when she'd come over to Cynthia's for a visit.

"You know that you're always welcome in my home," Cynthia said.

"I'm so proud of you, Cynthia. I've watched you grow so much over the past eight years. I knew that you were special the moment I first saw you. You just didn't believe how special you were."

"Don't talk like that, Hope," Cynthia said. "We're both going to start crying if you do."

"I can't help it. Everything turned out so beautifully for you and I can't help but be moved by it."

Cynthia remained still for a moment as Hope's words warmed her heart. She couldn't hold back her tears no matter how hard she tried. She embraced Hope because she had been truly instrumental in giving her a second shot at life.

Cynthia and Bryan had now been married for close to two years. Hester and Patty still didn't like Cynthia and from time to time they still tried to dip into her private life and find out about her past. Cynthia continued to ignore their inquiries and let them think whatever they wanted to. She no longer felt threatened by Patty and Hester the way she used to. Cynthia had Bryan all to herself and there was nothing they could do to change that.

Cynthia was now in her early thirties and for the first time she was concerned about her health.

Cynthia constantly felt fatigued. She was suffering from bad headaches and went to the bathroom frequently. She'd been feeling this way for several weeks but held off on going to the doctor because she thought her new ailments would pass.

"My ass is just getting old," Cynthia said to her reflection in the mirror one morning after she'd had a sleepless night. She picked up a laundry basket filled with dirty clothes sitting nearby and headed toward the basement. As she was about to go down the basement steps the telephone rang. Cynthia sat the basket down and answered the phone.

"Hello?" answered Cynthia.

"Is this Cynthia Howard?" asked a voice she didn't recognize.

"That's my maiden name, who is this?" she asked as she held the phone to her ear with her shoulder.

"You think you're better than me don't you?"

"Excuse me?" Cynthia asked confused.

"You're jack shit, and I'm going to let everyone around you know it."

"Who is this? Hester? This has to be an all time low for you. I can't believe you're calling my house acting like this. This is no way for a Christian woman to behave."

"This isn't Hester," said the voice and hung up. Cynthia tried to *69 the number but it wouldn't go through. A prerecorded message said she couldn't use the service to dial the number back.

"Whoever it was must have a block on their phone," Cynthia said aloud. She picked up her load of dirty laundry and continued on into the basement. As she stuffed clothes into the washer a horrible feeling washed over her.

"Oh damn," she whispered. "What if that was Johnny B? What if he's out of jail and wants to get even with me after all these years?" Cynthia began to panic and started pacing the floor. Her mind was running away with her.

"I can't allow Johnny B to do this to me. I've come too far to have the rug pulled from beneath me." Cynthia's thoughts were driving her crazy and she didn't know how to stop them from consuming her. Once again the telephone rang. Cynthia was hesitant, but finally answered it.

"Hello?"

"Hey, baby." It was Hope.

"Oh, Hope," Cynthia said exhaling a sigh of relief.

"What's wrong with you? Why do you sound like that?"

"I got a strange phone call a minute ago. I think it was Johnny B."

"Johnny B," Hope said loudly. "What in the hell did he want and how did he get your phone number?"

"Those are very good questions," Cynthia said now that Hope had caused her to think more rationally. "It probably wasn't Johnny B calling me up talking about how I think I'm better than him. That's not his style. That sounds like some dumb shit Butch would do."

"Butch, your ex-husband?" Cynthia knew she had Hope completely confused.

"Yes, Butch my ex-husband. I'll bet Anthony got in contact with him somehow and gave him our new phone number. Wait until I see that boy, I'm going to really let him have it."

"Are you sure Anthony would do that?" Hope asked. "I mean, that doesn't sound like something he'd do."

"It's the only logical thing I can think of, Hope. Butch called me up today to tell me I was jack shit, and I just don't appreciate that." Cynthia felt her anger swelling.

"Well, before you chew Anthony a new behind about your prank phone call, make sure he did give out the number."

"I will," Cynthia said. "So, what's going on?" she asked now that she'd resolved her little mystery.

"I was calling you to see if you still wanted to head over to the nursery to pick up some flowers for your garden."

"Yeah," Cynthia answered. "I'll come pick you up around noon. I just woke up not too long ago. Bryan and the kids left me in here all by myself so I decided to do some laundry while they're out."

"Okay, that's fine. I'll see you around noon," said Hope and then ended the conversation.

On Monday evening Cynthia was walking toward her car, which was parked in the employee parking lot at her job. As she approached the car, she saw that a note had been placed on the windshield.

"What in the hell is this about?" Cynthia said aloud as she picked up and read the handwritten note.

> You're jack shit, and I'm going to let everyone around you know it. I hate you, I hate you, I hate you!

"What the fuck!" Cynthia panicked. She looked all around her to see where Butch was.

"Butch!" she called out his name. "I'm going to call the police on you if you keep on doing this. I'm not playing with you." Cynthia continued to scan her surroundings to see if he was hiding behind a tree or peeping at her from around a corner of one of the apartment buildings near the school. However, she didn't see anyone.

"Damn idiot!" Cynthia cursed him for stalking her like this.

Cynthia drove directly to Anthony's school to pick him up from basketball practice. She hadn't spoken with him yet about whether or not he'd somehow contacted his father, but now she was about to. When she pulled up to the school he said goodbye to a few of his friends who were waiting for a ride home. As soon as he shut the car door Cynthia pulled off and then grilled him.

"I'm going to ask you a question, and I don't want you to lie to me." Cynthia's voice was edgy.

"I didn't do anything," Anthony quickly answered.

"Have you been in contact with Butch, your father?" Cynthia asked.

"No," Anthony quickly answered. "Why would I even want to talk to him? I don't like him and to be honest, I hate him." Cynthia swallowed hard.

"You shouldn't hate anyone," she said.

"Why are you asking about him anyway? He hasn't been around in all these years, why are you talking him up?"

"I don't know. I just thought somehow you were communicating with him, that's all," Cynthia said. She was now even more on edge because she began to question whether or not it was Butch who was scaring her like this. Later that evening, while lying in bed with Bryan, she told him about the phone calls and the note.

"So do you think it's Butch stalking you like this?" Bryan asked.

"I thought it was but I'm not so sure now. I just don't know who else it could be."

"What about your brother, Victor. You said the last time you saw him you guys were at war."

"That was so long ago. I haven't talked with or seen him since," said Cynthia.

"Maybe he's out of jail now and has somehow located

you. You always did say he was very immature and childish. This could be a prank he's pulling."

"You know. I wouldn't put something like this past him. My brother Victor is a real piece of work."

"Here's what we're going to do. In the morning we're going to drive over to the district police station. We'll explain what's been going on and let them tell us what can be done."

Cynthia relaxed a little and snuggled up close to Bryan. He stroked her hair and at that moment she felt safe and as if no harm would come to her.

The police department said they would patrol the area more often in search of any suspicious persons. As it turned out, no additional note was left on Cynthia's car and she breathed a sigh of relief.

Cynthia never fully allowed herself to relax because she didn't know if it was Johnny B, Butch or Victor who'd come up from her past to harass her. At times she found herself feeling paranoid and wondered if one of them was watching her, just waiting for the right moment to attack her. She tried to keep those unwanted thoughts out of her mind as much as she could, but from time to time they did pop up.

Cynthia also had continual problems with keeping food down and vomiting. Bryan finally put his foot down after a violent vomiting episode during the middle of the night.

"No, that's it, baby. We're going to the emergency

room," Bryan said as he exited the bathroom to go get dressed.

"No, Bryan. I'm fine. This feels like a pregnancy," Cynthia said.

"What? Are you for real?" Bryan quickly rushed back into the bathroom and embraced her.

"Stop. Just help me get back to bed," Cynthia said. "I'm not sure if I'm right, though. Tomorrow after church, I'll get a home pregnancy test and we'll find out for sure."

"Oh, Cynthia. This is such a blessing," Bryan said. "We're going to have a baby." Bryan began dancing around the bedroom with joy.

"Yes." Cynthia forced a smile onto her face, but it was hard to maintain because she was in such pain. She wondered why being pregnant this time felt so much different.

"Bryan." Cynthia wanted him to stop dancing and come lie beside her. "Let me lay my head on your chest," she said. Bryan quickly got back into the bed with her and allowed her to get settled. He began stroking her hair, and Cynthia welcomed the comforting feeling. She listened to Bryan's heartbeat and loved hearing how it matched her own. Cynthia closed her eyes and waited for sleep to come.

The following Sunday morning, Cynthia took her usual seat in the front row of the church. Hester Brown and Patty Pickett were seated behind her. Cynthia knew that they were up to something, but wasn't going to allow them to sour her mood. Bryan was going around whispering to the other deacons about Cynthia possibly being pregnant. Cynthia watched him as he walked around with Angel and Anthony. He was so proud and so happy with his family.

Cynthia had asked that he wait for her to take the pregnancy test before he made the announcement but Bryan couldn't hold back his joy, and she didn't blame him for wanting to share the good news.

The Sunday morning service went along as scheduled and before the pastor opened up the floor for testimonials, he allowed Bryan to make his announcement.

"I'd like to give praise to God Almighty for blessing me with a beautiful wife and two beautiful children, which I've adopted as my own. I want to also thank God for blessing my wife and I with another baby."

There was applause, and people sitting near Cynthia and her children congratulated her.

"I want you all to pray for us. I want you to pray that we have a healthy baby."

The congregation said amen and Bryan stepped aside so that the pastor could allow members to speak.

"I got something to say," a voice boomed out from behind. The voice was familiar to Cynthia but she didn't want to turn around in her seat to confirm that it was whom she thought it was.

"I want to speak!" The voice was sharp and raspy. Cynthia looked over her left shoulder and saw Hanna walking down the center aisle of her church. When Hanna made it to the front of the church she turned around to face everyone. She glared at Cynthia.

Cynthia was horrified by the sight and presence of Hanna. She looked so old and worn out. Hanna was very thin and bony. She looked as if she hadn't eaten in weeks, and her clothing was third-rate at best. Her skin didn't have a healthy glow; instead, it looked as if it were being cooked from the inside out. Her hair was matted down on one side and was shaved off on the other. The whites of her eyes were a mixture of red and yellow. The years of drug abuse were clear.

"Y'all have some hypocrites up in this church." Hanna began gyrating where she stood. Cynthia couldn't tell if she was dancing to some church song in her head or if she couldn't control her shaking.

"And you got one big one right here in the front row." Hanna pointed her finger at Cynthia. "I've been coming here, standing in the back of the church for weeks watching her. Watching how y'all treat her like she's royalty."

Hanna's voice was filled with heartbreaking emotion. Cynthia had no idea of what Hanna was talking about. She hadn't seen her in the church at all. However, she had to admit that if Hanna hadn't opened her mouth to speak, she wouldn't have recognized her.

"She didn't even invite me to her wedding." Hanna started crying. She smeared away her tears with the back of her hand. Cynthia noticed how her hands were black with dirt. My God, Cynthia thought. She looks like she doesn't even bathe.

Cynthia's heart broke. She had wanted Hanna to go to hell and, based on her appearance, it looked as if she had.

"She's not what you think she is."

The church was completely silent.

Angel snuggled up close to Cynthia and whispered, "Who is that crazy lady, Mama? She's scaring me."

Cynthia couldn't answer Angel right at that moment. Anthony, who was sitting on the other side of her, whispered, "Do we know her? She reminds me of Uncle Jo Jo."

It was at that moment, Cynthia realized that she'd kept most of her previous life hidden from not only her husband but her children, as well. She wanted no one to know about the deep secrets of her former life.

"I don't believe that this girl is up in my church," Cynthia said through gritted teeth. She threw daggers with her eyes at Hanna. She wanted to let Hanna know she wouldn't hesitate to beat her down in front of the entire congregation. Her secret was that important to her.

"Don't look at me like that," Hanna said. "I know you want to kick my ass. It's written all over your face."

Cynthia felt a thousand pairs of eyes suddenly studying her. She placed a plastic smile on her face to try to cover up her anger.

"You know what you did. You know what you did to me."

"She's about to tell all of your business?" Hester Brown leaned forward and whispered in Cynthia's ear.

"You know her don't you, Hester? You put her up to doing this, didn't you?" Cynthia snapped at her.

"Huh, I don't even know the girl," said Hester. There was a brief moment of silence and then Hester snapped her fingers. "Now I remember where I saw your face!" Hester said.

I didn't do a damn thing to you, Cynthia thought. At least, nothing that you didn't have coming to you.

"That woman right there is a hypocrite!" Hanna once again pointed to Cynthia.

"Ma'am..." the pastor said, trying to get Hanna's attention.

"No! Don't cut me off. Let me say my piece." Hanna swallowed hard. "She was a drug dealer!"

The entire congregation gasped.

"She sold drugs to me when she knew that I was pregnant. I lost my baby because of that."

Hanna was now speaking through her anguish and tears. "She did it because she was mad at me for taking her husband away from her. She was doing it to get even with me. She has the devil in her heart."

"Damn!" Cynthia heard Hester and Patty say in unison.

"You were part of that big police scandal a few years back, I remember seeing your face on the news and in the newspaper," Hester said. "You were a drug dealer. I knew there was something foul about you."

Cynthia glanced over at Bryan. The expression on his face was one of disbelief. She studied his eyes and they were asking questions she didn't want to answer.

"Oh, Bryan is going to leave you after this. You can bet your bottom dollar on that one," Hester Brown continued to taunt Cynthia.

"Oh, hell, no!" Cynthia shouted. She was furious; there was no way that she was going to allow Hanna to come into the safe world she'd created and destroy it.

Her heart was suddenly consumed with rage. She sprang to her feet to denounce everything that Hanna was saying and to drag her away from in front of everyone. Cynthia just couldn't deal with this type of exposure. The moment she sprang to her feet and moved aggressively toward Hanna, her mind short-circuited and she blacked out.

CHAPTER 26

When Cynthia awoke, she didn't know where she was. All she knew was that she felt horrible. She tried to lift her hand, but her movements felt restricted.

"Hey." She heard Bryan's voice and turned her head toward the sound of it.

"Why is everything so blurry?" Cynthia asked.

"You've been out for a while," Bryan said.

Cynthia sensed hostility in his voice.

"Give me your hand," she asked and noticed there was a long delay before Bryan delivered it.

"What happened?" Cynthia asked. "Where am I?"

"Baby, you're in the hospital. You blacked out."

"Blacked out? What to you mean? Did I faint?"

"Yes, what's the last thing you remember?"

"Angel said she was scared of somebody. Where is my baby at?"

"Hope is watching the children."

"What's going on, Bryan? Talk to me. What happened? Did I lose our baby?" Cynthia asked.

"No," Bryan answered. "The problems that you were experiencing were not because you were pregnant."

"They weren't?" Cynthia was more confused than ever.

"You've been feeling that way because you have diabetes and didn't know it."

"Diabetes? What are you talking about? I'm not a diabetic."

"Yes, you are. You just didn't know it. That's why you've been feeling so fatigued lately."

"Oh, God. If it isn't one thing, it's another." Cynthia's mind was still in a fog. "So what does this mean? I'm going to have to take shots or something? I don't like needles."

"I'm not sure about needles, but I do know that it's something that we'll have to keep a close eye on. The doctor spoke with me briefly about it, but to be honest all I wanted to know was if you'd be okay. Everything else just went in one ear and out the other one."

"How in the world did I get diabetes?" Cynthia asked.

"Do you have a family history of it?" Bryan asked.

"My grandmother had it, but I never had it. I didn't think that I could get it."

"Well from what I understand, you have Type II diabetes, which is the most common and the most treatable."

"Can I still have children?"

"I didn't ask that question. But when the doctor returns, you should ask that question."

"Oh, God. Why me? Why can't anything just go smoothly for me?" Cynthia whispered to herself.

"Is it true? Is what that woman said true?"

"Yes," Cynthia whispered.

"Oh, God. Everything is messed up now. You deceived me. You're not the person I thought you were. You're the very type of person I've always despised. The type of person I would spit on."

"Bryan, don't say that." Cynthia began crying. She tried to stop her tears, but she couldn't. His words were mean-spirited and it hurt her deeply that he was judging her instead of being concerned about her well-being. She was also concerned by how quickly his feelings for her had turned.

"I'm hurt, upset and angry. Perhaps I should've listened to Hester and Patty when they were trying to tell me something wasn't exactly right with you. I can't trust you Cynthia, you're a liar."

"I'm not a liar, Bryan, and you certainly don't need to listen to Hester and Patty." Cynthia felt her blood pressure rising. "I can't believe you're coming at me like this during a time I need to be comforted by you. Who are you and what did you do to the man who loved me?"

"I don't know how much I love you anymore. I can't love someone who has done what you've done. My heart isn't that forgiving. Besides, it wasn't just Hester and Patty who warned me, there were others in the church who were also trying to caution me about you."

"Baby, you have to let me explain things." Cynthia's voice cracked. She now realized the severity of the situation and how Bryan's knowledge of her seedy past changed everything. Her life, her marriage and her very happiness were now threatened.

"Please, you have to let me explain," Cynthia pleaded with him. She squeezed his hand hoping he'd squeeze back, which she would have taken as confirmation that he was at least willing to listen to her.

"You should have told me about this a long time ago. You've embarrassed me. I don't want to know all of the sleazy details of your life as a drug dealer. I have to make some choices about this marriage, and how I feel about you. This is insane. What else have you lied to me about?"

"Bryan, listen to me. I didn't mean to deceive you. And I swear to you that there is nothing else in my past that would upset you to this degree. Baby, I only wanted to make you happy. I wanted to be everything to you. I didn't want you to know about my past because it was painful for me. It wasn't easy selling poison to people. It was horrible and I feel awful about what I've done. I was a much different person then." Cynthia paused for a long moment waiting for Bryan to say something but he didn't. She squeezed his hand again but he didn't squeeze back.

The following day, Cynthia was feeling much better, and her blurred vision was all but a thing of the past.

As she scanned her surroundings she was surprised to see Hope sleeping in a nearby guest chair.

"Hope," Cynthia called to her. Hope woke up and smiled at her.

"Hey. I must have dozed off. I haven't gotten much

sleep lately because I've been so worried about you." Hope stood up and walked over to Cynthia's bed. She took Cynthia's hand and placed it in her own. "I've got to nurse you back into good health," said Hope.

"I thought you were with my kids. Are they with Bryan now?"

"They're with your uncle Jo Jo," said Hope and began to rub her hand frantically. Hope had a worried smile on her face and Cynthia instantly sensed something was wrong.

"Why are they with Uncle Jo Jo? Where is Bryan at?" Cynthia demanded to know.

"Sugar, I don't know where he is. He called me up talking crazy."

"Talking crazy? What did he say?" Cynthia asked as she sat up and repositioned herself on the bed.

"Baby, you need to get your rest and get well. You shouldn't worry about him right now."

"Hope, he's my husband, it's my job to worry about him. Now, where is he? You know something but you're not telling me," Cynthia said as she continued to read the sad expression in her eyes.

"He left didn't he?"

"I don't know for sure," Hope admitted. "He said that he couldn't watch the kids because he needed to get away for a while. He was very upset about being deceived and about how and why you kept your secret from him. He didn't know if he could trust you."

"Trust me? Of course he can trust me."

"I know, and I tried to tell him that everyone deserves a second chance but he just couldn't see that. It's a right-versus-wrong issue for him. He's badly hurt by all of this and he's having trouble dealing with it."

"I should have told him, Hope." Cynthia closed her eyes. "I should've never kept my life with Johnny B a secret."

CHAPTER 27

Cynthia was released from the hospital on Tuesday. Hope picked her up during the morning while the kids were at school. As Hope drove her home she talked about how Anthony and Angel had spruced up the house and made her a giant get-well card.

"They can't wait to see you when they arrive home from school," said Hope. "They were so afraid of losing you. Especially Angel. She was upset when she couldn't come into your hospital room."

"I spoke to both of them on the phone and told them not to worry," Cynthia said.

"You scared them half to death when you fainted in church. Incidents like that have a way of traumatizing kids."

"Do you think my episode at the church had a really negative impact?" Cynthia asked.

"I hope not, but one can never tell. I think you need to be reassuring to them. Anthony and Angel will need that."

"I was furious with Hanna and Hester. They were pushing my buttons at the same time. I swear to you, Hope, I've never really wanted to kill anyone in my life, but if I'd had a gun the day Hanna walked into the church I would have shot her cemetery-dead."

"Cynthia, you were in the House of the Lord. You can't shoot someone in church."

"I know. I've been praying for forgiveness for my thoughts."

"I can understand how you felt that way. Hanna seems like a vindictive woman and she was out to destroy your good relationship with Bryan."

"Hanna is low-down," Cynthia said. "I now realize it was Hanna who was stalking me." Cynthia gazed out of the car window for a moment as they approached a stop signal. "So, what happened to Hanna?" Cynthia finally asked.

"The pastor wasn't very happy about how she conducted herself. He said that she had hell in her heart and Evil should be her name. He asked her to leave or risk being escorted out. After a long moment she left."

"Where did she go?"

"Just outside. She waited and watched the church from a park across the street. I think she was waiting to see what was going to happen next. When the ambulance arrived for you she watched as they took you away." Hope paused in thought. "Let me ask you a question."

"Go ahead."

"Do you still hate her? I mean, I don't have to worry about you killing the woman or anything, right?"

"Yes and no," Cynthia answered. "The human part of me wants revenge but my spiritual side is telling me to let it go and forgive her for her sins and pray for her salvation. Hanna is just an accident looking for someplace to happen. The situation she was in when I turned my life around was tragic and frankly it still is tragic. Now things are so twisted around in her mind that she wants to blame me for everything that has gone wrong in her life, and that's just crazy."

"I guess the old saying is true. Misery does love company."

"It may be true but right now, I'm not even trying to hang out with Misery. I've been there and done that already. I have to figure out how I'm going to fix the trust between Bryan and I. He has to give me a chance to make things right. I have to get him to listen to me. I don't want him to end our marriage over this. I don't want him to leave me."

"I wish I could tell you where he was so you can go to him," Hope said. "But I haven't seen him at all."

"He'll show up," Cynthia said with confidence, "and when he does I'll be waiting to explain everything to him."

Cynthia's nerves and worrisome thoughts had gotten the best of her. It was now Thursday and Bryan still hadn't returned home.

"This is so unlike him," she said aloud as she paced back and forth in the kitchen. Every so often she'd stop and glance out of the kitchen window at a passing automobile hoping it was Bryan returning home. Her thoughts and imagination ran away with her by suggesting the possibility he had been in some horrific accident and was unable to communicate with her. To ease her mind, Cynthia spent a good portion of the day calling local hospitals to make sure he wasn't a patient. Thankfully, he wasn't in any of them. Cynthia didn't sleep at all on Thursday night and, before she knew it, Friday morning had arrived. She got out of bed when she heard the kids fumbling around in the kitchen. She headed downstairs to prepare breakfast for them.

"Where is Bryan at?" asked Angel.

"Shut up. Why are you asking such a dumb question?" Anthony scolded his sister.

"Who are you calling dumb, Mister, I'm not the one failing history class." Angel put Cynthia on notice about Anthony's poor performance.

"Will you two please stop fighting! I don't want to hear your squabbling this morning!" Cynthia shouted at them.

"She started it." Anthony placed blame on Angel.

"No I didn't," Angel shot back.

"I want silence, right now!" Cynthia hollered. This time Angel and Anthony complied. Cynthia prepared breakfast for them and then made sure they got on the school bus. She thought for sure Bryan would contact her but he didn't. Cynthia decided enough was enough and she was going to find him.

"I know he's just hiding out in some nearby hotel," she reasoned with herself. Cynthia pulled out the yellow pages and contacted every hotel within a twenty-mile radius. Bryan wasn't at any of them. Saturday morning came and Cynthia's body and mind were exhausted from a string of sleepless nights. She slept all day Saturday and didn't wake up until 8:00 p.m. Saturday evening. She walked into the family room and found Angel and Bryan behaving themselves and watching a program on television.

"Are you guys okay in here?" she asked.

"Yeah, we're fine," Anthony said. "Don't worry about cooking dinner for us. I fixed chicken strips, corn and a side salad for us earlier."

Cynthia was shocked when she heard that.

"Who are you and what have you done with my son?" Cynthia smiled. Anthony got up and walked over to her.

"Are you okay?" he whispered to her.

"I'm fine," Cynthia answered.

"Well, I just want you to know I'll never leave you like my dad and Bryan have. I'll always be with you." Cynthia wasn't prepared for Anthony's sudden maturity.

"Honey." Cynthia embraced him. "Thank you."

"I don't want you to be sad," Anthony said.

"I'm not sad. As long as I have you and Angel, I could never be sad." Angel joined them to be hugged as well. After a long moment, Cynthia broke the silence.

"I want you guys to lay out your clothes for church tomorrow morning. I want to get there early to get a good seat."

"Okay," Anthony said and then took Angel by the hand and led her upstairs to do just what Cynthia had asked.

* * *

Cynthia made it to church in plenty of time to get a seat up front. She was welcomed back by many of the members who were happy to see she had recovered and was healthy enough to return. Once the church seats were filled the pastor came up to the podium. He glanced down at Cynthia and her children and smiled at them.

"Marriage is hard work," the pastor began his sermon. "Even on a good day, marriage is hard. It amazes me when young couples come to discuss complications within their marriage. Many of them act as if marriage is supposed to be free of problems, complications and setbacks."

"Come on now, preach!" Cynthia heard someone from behind her shout out.

"If you purchase a car, you know that down the line you're going to have car problems. When you purchase a home, chances are that at some point, you're going to run into a problem that needs to be fixed. Am I wrong?"

"No," the entire congregation answered.

"So it's safe to say that any couple who is married is eventually going to have to deal with problems in the marriage. You see, the bible explains and gives direction on how to overcome marital problems. Both partners must want the marriage to work. Couples have to communicate and understand each other. Just wanting the marriage to work isn't enough. You have to work at it. And when I say work at it I mean maintain it properly. Let me give you an example. If you're driving a Lexus and using a Chevy manual to maintain it, that Lexus is going to break down. If you're married to a person and don't have their well-being as your highest priority, the marriage is going to break down. Too many of us go into a marriage with pre-conceived notions. Too many of us enter into marriage carrying baggage filled with problems and unrealistic expectations. We head into marriage wanting our spouses to be perfect when we're not perfect ourselves. There are many of us in here who have placed our souls in the pawnshop of sin because we were misguided in some way. But even sinners are loved by God, and regardless of what sins have been committed God still loves you and offers deliverance and salvation from the mess you get yourself into. If God has delivered you, let me hear you say amen."

"Amen," Cynthia uttered.

"When you look at your husband or wife, understand that we're imperfect and human. When you marry a person love them for who they are not for what you want them to be. Communicate with each other, talk to each other and understand one another." After the pastor said that the choir stood up and began to sing. Cynthia, Angel and Anthony sang along with the choir and congregation. The three of them were so completely caught up in the rapture of the music they didn't notice Bryan coming toward them via the center isle. When Cynthia finally did see Bryan he was standing next to her. Cynthia captured his gaze and held onto it. She was trying to communicate with him through the windows to her soul. She wanted him to understand she loved him and needed him. She wanted him to know she'd made a mistake and she was sorry for it. Bryan embraced her and Cynthia held on to him.

"I'm sorry I haven't called or been home," Bryan said. "I love you, and I forgive you."

Cynthia whispered purposely in his ear, "That is the first, only and last time I will allow you to disappear like that without contacting me. If you ever do it again, I may not be home for you when you return." After Cynthia said what she needed to say she kissed his ear to ease the sting of words.

"Agreed," Bryan said.

"Do you sill want me and our marriage?" Cynthia asked.

"Only if you're willing to work and never give up on us," Bryan answered.

"I'll never give up on us," Cynthia pulled away from him and trapped his gaze within her own once again. "Never, ever will I give up on you or us."

CHAPTER 28

The following summer, Cynthia was eight months pregnant with Bryan's first child. She loved the way that Bryan attended to her every need. He made sure that he was available to her in every possible way. Cynthia also enjoyed this pregnancy much better because it was planned, and she had more than enough space to welcome in the new addition to the family. Angel helped her pick out the perfect color for the baby's room and even helped her to paint it.

Cynthia was now lounging around in her backyard. She and Angel had become avid readers and enjoyed spending summer afternoons drinking iced tea and reading to each other. They'd just finished reading Lorraine Hansberry's play, *A Raisin in the Sun,* and Angel was giving her thoughts on why one of the characters had given a large sum of money to his friend.

"That was just dumb," Angel said. "I mean there is no way I'd give six thousand dollars to my friend and tell him to drive down state to get a liquor license while I wait here. I mean, he had six thousand dollars. Why didn't he just go and get the license by himself?"

"That's a very good point," Cynthia said, "but remember that the son had an alcohol problem and was depressed. Depression can make a person do strange things."

"Well, I hope that I never get depressed enough to give someone six thousand dollars."

"I hope that you never get that depressed, either, sweetie."

"So, Mama, are we still going to Uncle Jo Jo's birthday party tomorrow?" Angel asked, changing the subject.

"Yes. Uncle Jo Jo will be turning seventy. That's a big age, and all of the family will be there."

"I just hope that it's not boring."

"There will be other children there. Besides, you'll get to meet cousins that you've never met before."

"Girl cousins, right? Boys are just too silly and dumb."

"Yes, Angel. There will be plenty of girl cousins for you to hang out with," Cynthia said, laughing. Then she stopped because she felt the baby kick.

"Ooo," she cried out.

"Let me feel it," Angel said and then touched her mother's stomach. "Man, she's kicking you hard."

"Tell me about it," Cynthia said.

"Does it hurt?"

"No, it just feels strange, that's all. I'm fine."

"We're going to name the new baby Elaine if it's a girl, right. She'll be named after my grandmother."

"That's right," Cynthia answered as she tried to relax on her lawn chair.

"Tell me about Grandma again," Angel said.

"Well, for one thing, she knew that you were a girl before I did. When she'd gotten really sick, before you were born. She kept telling me how beautiful you were."

"How did she know that I was a girl and you didn't?"

"Because your grandmother was special like that," Cynthia answered. "She was very, very special.

CHAPTER 29

The next day, Cynthia, Bryan, Anthony and Angel were enjoying themselves at Uncle Jo Jo's seventieth birthday party. The gathering was held at a forest preserve and all of the family came out to wish him well. For Cynthia, it was the first time she'd seen a lot of her family since her wedding and some she hadn't seen since her mother had passed away. Everyone was happy for Cynthia and Bryan and couldn't wait for Cynthia to deliver her baby.

"I want to spoil the baby rotten," Uncle Jo Jo said. He and Cynthia were sitting at one of the picnic tables which was filled with food and drinks. Anthony, Angel and Bryan were recruited by several other family members for a friendly game of sixteen-inch softball.

"I'm so glad that you're doing so well." Uncle Jo Jo placed his hand on top of Cynthia's. "I was really worried about you for a while, but things turned out real good for you. And Bryan, what a good man he is. He's a good father, much better than that Butch fella."

"Oh please, don't even mention his name," Cynthia said. "The last person I want to think about is Butch. He hasn't been around in years and I just don't feel like talking him up."

"It's funny you should say that." Uncle Jo Jo twisted the cap off of his drink. "I ran into Butch about three months ago."

Cynthia raised her eyebrow. "Oh really."

"Yeah, ran into him on the street, begging me for money as I was pumping my gas. He's pretty bad off. But you might find this funny. He actually asked me if I'd talk to you about getting back together."

"Uncle Jo Jo, stop lying."

"No. I'm serious. He actually fixed his mouth and asked if I would talk to you about taking him back."

"What did you tell him?"

"Shit, I told him the truth. I told him that he messed up and that you were now married with a big house and a man who loves you."

"Did he ask about the children?"

"Briefly. He said that he'd come around more, but his money isn't right and he didn't want to show up empty-handed. I told him not to bother. I told him to leave you and the kids alone or I'd be delivering him a message."

Cynthia laughed. "I can't believe that you still have that much spunk in you at the age of seventy."

"You should see how much spunk I have when I take my Viagra pills."

Both Cynthia and Uncle Jo Jo cracked up laughing.

"What's so funny? What did I miss?"

Cynthia glanced up and saw Hanna standing in front

of them. Cynthia didn't say anything, she just looked at Hanna for a long moment.

"Hello, Cynthia," Hanna said. "You look good."

"Uncle Jo Jo, I have to go. I'll let you and Hanna visit with one another." Cynthia stood up to leave.

"You know, before you go I want to mention something to you," said Uncle Jo Jo.

"What is it?"

"People make mistakes. And when a person makes a mistake and corrects it, he's a better person. It takes a lot for a person to say, I'm sorry. It takes an even bigger person to forgive those who have done them wrong. You, of all people should understand what I mean."

Cynthia was caught off guard by the way Uncle Jo Jo made her think about her crippled relationship with Hanna. But he was right. She'd been carrying around hate for Hanna for far too long. Cynthia turned and acknowledged her cousin.

"Hello, Hanna," Cynthia said as she swallowed hard.

"I, uh..." Hanna paused and Cynthia saw tears forming in her eyes. Cynthia swallowed hard again because she and Hanna shared the same pain, the same wounds and the same scars.

"I'm so sorry, Cent." Hanna got the words out, but not without crying first. She quickly smeared away her tears with her hand. "I'm so very, very sorry."

Cynthia studied Hanna's eyes and saw sincerity in them. She exhaled hard, because all she had really wanted from Hanna was an apology.

"I'm sorry, too," Cynthia said and began crying.

"You're my sister. And I've hurt you and I want you to know that I wasn't in my right mind."

"I know," Cynthia said and stepped toward Hanna and embraced her. "I wasn't in my right mind, either."

"I love you, Cynthia."

"I love you, too, Hanna. And I forgive you."

"See, now that's the best birthday present I've ever gotten," said Uncle Jo Jo.

CHAPTER 30

Cynthia and Hanna found an empty picnic bench where they could talk in private.

Hanna looked much better than when Cynthia had last seen her. Her clothes were clean and she looked as if she had cleaned herself up from the years of substance abuse.

"My life with Butch was a blur," she explained. "Now that I'm clean and have had time to reflect on it, I think I was just insane. That's really the only way that I can explain it."

"Let me tell you something that my pastor told me that has really stuck with me. He told me that at some point, many of us put our souls in the pawnshop of sin, but we should always remember that God is always there and willing to save us. All we have to do is ask."

"I know. Believe me, I know. When I came to your church, all I knew was that I wanted to be saved. I wanted to turn my life around. I wanted to be like you. When I saw how happy you were and how well things were going for you, I just wanted my life to be as happy as yours was."

"So how are things going for you now?" Cynthia asked.

"Really good. I've been clean now for almost a year. It's not easy, but being strung out wasn't easy, either. Cent, I've done things that are just beyond words. The drugs just had me mentally screwed up."

"I owe you an apology, too. When you told me you were pregnant, I knew that I should have gotten you help, but I didn't and—"

"Cent, it's okay," Hanna said. "We're past that now. Perhaps one day, I'll meet a good man and we'll have children. This time, I won't take the gift of being pregnant for granted."

Cynthia smiled at Hanna. She had to admit that being around the Hanna that she used to know felt good.

"Did you know that your brother Victor had gotten out last year?"

"No. I had no idea," Cynthia said. "How is he?"

"Well, he didn't stay out for long. He was locked up again like three weeks after he'd gotten released."

"What did he get locked up for?" Cynthia asked.

"He bought drugs from an undercover agent named Lisa Granger."

"You're kidding."

"I wish that I was. I also heard that Johnny B went completely insane while in jail. They have him in a special detention center for the mentally unstable."

"Wow," was all that Cynthia could say. "So where are you staying at now?"

"I was living with my dad for a while but just two weeks ago, I got my very first apartment and it feels wonderful. I went through a program that helped me beat my addiction as well as taught me some job skills."

"Who do you work for now?"

"I work for a group home that helps teenage girls fight addiction. It's one of the most rewarding jobs I've ever had because I understand what they're going through. So far, I was able to really reach one girl who has been doing well."

"I'm proud of you, Hanna. That's such a selfless and honorable thing to do."

"Well, some days are better than others, but overall I really love what I do."

"And I'll bet those teenage girls really appreciate you for all the you're doing for them."

"Yeah. They're like my babies," Hanna said with a smile.

"Hanna, come take a walk with me over to the softball field. I'd like to introduce you to my family."

Hanna smiled.

"I was hoping you'd introduce me," Hanna said.

Hanna and Cynthia stood up and looped their arms around each other before heading over to the baseball field where the rest of the family was.